YESTERDAY NEVER DIES

Borgo Press Books by BRIAN STABLEFORD

Alien Abduction: The Wiltshire Revelations * *Asgard's Conquerors* (Asgard #2) * *Asgard's Heart* (Asgard #3) * *Asgard's Secret* (Asgard #1) * *Balance of Power* (Daedalus Mission #5) * *The Best of Both Worlds and Other Ambiguous Tales* * *Beyond the Colors of Darkness and Other Exotica* * *Changelings and Other Metaphoric Tales* * *The City of the Sun* (Daedalus Mission #4) * *Complications and Other Science Fiction Stories* * *The Cosmic Perspective and Other Black Comedies Critical Threshold* (Daedalus Mission #2) * *The Cthulhu Encryption: A Romance of Piracy* * *The Cure for Love and Other Tales of the Biotech Revolution* * *The Dragon Man: A Novel of the Future* * *The Eleventh Hour* * *The Fenris Device* (Hooded Swan #5) * *Firefly: A Novel of the Far Future* * *Les Fleurs du Mal: A Tale of the Biotech Revolution* * *The Florians* (Daedalus Mission #1) * *The Gardens of Tantalus and Other Delusions* * *The Gates of Eden: A Science Fiction Novel* * *The Golden Fleece and Other Tales of the Biotech Revolution* * *The Great Chain of Being and Other Tales of the Biotech Revolution* * *Halcyon Drift* (Hooded Swan #1) * *The Haunted Bookshop and Other Apparitions* * *In the Flesh and Other Tales of the Biotech Revolution* * *The Innsmouth Heritage and Other Sequels* * *Journey to the Core of Creation: A Romance of Evolution* * *Kiss the Goat: A Twenty-First-Century Ghost Story* * *The Legacy of Erich Zann and Other Tales of the Cthulhu Mythos* * *Luscinia: A Romance of Nightingales and Roses* * *The Mad Trist: A Romance of Bibliomania* * *The Mind-Riders: A Science Fiction Novel* * *The Moment of Truth: A Novel of the Future* * *Nature's Shift: A Tale of the Biotech Revolution* * *An Oasis of Horror: Decadent Tales and Contes Cruels* * *The Paradise Game* (Hooded Swan #4) * *The Paradox of the Sets* (Daedalus Mission #6) * *The Plurality of Worlds: A Sixteenth-Century Space Opera* * *Prelude to Eternity: A Romance of the First Time Machine* * *Promised Land* (Hooded Swan #3) * *The Quintessence of August: A Romance of Possession* * *The Return of the Djinn and Other Black Melodramas* * *Rhapsody in Black* (Hooded Swan #2) * *Salome and Other Decadent Fantasies* * *Streaking: A Novel of Probability* * *Swan Song* (Hooded Swan #6) * *The Tree of Life and Other Tales of the Biotech Revolution* * *The Undead: A Tale of the Biotech Revolution* * *Valdemar's Daughter: A Romance of Mesmerism* * *War Games: A Science Fiction Novel* * *Wildeblood's Empire* (Daedalus Mission #3) * *The World Beyond: A Sequel to S. Fowler Wright's The World Below* * *Writing Fantasy and Science Fiction* * *Xeno's Paradox: A Tale of the Biotech Revolution* * *Year Zero* * *Yesterday Never Dies: A Romance of Metempsychosis* * *Zombies Don't Cry: A Tale of the Biotech Revolution*

YESTERDAY NEVER DIES

A ROMANCE OF METEMPSYCHOSIS

BRIAN STABLEFORD

THE BORGO PRESS

MMXII

YESTERDAY NEVER DIES

FIRST EDITION

Published by Wildside Press LLC

www.wildsidebooks.com

DEDICATION

For the mysterious Tom Dean,
with thanks for his assiduousness
in maintaining my public image.

CONTENTS

AUTHOR'S NOTE

Although this story is complete in itself, frequent reference is made to earlier stories in the series to which it belongs, whose substance has inevitably come to account for a gradually increasing part of the characters' personal histories and relationships. The earlier stories, in order of the series' internal chronology, are: *The Legacy of Erich Zann* (first published in the Perilous Press volume *The Womb of Time*, reprinted in the Borgo Press collection *The Legacy of Erich Zann and other Tales of the Cthulhu Mythos*); *Valdemar's Daughter* and *The Mad Trist* (published as complementary halves of a Borgo Press Double); *The Quintessence of August*; *The Cthulhu Encryption*; and *Journey to the Core Of Creation* (issued as Borgo Press novels).

"All which I bid you remember (for I will have no such Reader as I can teach) is, that the Pythagorean doctrine doth not only carry one soul from man to man, nor man to beast, but indifferently to plants also, and therefore you must not grudge to find the same soul in an Emperor, in a Post-horse, and in a mushroom.... And therefore though this soul could not move when it was a Melon, yet it may remember, and now tell me, at what lascivious banquet it was serv'd. And though it could not speak, when it was a spider, yet it can remember, and now tell me, who used it for poison to attain dignity. However the bodies have dull'd her other faculties, her memory hath ever been her own, which makes me so seriously deliver you by her relation all her passages from her first making when she was that apple which Eve eat, to this time when she is he, whose life you shall find in the end of this book.

John Donne, "Epistle" to *Metempsychosis*
(dated 16 August 1601 by the author)

"The parasitism of the infinitely small is the cause of nine-tenths of our diseases. It is against this cause, more especially, that our new method of treatment is directed, and, we are happy to add, with the most perfect success."

François-Vincent Raspail,
Histoire naturelle de la santé et de la maladie (1845)

Oberon the Fay. A humpty dwarf only three feet high, but of angelic face, lord and king of Mommur. He told Sir Huon his pedigree, which certainly is very romantic. The lady of the Hidden Isle (Cephalonia) married Neptanebus, King of Egypt, by whom she had a son called Alexander the Great. Seven hundred years later, Julius Caesar, on his way to Thessaly, stopped in Cephalonia, and the same lady, falling in love with him, had in time another son, and that son was Oberon. At his birth the fairies bestowed their gifts—one was insight into men's thoughts, and another was the power of transporting himself to any place instantaneously. He became a friend to Huon, whom he made his successor in the kingdom of Mommur. In the full-ness of time, falling asleep in death, legions of angels carried his soul to Paradise. (*Huon de Bordeaux, a romance.*)

E. Cobham Brewer,
The Dictionary of Phrase and Fable
(Revised and Updated Edition, 1890)

CHAPTER ONE:
ROBERT LE DIABLE

I had been to the "new" Salle Favart several times before the evening of the thirty-first of October 1847, when I went there to see the première of the latest revival of *Robert le Diable*. Indeed, I had gone to see Hector Berlioz's *Damnation de Faust* there the previous year, whose relative failure had been one of the factors determining the Opéra-Comique's recent policy of favoring known crowd-pleasers rather than risking too many new productions. Anxiety about the political situation played a part in that too; in turbulent times, esthetes often develop an exaggerated nostalgia for relatively recent pasts that have taken on a golden edge in retrospect.

I must admit that I felt a trifle embarrassed settling into one of the three seats in the box on my own, and could not help feeling a trifle resentful of Auguste Dupin, who had insisted on my reserving the three seats while leaving one of them unfilled, and had then sent me a note on the very afternoon of the performance, saying that he had been "unavoidably delayed," but that he hoped to get to the theater by the interval—which was scheduled to take place after the second act.

I felt even less comfortable when, on glancing around the auditorium, I saw Pierre Chapelain sitting in the middle seat of the similar box directly opposite. Dupin and I had not seen much of Chapelain of late, but I would certainly have invited him to take the third seat in our box had Dupin not forbidden me to do so. It was not much consolation to observe that there was an empty seat in his box too, to the physician's left. Strangely enough, the seat to his right was occupied by a woman wearing a domino, complete with half-mask.

It was by no means unknown for Parisiennes to wear dominoes as fashion accessories on other occasions than masked balls, in the days before the 1848 Revolution, although I associated the habit more with spring than autumn, because Shrove Tuesday and Mid-Lent were the peak times for such indulgences. I wondered momentarily whether the woman might possibly be an American, for All Hallows' Eve tends to be a more important occasion there than the following day—Toussaint, in France—because of the customs imported by poor Irish and Scottish immigrants. Having been taken up by the general populace and Americanized in its social democracy, its celebration was now often associated with costuming and the wearing of masks.

There was no way to know who the woman was, however, although I took note that the lower part of her face, as seen by means of a rapid peep through my opera-glasses, suggested that she must be in her forties: much the same age as Chapelain. That, coupled with their appearance together in a box at the Opéra-Comique, always a popular exhibition-hall for relationships on the brink of formality, inevitably led me to wonder whether the physician might be thinking of marrying again, perhaps to some prosperous widow. If that were so, it would have helped to explain his recent neglect of the company of Dupin and myself, which had been such an important aspect of his social life a year before. On the other hand, it still left the empty seat to Chapelain's left unexplained.

Chapelain saw me too, of course, and we exchanged polite nods of the head, although his expression seemed to me to be a trifle distracted, almost bordering on the sullen.

There was still some ten minutes to go before the curtain was due to go up when the door of my box suddenly opened, and someone came in. I turned my head gratefully, expecting to see Dupin, his unavoidable delay happily terminated, but it was the so-called Comte de Saint-Germain.

He did not sit down in either of the vacant chairs. Indeed, he plastered himself against the far partition of the box, seemingly concealing himself behind the curtain—which had not been drawn back to ensure maximum visibility to a hypothetical observer sitting in the right-hand chair, because there was no one in the chair in question—at least until he moved it slightly across to give him better cover.

"What the devil do you think you're doing, Saint-Germain?" I said. "This is a private box."

He did not even look at me, being too busy peering surreptitiously out into the auditorium. "I know," he said, "but we're friends, are we not? What is more natural than friends dropping into one another's boxes before a performance to say *bonjour*? Except that Chapelain is all the way over the far side of the hall—why is that?"

"No," I said, coldly, deciding to focus on his first question. "I don't believe that we are friends."

"Don't be ridiculous," he said. "It's only a matter of months since I saved your life—that's a bond that lasts a lifetime. Pass me those opera-glasses, would you?"

So ingrained are habits of politeness that I actually reached across to hand him my opera-glasses, even as I replied to him, in an even colder tone: "As I remember it, Monsieur de Saint-Germain, it was the Breton who called himself Oberon Breisz who saved my life in Saint-Sulpice—after you had endangered it, by enticing me there."

Still hiding behind the curtain, but still peering out clandestinely, he put the opera-glasses to his eyes and focused them on the opposite box. I could not believe that he was using them to study Chapelain, and drew the natural conclusion.

A distinct grimace of disappointment crossed his face

"Let's not quibble," he said, by way of a response to my objection. "Do you know who that woman is in Chapelain's box, perchance?"

"No," I said, shortly—but I looked at her again, automatically, and saw her turn to greet someone who had just stepped through the door of her own box: two people, in fact, both men who would presumably have preferred to think of themselves as still just about in the prime of life rather than merely old.

With four people temporarily crammed into a three-chair box, the small space seemed crowded, but the occupants did their best to exchange polite formal greetings while maintaining a respectable distance between them. My impression was that Chapelain had not met either of the older men before, but that the lady knew them well.

"That's odd," Saint-Germain murmured.

"What's odd?" I asked, reflexively, still in a state of some confusion as to how to put an end to the importunate visitation.

"Meyerbeer and Scribe obviously know who she is," he said. "Meyerbeer must have come all the way back from Vienna to see the performance. Maybe's he's come to make sure that there are no unauthorized alterations. Last time *Robert* was produced here—well, not here exactly, but in the old hall, before it burned down—the piece was considerably revised. That was thirteen years ago, before my time, of course, but I heard a couple of the members muttering something about mystery and sacrilege while reading the theater notices, and naturally pricked up my ears. Meyerbeer took umbrage, apparently, although...."

He was cut off abruptly when the door opened again, and this time we both turned, presumably both expecting to see Auguste Dupin appear.

Again, it was not Dupin. It was Lucien Groix, the Prefect of Police. He seemed even less pleased to see Saint-Germain than Saint-German was to see him, and I sensed a flare of mutual hostility, although I thought it possible that both men were merely disappointed that the other was not Dupin. At any rate, the fake Comte's eyes narrowed slightly, and he blurted out—unwittingly, I'm sure: "Are you following me?"

Groix collected himself with the rapidity that one would expect of a man in his position. "Don't be absurd, Monsieur Falleroux," he said with deliberate disdain. "I have people to do that sort of thing for me."

I could see that the comment stung, and not merely because the Prefect had used the charlatan's real name. Saint-Germain/Falleroux had no time for a reply, though, for Groix had immediately turned to me.

"Where's Dupin?" he asked bluntly. His customary urbanity seemed to have gone missing.

"I don't know," I confessed. "He sent me a note saying that he'd been unavoidably delayed and couldn't get here before the interval. I'd rather assumed that it was you who had detained him." That had been my natural assumption, although the Prefect, like Chapelain, had been conspicuous by his absence from Dupin's life of late.

Groix evidently wanted to ask more questions, but was obviously inhibited by Saint-German's presence. I could not help noticing the way that the prefect was clutching his walking-stick with his gloved hand, almost as if it were a weapon, although it was a light and slender black-lacquered affair, far less use than ornament. Probably without realizing it, Saint-Germain had raised his own cane slightly, although it was a similarly elegant model, made of Chinese bamboo, as useless for sturdy defense as for reckless aggression.

I reflected that all our standard masculine accoutrements had become useless, in spite of their stubborn survival. Canes no longer function as swords, hats as helmets, or gloves as gauntlets, but we cling to them nevertheless, as symbolic residues of the past, reluctant to let go of them in spite of their redundancy—almost as if they still had potency as talismans, if not as instruments. Saint-German was not clutching his own stick as convulsively as Groix was gripping his, but even he seemed unusually tense, and I judged that their present fit of animosity had been generated on the back of an existing ill-humor in each case.

"Monsieur de Saint-German was just leaving," I said, hoping that the Comte would take the hint. "He just stopped in to say *bonjour*, even though we are not really friends."

Saint-Germain showed not the slightest sign of retreating,

however; he obviously wanted to get back at the Prefect for the casual slight.

"I'm surprised that you have time to visit the theater, Monsieur Groix," he said, snidely, "with the regime and the administration tottering around you. Shouldn't you be busy making preparations to emigrate? Or do you imagine that your bulging files contain enough blackmail material on Monsieur Raspail and his friends to allow you to survive a Republican revolution?"

I was shocked by his rudeness, but Groix seemed unsurprised. He was probably all too keenly aware of the precariousness of his position, and well used to the diminution of respect that had been suffered by the court and the administration alike. It had always seemed to me that Lucien Groix was more interested in the criminal aspects of the prefecture's work, in which he often employed Dupin as an unofficial consultant, but as Prefect, he had responsibility for the political police too, and the Republican orators of Paris had every reason to detest as well as to fear him. If Louis-Philippe were toppled—and there were few people in Paris who thought him capable of clinging to the throne for another year—then Groix would surely have to leave Paris, and perhaps France, if he were not to run the risk of ending up in one of the prisons to which his agents had sent so many others.

"Are you sure that your own organization will survive, Monsieur Falleroux?" Groix countered. "You might be a man devoid of faith yourself, but the majority of your members are royalist through and through."

"The Harmonic Society is above politics," Saint-Germain stated, airily. "We are seers and sages, and we are irreplaceable. This time next year, I shall still be here, while you are in hiding in London."

Groix must have been under a great deal of pressure, for I saw him snap then, as I had never seen him snap before. It was his turn to let his mouth get ahead of his mind. "What makes you think that?" he said, his voice almost reduced to a hiss as he fought to control his wrath. "Have you cast my horoscope?"

"Don't be ridiculous, Monsieur Groix," Saint-German retorted, with a smile of smug self-satisfaction. "I have people to do that sort of thing for me."

Groix's eyes glittered, but his face did not turn red. He made no explicit threats, but I had the distinct feeling that if he were still in place this time next year, Saint-Germain might be the one hiding in London, for fear of being sent to the *bagne*.

The Prefect turned back to me. "Would you be so kind as to ask Monsieur Dupin to come to see me tomorrow morning, without fail, Monsieur Reynolds," he said. And with that, he stalked out. He did not slam the door, but I believe that it was a testament to his powers of self-restraint that he did not.

Saint-Germain let out his breath and sat down in the right-hand chair. He reached out across the empty chair to hand my opera-glasses back. He no longer seemed anxious about the possibility of being seen, although I could not imagine that it was the Prefect from whom he had been hiding in the first place.

"Something's going on," he said, with a hint of malicious delight in his voice. "Where's Dupin?"

I hesitated over giving him an explicit order to leave, because I was not sure what I could do if he simply refused. The idea of a public quarrel in the quality section of the Opéra-Comique, which would immediately attract the attention of the *hoi polloi* and journalists in the stalls, was distinctly unattractive.

"The curtain will be going up in two minutes," I told him, feeling like a coward for settling for such a weak-kneed hint.

"No it won't," he said. "It's always late on the first night—and Meyerbeer's still chatting to the mystery woman. They won't dare to start before he's back in his own box. The director would doubtless have rather he'd stayed in Vienna, but since he's here...he is the composer, after all."

I glanced across at the other box. The two men—the composer and one of the librettists, I now knew—were, indeed, still conversing with the woman in the domino. Chapelain, however, was looking across the space of the auditorium at our box, and frowning, He had seen Saint-Germain now that the President of the Harmonic Society was no longer lurking behind the curtain, and obviously found his presence no less welcome than I did.

Saint-Germain was obviously right—something *was* going on; but I had not the slightest idea what it might be.

When he saw that I was not about to give him any more information, Saint-Germain continued talking, as was ever his wont. "If the Prefect had simply wanted Dupin to visit him tomorrow," the charlatan said, "he would have sent a messenger. If he wanted to see him on Prefecture business, he would not have come to the theater to do so. When he first came in, I assumed that the third seat must have been reserved for him, but that was obviously mistaken. Besides which, he really cannot afford to be wasting time at the opera with things falling apart around him...unless he has a very strong personal reason. Was it your idea to come here tonight, or Dupin's?"

I had to clench my teeth to avoid polite reflex giving him the answer. Eventually, I managed to say: "That really is none of your business, Monsieur Saint-Germain."

"It's foolish of you to make a game of it, my friend," he said. "You know me well enough to know that I can't resist a challenge. If there's a mystery here, I'll not rest until I get to the bottom of it. Do give my regards to Monsieur Dupin, when he arrives...*if* he arrives. I consider him a dear friend too, of course, even though there's a sense in which he got me into this mess."

"What mess?" I asked, utterly confused.

He stood up, shaking his head. "No, no," he said. "If you won't confide in me, I'm not going to confide in you. It is, to borrow your phrase, none of your business. *Bonsoir.*"

And he left. He closed the door very quietly—which was perhaps as well, as the curtain was going up, only a couple of minutes late. Giacomo Meyerbeer was no longer in Chapelain's box, and the company obviously felt ready to begin, in spite of the inevitable first night nerves.

Alas, I was no longer in a fit condition to pay much attention to Robert and Bertram's unfortunate encounter with the minstrel; my mind was all at sea. Fortunately, I had seen *Robert le Diable* before, and knew that I would be able to pick up the plot easily enough, once I had collected myself—not that *Robert* has much of a plot, being even more of a hotchpotch than most operas.

Oddly enough, I knew that Dupin had seen the opera before too, and until he had been so insistent that I take a box for tonight's performance, my impression had been that he did not care for it overmuch. When I had invited him to accompany me to see *La Damnation de Faust* a year before, he had been rather rude about "devil operas" in general, and he had been unimpressed by my insistent claim that Berlioz was an as-yet-unappreciated genius. Although he seemed to have made more of an effort to reacquaint himself with modern music after the unfortunate affairs of the lost Stradivarius and the haunted cello, he was still a trifle sensitive about the darker properties of music, as outlined in the book that had once obsessed him—*Les Harmonies de l'enfer*—but which he now seemed reluctant even to open.

Why then, had he been so enthusiastic to see this particular play on this particular night? Whatever the reason was, did it have something to do with Groix's presence—and, for that matter, the presence of Chapelain's masked lady?

The deepest mystery of all, of course, from my own point of view, was why I could not even begin to venture an answer to those questions. Why, if Dupin had had a particular reason for wanting to be here tonight, in company with me and an empty seat, had he not told me the reason? If "something was going on," why was I not party to it?

And where was Dupin? If it was not a summons from the Prefect of Police that was keeping him away, when he had seemed so enthusiastic to be here, what could it be?

I knew that racking my brains over such questions was futile, not merely because I had no chance of working out the answers at present, but because I knew that I only had to be patient until I was able to ask Dupin, perhaps in the interval or—if Saint-Germain turned out to be right about the possibility of him not turning up at all—tomorrow. The sensible thing to do, for the time being, was to concentrate on the opera. That was, after all, why I was here.

I tried to do that, but my ill-humor overflowed, transforming itself into criticism of what I was seeing and hearing.

I was not one of the many music-lovers who considered Meyerbeer to be the greatest composer of the era, of a stature only slightly less than his great forebear Rossini. Chopin, who had allegedly taken great inspiration from the original version of *Robert*, way back in 1831, had, in my opinion, far surpassed him, as had Berlioz, not to mention Wagner. It was no surprise to me that, in spite of its awesome reputation as the grandest of early grand operas, few works had been more extensively revised in its various revivals than *Robert le Diable*, sometimes involving music written by other hands—much to the composer's displeasure.

The problems with the piece had, I knew—although it was all ancient history from my viewpoint, unfolding long before I had come to Paris—arisen long before its completion. Meyerbeer and Scribe had initially planned it as a three-act comic opera for the old Opéra-Comique in 1827, more as a parody of than an homage to the first of the great "devil operas," Weber's *Der Freischutz*, which had had a phenomenal success at the *other* Opéra in 1824. The Opéra-Comique had run into acute financial difficulties, though, and when the collaborators had finally been able to go back to the piece, Meyerbeer, Scribe, and Casimir Delavigne had been commissioned to rewrite it as a five-act grand opera instead.

Eugène Scribe was by now famous as a writer of "well-made" plays, but he had not been able to do much, even with the help of Casimir Delavigne, to adapt a short comedy that had already played fast and loose with its supposed legendary source into a substantial drama. What remained of the original plot had evidently been twisted out of shape, and the story had been blatantly padded by the addition of the entirely gratuitous sensational episode that had done much to secure the work's success: the so-called dance of the nuns, the highlight of the third act.

I could not help thinking, churlishly, that it had been unjust as well as foolish for Scribe and Delavigne to identify the legendary Robert the Devil—as featured in the folktale prominently reproduced in the *Chronique de Normandie* and various other metrical romances, about a boy sired by the Devil who eventually represses his inherited evil ways to become a good Christian—with the historical Robert the Great, Duke of Normandy. The identification had apparently been forged by mistake, because seventeenth-century reprints of the "original" *Robert le Diable* had often been juxtaposed it with *Richard sans peur*, a completely different story about the son of Robert the Great.

Having researched the question in a desultory fashion the first time I had seen the opera, I suspected that the confusion might extend even further, given that the name Robert had also been attached, by subsequent Norman chroniclers, to the much earlier Viking founder of the province that had become the Duchy of Normandy: a pirate who had sailed up the Seine to attack Paris and run riot in the surrounding territory on two occasions, and whose real name had been Hrolf. At least Hrolf really had undergone a repentance of sorts, promising to convert to Christianity as the price for being granted legal title the province of Normandy by Charles the Simple—the least of Charlemagne's namesake descendants—although he had subsequently reverted to the bloody worship of his pagan gods.

I tried hard to put such pedantic ruminations out of my mind, however, and concentrate on the opera itself.

As I watched the first and second acts unfold, gradually revealing Robert of Normandy's difficulties in wooing Isabelle, Princess of Palermo, his accidental disruption of his half-sister Alice's romance with the minstrel Raimbaut, and the virtuous Alice's attempts to redeem him from the road to ruin along which he is being prompted by his "friend" Bertram, I could not help seeing all of it as a mere prelude to the dance of the nuns—

much more so at any rate, than a preparation for the denouement, in which Bertram, who is actually Robert's father, fails to
keep the bargain he has made with the Devil to deliver his son's
soul, and is dragged off to hell, like all the other devil-led fools
of the genre, in imitation of the prototypical *Don Giovanni*.

The dance of the nuns actually adds nothing to the opera's
plot, being merely an arbitrary intrusion of a scene in which
Robert has to recover a magic branch from the ruined convent
of Saint Rosalia, in order to render himself invisible—which
will allow him to gain the access to Isabelle that he has been
forbidden. The ballet does, however, add a strong, and arguably
unhealthy, dose of eroticism to the story, because the ghostly
nuns dance in remembrance of a debauched past grotesquely
unbefitting their vocation. Knowing that the erotic ballet was to
come, it was difficult to see the machinations of the first two acts
as anything but teasing foreplay, or mere delay. I told myself,
however, that it was merely my annoyance at Saint-German and
Dupin that was making me impatient, and that I really ought to
try to enter into the true spirit of the piece, savoring the music
as if I were hearing it for the first time.

I could not do it. Other thoughts kept getting in the way, in
spite of all my efforts—not merely the question of where Dupin
was now, but the question of exactly when and where he had
seen the play before. Obviously, it had been before my arrival
in Paris, and if it had been at the Opéra-Comique, it must have
been before the fire in 1838, quite probably the 1834 revival
to which Saint-Germain had made oblique reference. That had
been some while before Lucien Groix had worked his way up
to his present position, but he and Dupin had already been old
friends. Was it possible that Dupin and Groix had seen the opera
together thirteen years ago? Did that have something to do
with the singular circumstance of Groix coming here tonight,
expecting to see Dupin?

Tormented by such unanswerable questions, I could not even
keep my eyes on the stage. I looked across at Chapelain's box
repeatedly—and then looked away again, ashamed of my rude-

ness, scanning the upper galleries as if I were merely parading my gaze around the entire house. In spite of the poor light, I was convinced that I saw Saint-Germain on the far side of the upper gallery, in one of the worst seats in the house. That would have been extremely atypical of him, but the abormality did not make me any less certain of the identification, which I checked with further glances every time the lighting of the stage was bright enough to allow the possibility of a glimpse.

My restlessness lasted all the way to the interval, when I remained in my seat rather than going down to the foyer, hoping that Dupin might appear at any moment, having been waiting outside for the opportunity to come in without creating a disturbance—but he did not, and after ten minutes, my patience ran out.

If the Comte de Saint-German and Lucien Groix thought that it was acceptable behavior to burst into other people's theater-boxes uninvited, I thought—atypically, I ought to say—then why should I not do the same? If all the other mysteries of the evening were insoluble, one, at least, was within my potential grasp.

Pierre Chapelain and the masked woman had also remained in their seats, and showed no sign of budging—so I got up, stamped around the circular corridor behind the boxes, and barged into theirs.

CHAPTER TWO: THE PHANTOM OF THE OPERA

Having seen me leave my box, and perhaps having deduced my reason for doing so, Chapelain was by no means as startled by my appearance as I had been by Saint-Germain's or the Prefect's—and unlike them, I had had the grace to knock and wait to be admitted.

Chapelain's greeting, although polite enough, was more than a trifle frosty—perhaps because he had caught a glimpse of Saint-German in my company, although I remembered that he had seemed sulky even before then. He was obviously curious, though—perhaps almost as much as I was.

"Is Monsieur Dupin not with you?" he asked.

The question was in no way surprising in itself, but the fact that it had been asked before I had been introduced to the masked lady was. My surprise must have shown, because Chapelain blushed, thus revealing an honesty of expression that neither Saint-German nor the Prefect had condescended to do.

"My apologies," he murmured, "but you will appreciate, I think, that as a physician, I have a duty of confidentiality to my patients, and I regret that I am unable to introduce you to my companion."

I had, in expecting the introduction, reflexively turned toward the lady, who was studying me carefully from behind her mask. "You are a friend of Monsieur Dupin?" she asked. Her voice immediately dispelled any suspicion that she might be an American, although it was very difficult to identify an alternative place of origin from such a brief sentence

"Yes, I am," I told her.

"And he was supposed to be here tonight?"

"Yes, he was—and still is, although he is very late. Do you know him, Madame?" That was slightly impertinent, but I thought that the circumstances permitted me a certain license.

"We met once, very briefly," she said, "in 1834—here at the *Comique*, as it happens...or rather, in the old theater...in the Green Room."

That surprised me; I had not thought Dupin the sort of person to visit the Green Rooms of theaters in order to socialize with the artistes after a performance. Lucien Groix, on the other hand, in his younger days....

I ventured a further impertinence. "I would be happy to remember you to him," I said, "if I knew your name."

"If even half of what Monsieur Chapelain has been telling me about him is true," the lady said, with a slight chuckle, "he will be able to deduce my identity from what I have already told you. Monsieur Groix could not stay for the performance, I assume? Pierre tells me that he is now the Prefect of Police. And poor Professor Thibodeaux is dead, alas."

It was not the first time I had heard the name of Thibodeaux mentioned, but I could not for the life of me remember when I had heard it before, or in what context. The calculus of probability suggested that it must have been Dupin who had mentioned it to me—but he mentioned so many names, while he was using me as a sounding-board in helping himself to organize his ideas.

My own powers of ratiocination were no match for Dupin's, but my long acquaintance with him had taught me something of his methods, and perhaps even communicated a little of his ingenuity...or perhaps not.

"Perhaps it was in memory of Monsieur Thibodeaux's death that Monsieur Dupin asked me to hire a three-seater box, but to leave one of the seats empty," I suggested.

The lady's surprise was half-masked, but Chapelain's was not. "But what about Groix?" He said. "Was he not taking the third seat? I assumed that he was making his apologies to you, because he had been called away."

I realized my mistake too late, but tried to gloss over it as best I could. "The plot thickens," I remarked—in English, because the phrase has no exact equivalent in French. I switched back to French in order to explain my meaning, however, even though I had deduced by now from the lady's indeterminate accent that it was probably not her first language. "Monsieur Dupin did not ask me to invite Monsieur Groix, and I had no idea that the two of them had seen the opera together thirteen years ago, or that there had been a third party present."

"But surely Dupin told you...," Chapelain began—and then shut up abruptly, not so much because it was obvious that Dupin had not told me what he thought I ought to know, but because he had realized that he could not tell me either; the information had evidently come from his patient, and was thus protected by the veil of confidentiality.

"Did you deliberately leave a seat in your own box empty?" I took the risk of asking.

The question was aimed at Chapelain, but it was the lady who answered.

"Our intended companion is slightly indisposed," she said. There was a slight edge of sarcasm in her voice. The masked woman was not showing any obvious signs of physical illness, but there was definitely a certain strain in her attitude and her voice. I thought that she might perhaps be nervous, in spite of her determination to appear calm—more fearful than expectant, I guessed. I knew that I had taken impertinence far enough already, however, and could not possibly raise the subject of her possible anxiety. Chapelain was, in any case, eager to change the subject

"I assume that you did not invite Saint-Germain to your box either?" he said, bluntly.

"I certainly did not," I replied, "and I apologize for having unwittingly permitted him to use it in order to spy on Madame. A braver man would have thrown him out on his ear."

"A less polite man, perhaps," said Chapelain. "I don't blame you—but I would not like you to take the wrong inference. He was not spying on Madame."

I stopped myself querying that statement just in time, as my fledgling talent for education caused me to glance at the empty chair. Saint-Germain had been disappointed because the person he had hoped to see in the box was not here. Who could it possibly have been? I had an inkling—but that was certainly not a question I could ask Chapelain.

I was tempted to fish for more information about the mysterious Thibodeaux, but it was neither the time nor the place—and, as if to confirm that, the bell rang to request the audience to take their seats again. I bowed to the lady, shook Chapelain's hand, and apologized for having disturbed them. Neither made any reply, thus suggesting that I really had disturbed them, and that they would rather I had not done so. A glance across the auditorium told me that Dupin had not arrived. His unavoidable delay had obviously been more protracted than he had hoped.

As I opened the door to the box, however, I almost collided with someone coming in—a young woman wearing a domino identical to that of the woman who was still in her seat. In spite of the mask, I recognized her immediately; it was Jana Valdemar.

Because her head was down and the range was too close, she cannot have seen anything, to begin with, but my stereotypical black jacket, shirt-front, and cravat.

"I'm truly sorry, Pierre," she said "But I feel a little bet...oh!"

She had looked up. Evidently, she had not only realized her error but had recognized my face. Her exposed cheeks were pink, and she froze, utterly nonplused.

Instinctively—we were, after all, in the corridor of a prestigious theater, where etiquette rules supreme—I bowed. "An understandable mistake, Mademoiselle," I murmured—and, moved by an irresistible influence, continuing murmuring, with urgent rapidity: "Obviously, since you are masked, I have no idea who you are, but it might interest you to know that the Comte de Saint-Germain is in the house, sitting in the upper gallery on this side of the auditorium. He came into my box uninvited before the performance and stared into this box, but I doubt that he will do it again. If you are discreet, you should be able to remain invisible."

Then I stepped aside, holding the door open for her. I caught a glimpse of Chapelain standing up inside and looking out, a picture of anguished embarrassment. I nodded to him again, closed the door behind Jana Valdemar, and hurried back to my seat.

As I passed the stairway leading up to the gallery in which I had glimpsed Saint-German, I looked up reflexively. I did not see Saint-Germain, but I did see Lucien Groix standing at the top peering into the gallery as if he were looking for someone. I could not believe that he really had been following the fake Comte, given that he did, indeed, have agents to do that sort of thing for him, but he was nevertheless there. Why? Clearly, in spite of the fact that the regime and the administration were falling apart, Monsieur Groix still had time to "waste" at the theater.

Perhaps, I thought, *he doesn't want to miss the dance of the nuns.*

Neither did I, of course; it was the highlight of the opera.

Whether or not it was due to Meyerbeer's presence, the music and the choreography of the third act seemed to me to be exactly as I remembered them. I knew that other versions of the opera had expanded the ballet, sometimes replacing Meyerbeer's music with something more bacchanalian, but this one seemed strictly orthodox.

The idea of the piece is simple enough. When Robert and Bertram go into the ruined Convent of Saint Rosalia—named for the patron saint of Palermo—in order to search for the magic branch, their intrusion awakens the ghosts of long-dead nuns buried in the crypt, whose silent ballet recalls, not the sanctity and placidity of their convent life, but the supposed erotic adventures of their remoter youth.

To be perfectly honest, the version of the ballet featured in the present performance seemed a trifle tame by the standards of 1847, although I could imagine that it must have seemed considerably more risqué in 1831; the art of ballet had undergone a considerable evolution in the interim, and so had notions of the kinds of debauchery that could be accommodated on respectable stages like that of the Opéra-Comique. Romanticism had a lot to answer for—or to be congratulated on—in that respect.

In spite of the fact that he was an exceedingly staid and bourgeois king by comparison with the Bourbons, Louis-Philippe's reign had seen a considerable relaxation of moral restraint in the theater. Perhaps it was because of his supposedly democratic credentials that outrageous behavior once confined to the private lives of courtiers—at least according to scurrilous rumor—was now considered entirely appropriate for representation on the popular stage. I had never actually been to Bobino, but reportage suggested that far worse debauchery could be seen there every night than was delicately suggested in Meyerbeer's ballet, and attributing such behavior to nuns was now entirely typical of the anti-clerical sentiments that were loudly running riot in Republican ranks—not that there was anything unusual about the suggestions themselves, which were as old as convent life.

Even so, as I watched the ballet through my opera-glasses, I could not help feeling that, just as identifying Robert the Great as the legendary Robert the Devil, even while allowing him to remain fundamentally virtuous, was something of an insult, Scribe's invention was an even more blatant insult to poor Saint Rosalia, who had allegedly been one of the relatively few female hermits, and highly unlikely to have participated in any orgies. So far as I could tell, she was only cited in the story because of her connection with Palermo, where the action was set, although I knew—as Scribe and Delavigne has presumably known—that she was descended from a Norman family. That had presumably been the hook on which the librettists had hung Duke Robert's entirely imaginary romance. The actual Saint Rosalia had dated from at least a century later than Robert the

Great, and could not possibly have had a convent named after her during his lifetime, let alone a ruined one.

As the ballet drew toward its close, knowing that the plot was about to return to the romantic entanglements of Robert and Alice, and Bertram's doomed attempt to complete his diabolical bargain, I lowered my opera-glasses and sat back in my chair, expecting the opera to become even less interesting to me, given my confused state of mind. Had Dupin been there, the situation would have been different, but I was on my own, and feeling increasingly awkward in my isolation...except that, all of sudden, I realized that I was no longer isolated.

I honestly do not know how long the ghost had been there, and in a strange way, the fact that it might have been there throughout the ballet without my realizing it—perhaps without my ever realizing it, had I not sat back at that particular moment—was more alarming than the specter's presence. I had been associated with Dupin for so long, and had seen so many bizarre things in consequence, that my awareness that I was looking at a ghost seemed almost run-of-the-mill; and what shot through my mind was neither terror nor amazement, but the thought that Dupin would never have forgiven me if I had not seen it. Not that either of us would ever have known, if I had let it pass unnoticed...but the principle remained the same.

Perhaps that thought was itself bizarre, but from the instant I caught sight of the ghost, I thought I knew why Dupin had instructed me to hire a three-seater box for an audience of two. He had surely known—or at least, suspected—that the ghost would appear, and that was why he had wanted to come.

But he had missed it.

He had been unavoidably detained.

The ghost was not phosphorescent, but nor was it entirely a creature of shadow. It reflected the distant lights of the stage just as an ordinary person would have done, in spite of the fact that it was not really solid, that it was the mere *appearance* of a person. I was not in doubt about that, and not merely because I had not heard anyone come into the box. There was something about the presence that was unmistakably spectral, although I could not pin down exactly what it was. It was not transparent any more than it was phosphorescent, but it was not truly present either; it had no mass; it did not belong.

There was, however, something odd even about the quality of its unbelonging. It did not seem *out of place*. It seemed, in fact, to be exactly where it ought to be, in the empty seat next to mine...but if it was not out of place, it was definitely out of time. It belonged to the past—perhaps not to a very distant past, but one that was definitely dead.

It was wearing spectral clothes, in a style that might still have passed muster even today, and there was nothing unusual about the cut of its black hair and beard, but there was something in its attitude and its gaze that spoke of displacement. Even before it turned to look directly at me, I could measure a peculiar puzzlement and disorientation in its perception, as if it could not quite understand why everything around it was different. When it did turn its head, the movement was slightly awkward—and it was then that I noticed that its hands, positioned on the handle of a wooden walking-stick wedged vertically between its knees, were gnarled by arthritis—an arthritis that probably affected its neck too.

Ghosts, I presumed, did not usually suffer from arthritis, so I deduced that this one must be more like some kind of strange echo of an arthritic person who really had sat in an equivalent chair in an equivalent box, perhaps in 1834. If the image really had been displaced in time, I thought, then of course everything looked different. This was still the Salle Favart, but it had been completely rebuilt after the fire of 1838. And *Robert le Diable* was still *Robert le Diable*, but this was not the same version of the opera that had been played here in 1834, if what Saint-Germain had said could be trusted. Not only were the dancers different, but so was the dance, and the music accompanying it.

The ghost was that of a man of about sixty, probably a little older than Meyerbeer and Scribe, but when he turned to look at me and I stared into his dark, ungleaming eyes, I had an impression of much greater antiquity than that. His overall appearance, I felt sure, dated from 1834—I was even convinced that I could guess the name of the man at whom I was looking—but there was something within and beyond that appearance that was much older, and much less human.

The Devil himself?

I thought not; the gaze did not seem particularly friendly, but it did not seem to be malevolent either—mischievous, perhaps, or at worst slyly malicious. Even so, I told myself, it might conceivably have been one of the many pale simulacra of the Christian Devil that haunted the interstices between our material world and what some people called the dream dimensions. There are, as Hamlet remarked, more things in heaven and earth than were dreamt of in Horatio's philosophy.

I almost contrived to unfreeze my throat in time to speak, although I have no idea what I would have said. Instead, the ghost spoke, perhaps thus proving that it had some small measure of material presence.

"Yesterday never dies," it said, "but such is the rhythm of time that one has to grasp its echoes on the wing."

There was a measure of melancholy in the words—as, I suppose, befitted their content—but there was also an odd note of satisfaction, of intellectual triumph. The latter was a note that I had heard before, in Auguste Dupin's voice, when he had solved a puzzle of some sort.

"Can you see me?" I enquired, interestedly.

I could not see any sign in the phantom's expression that it had heard what I said, but it did give the impression that it could see someone sitting where I was sitting...or had been sitting in a chair alongside his own, in 1834 or some other time: Auguste Dupin, I guessed, if this really was an echo of 1834 caught on the wing...with how many other undying yesterdays caught in its uncanny net?

Seized by a sudden intuition, I looked across the auditorium, wondering whether Chapelain, the mystery woman, and Jana Valdemar could also see the phantom. Chapelain was staring at the stage, his profile reflecting the distant limelight—but both masked women were ignoring the final steps of the ballet and looking across the auditorium. The combination of the masks and the angle of the feeble lighting made it impossible to judge their expressions, or to see where their gazes were focused, but I was immediately convinced that they could see that I was not alone, even if they did not know that my companion was not human.

I immediately looked back at the ghost again, in order to estimate how much they might be able to see of it by the light reflected from the phantom visage—at least, I tried to. As unobtrusively as it had appeared, the specter had vanished again.

Perhaps they didn't see it, I thought. *Perhaps they were merely looking at me.* I did not believe it.

Strangely enough, even though I had not felt frightened—and ironically, in view of the observations I had earlier made of Lucien Groix—I found that my hand was convulsively closed on the pommel of my own walking-stick, although I had no memory of even having picked it up. Even though I had not yet shown any sign of arthritis in my knuckles, the grip was so tight and painful that I had difficulty relaxing the fingers in order to lie the cane down again—but I had no sensation of wielding it, even symbolically, as a weapon of defense; it was more a matter of clutching an amulet or a talisman: an echo of a time even more remote, I supposed, than the heroic age of swords and chivalry.

If the rest of the opera would have been an anticlimax after the dance of the nuns in any case, it was doubly or triply so after the manifestation of the ghost: the ghost, I presumed, of the mysterious and long-dead Professor Thibodeaux. I suppose it ought still have been possible for me to obtain a thrill of sorts from Bertram's summons to Hell, if not from Robert's marriage to Isabelle, all the more so having been given the glimpse of something even more enigmatic than the problematic overlap of 1834 and 1847 in the spectral eyes, but it was not.

I was by now, it seemed, too experienced a ghost-seer to be

thrown off my stride by such a subtle hint of diabolism, and too seasoned a dealer with entities mistaken for and conflated with the imaginary devils of Christendom to find their occasional intrusion into our world anything more that a fact of life. I had been beyond the limits of the world, and had been possessed in my own flesh by an entity that most people would have identified as a demon. I was not a novice in such matters.

Indeed, I had sufficient second-hand expertise, by virtue of many long conversations with Dupin, to know that my sighting of the ghost was highly atypical in several respects. Most ghost-seers, according to Dupin, only see ghosts that they are half-expecting to see: ghosts of people that they knew in life, or ghosts of their ancestors, or anecdotal ghosts with whose stories they are familiar—because, of course, the experience of seeing a ghost is mostly, and often entirely, subjective. It was obvious to me now that the reason that Dupin had not breathed a word about what he half-expected to see tonight was his curiosity to know whether I would be able to see anything at all, given that I had never met Thibodeaux and had only heard his name in passing. He would doubtless be very interested to know that I had.

But where was Dupin? If he had half-expected to see a ghost tonight, that made it more than doubly surprising that he had missed the opportunity. Any number of things might have kept him away from a mere opera—especially one that he considered second-rate—but to keep him away from a manifestation that anyone but him would have considered supernatural...that was a different matter.

I could not help wondering whether his absence might have anything to do with the "slight indisposition" of the person originally intended to occupy the third seat in Chapelain's box, although *she* had managed to arrive at the interval, even if he had not; but I knew that I had to be cautious about placing too much credence in any "deduction" in that regard. I had to remember that I was only a pupil, not a master, in Dupin's arcane arts.

On the other hand....

Pierre Chapelain was a magnetizer: a physician who employed treatments based in the science of suggestion. He used magnetism—or hypnotism, as it was increasingly being called nowadays—as both an aid to diagnosis and an aid to make his patients feel better, whether to suppress dolor or to mobilize their innate resistance to disease. In objective terms, most of his prescriptions were elementary, with more emphasis on physical exercise than drugs; he was an opponent of sanguination, and was even suspicious of antisepsis—of which Dupin approved wholeheartedly, being a covert to François Raspail's theory of disease. Chapelain's opinion was that many ailments, not excepting the most familiar infectious diseases, were best treated by attempting to encourage the power of mind over body, although that was frustratingly difficult with many patients, whose habits, tastes, convictions, and petty manias were often unwittingly antithetical to that kind of natural self-defense.

Chapelain had the reputation of being a good physician, and what little I had seen of his treatments supported that contention, but he suffered from a certain lack of self-esteem, and was often frustrated by the imitations of his hypnotic technique. He had told me more than once that the best physicians of his sort worked in pairs, employing what modern parlance was beginning to call "mediums"—hypersensitive individuals who, when entranced themselves and guided by a magnetizer, sometimes had more far-reaching insight into a patient's mental state than either could have achieved alone. He was as insistent as Dupin that there was nothing supernatural about such intuition, which was based in a capacity for sympathetic identification with others that most women, and even a few men, possessed to some degree.

In that respect, the doctor made no secret of the fact that he deeply regretted the loss of the best medium with whom he had ever had the opportunity to work: Jana Valdemar. At least, he made no secret of that to me—but he had not been nearly so ready to confess it to Dupin, who had once got into a contest of wits with the young woman in question, and did not approve of the manner in which she had attempted to deploy her undoubted talents. The Comte de Saint-Germain, I knew, also had a strong interest in her, having once been her mentor, and had been enthusiastic to renew that situation for some time. Now I knew that she was the person who should have been in Chapelain's box when the fake Comte barged into my box, it explained why Saint-Germain had been so eager to spot the absentee, and so disappointed to find the seat empty. If Chapelain were associated with the medium again, that might also explain why he had been keeping us—or, more specifically, Dupin—at some distance of late, fearful of Dupin's disapproval.

I took a certain pride in having worked all that out long before the fifth act came to an end, but I was still deeply frustrated by the questions into which I had no insight at all, however hazardous. Why was Chapelain's patient here, along with Lucien Groix, both of whom had apparently seen the 1834 performance—and along with Thibodeaux, who had turned up in spirit, and Dupin, who should have turned up but had not? Something was, as Saint-Germain had readily observed, *going on*—something of which I had only scratched the surface thus far. And now that Saint-Germain's curiosity had been piqued, presumably by virtue of a mere coincidence, how might his potential involvement complicate the situation?

Such preoccupations were still weighing upon me as I made my way out into the street. Convention demands that the first waves of fiacres parked outside the theater waiting for the *sortie* should go to ladies and their escorts. Many unaccompanied males dispersed to look for cabs a little further afield, but I always waited, knowing that once the first fleet of fiacres had taken off like a flock of startled birds, others would begin to arrive to pick up the stragglers. I moved some forty meters along the *trottoir*, in order to find a deserted spot, but I took up a station under a *réverbère* so that I would be clearly visible when I got the chance to flag a cab down. I knew that I would have at least ten minutes to wait, so I sank into an absent-minded reverie—or, rather, sank back into the same one that had possessed me ever since my sighting of the ghost.

After two minutes or so, a private carriage drew up along-side me and stopped. I recognized Pierre Chapelain's carriage, but it was the older masked woman who put her head out of the portiere.

"May we offer you a lift, Monsieur Reynolds?" she asked. Obviously, Chapelain had told me her name, even though he had shirked the formal introduction. Chapelain and Jana Valdemar were presumably inside the carriage, but neither showed their face.

"Thank you, Madame, but no," I said. "It would take Dr. Chapelain out of his way."

The carriage did not draw away. "Forgive me for asking," said the masked woman, "but are you feeling ill?"

I was slightly surprised by that, although it was easy enough to guess what she was getting at. Evidently, she had seen someone else in my box, briefly. She was curious.

"Quite well, thank you, Madame," I assured her. Until she asked, I had not suspected otherwise, but I realized that I did feel a trifle queasy. We were still in the precincts of the *Comique*, however. Etiquette still ruled.

Still the carriage did not pull away, although more fiacres were now beginning to arrive, and it would soon be causing an obstruction.

"Forgive me again," the lady persisted, "but you really do look as if you've seen a ghost."

The game was obviously up. Even etiquette could not excuse a blatant and transparent lie.

"As a matter of fact, Madame," I said, "I have—but the expe-rience was transient, and the phantom did not appear to mean me any harm." I looked her in the face then, almost challenging her to find a permissible conversational countermove.

"In that case," she said seemingly quite unperturbed, and probably having obtained the conformation she wanted, "I'll wish you *bonsoir*. Sleep well, Monsieur Reynolds."

The masked face disappeared from the *portière*. I heard

Chaplain rap twice on the wall of the carriage's compartment with his cane, and the coachman, meekly obedient, flicked the horses lightly with his whip, instructing them to move off. They obeyed.

I was, however, in no mood to go meekly home to my bed, to sleep—if I could—and then to wait for Dupin to call on me at his leisure. I wanted to see him, and I wanted to see him right away, if I could find him. I was not so certain of my powers of deduction as to take it for granted that I could find him, but there was only one place I could think of to look, and I certainly intended to try it before admitting defeat.

When the fiacre finally collected me, I told the coachman to take me to the Rue Dunot, where Dupin's lodgings were. I did not expect to find him at home, in the strict sense of the term, but I did think that he would be in the house, and that he would open up to me, even if he would not do so to anyone else.

CHAPTER THREE: THE THREAT OF INFECTION

When I got down from the fiacre, I paid off the driver. There was no point asking him to wait. If it turned out that I could not find Dupin, I could walk home easily enough; the night was fine and mild, considering the time of year, and brightly moonlit. I was not afraid of footpads at such a distance from Montmartre and Belleville.

I went to the door of the concierge's lodge at the coaching entrance of Dupin's building, and knocked on it with the pommel of my stick, in a peremptory manner. There was no answer—which did not surprise me. I knocked again, and waited a further half minute before calling out: "It's me, Dupin—let me in."

I would have added an extra incentive had I got no response with my self-identification alone, but I eventually heard movement on the other side of the door, and then a voice said: "Go home. I'll come to see you tomorrow afternoon."

"I need to talk to you," I said.

"It's not a good time," he replied. "I'm sorry I couldn't get to the theater. Tomorrow afternoon, without fail."

It was obvious that I had to deploy the extra incentive after all. "I saw the ghost," I said, and baited the hook further by adding: "Thibodeaux's ghost."

Had I been wrong in that deduction, the cast of the hook and line would have gone wrong, but I knew before he had finished hesitating that I could chalk up one hit, at least.

"Are you wearing gloves?" he asked, finally, unable to prevent himself yielding to temptation.

"Of course," I said.

"Don't take them off," he instructed. "In fact, stay in the vestibule, such as it is. Believe me, my friend, you really won't want to come any further."

The stink hit me as soon as he opened the door. He was right; I really didn't want to go any further—but I did want to talk to Dupin. I stepped inside, and let him close the door behind me. He moved swiftly then to take up a position on the threshold of the inner doorway of the minuscule vestibule—one of only two others inside the lodge—but not swiftly enough to prevent me catching a glimpse of the bed-alcove at the far side of the inner room into which the vestibule opened.

Madame Lacuzon, Dupin's concierge and protective dragon—the "old witch," as she was known in the neighborhood—was lying on the bed, quite inert. Her eyes were closed, but her face, although drawn, seemed peaceful enough.

The stink was many-layered, but the sharpest stratum was a combination of cleaning fluids, including phenol. I could also smell camphor, and I could identify the distinctive label of a bottle of Raspail's Elixir on the bedside table. To judge by the other odors, the old woman had suffered from both vomiting and diarrhea, over a fairly protracted period of time—but Dupin had had an opportunity to clean up, and to deploy the measures against the threat of infection that Raspail recommended in his manual of hygiene.

I was profoundly glad that I had not arrived a few hours earlier.

"What wrong with her?" I asked.

"I don't know. As François Raspail insistently points out, the same symptoms can often be generated by different causes. It might have been picked up by contagion, or it might have been something she ate—thanks to two consecutive bad harvests and the consequent economic problems, the quality of food in Paris has deteriorated markedly of late. I feared for her life at one point, but I think she is over the worst now; if there is no recurrence of the symptoms, I should be able to get her to take an adequate supply of liquids over the next few hours."

"Did you call a doctor?" I asked.

"No," he replied, curtly. Madame Lacuzon, I suspected, was not the kind of person to put her trust in licensed physicians—or, indeed, anyone at all apart from Dupin.

"Was it one of Raspail's tiny parasites, do you think?" I asked. I had always been uncertain as to whether Raspail's theory of infection was really credible, given that every orthodox physician in Paris, and many of the unorthodox ones, were dismissive of it—especially the Royalists, who hated Raspail's Republican guts.

"I don't know, I tell you," he retorted, with more asperity than might have been warranted. "Any physician would doubtless be able to conjure up some Latin name to pass off as a diagnosis, but it would merely be a device to cover up his ignorance. We have no means, as yet, to search for and identify microbes, if they are indeed the primary agents of infectious diseases—but I was sufficiently familiar with the symptoms to know that it was vitally necessary to settle her gut and protect her from dehydration. I've contrived to keep feeding her water, and eventually managed to dose her with kaolin and morphia to line her stomach and settle its spasms. She might yet have another fit—for which reason I will not leave her, at least until morning. With luck, though, she will sleep now until the blight has passed. How did you know that she was ill?"

"I guessed," I told him. "Once I knew that you had expected to see more at the theater than the opera, I could only think of one thing that could keep you away: mortal danger to someone you would never trust to anyone else's care. I don't know exactly what Madame Lacuzon—Amélie—is to you, but I know that she's no mere concierge."

"She would do the same for me, and more," Dupin said, stiffly. "Who told you about Thibodeaux?"

"A woman clad in a domino sitting in a box opposite mine, with Pierre Chapelain and Jana Valdemar. He would not introduce her, on the grounds that she was his patient; evidently, she wanted to remain incognito, or she would not have been wearing the mask. She said that she met you at the theater—the old theater, that is—in 1834, in the Green Room, with Lucien Groix and someone named Thibodeaux, She said that you would be able to deduce her identity. I hope that she did not spoil your experiment by letting the name slip. That is why you were keeping me in the dark, I take it—as an experiment?"

"I'm sorry," he said—but it was only a reflex. He was not sorry; and, in truth, I could not see why he should be.

"You have your result," I said. "Even in your absence, with no expectations at all, and without having any more knowledge of Thibodeaux than a vague memory of hearing you mention the name, I saw the ghost in the box. So, I believe, did the lady in the domino—and she, too, knew that it was a ghost. Remarkable, is it not?"

"Remarkable," he agreed, pensively. "I hardly expected to see it myself, given that the theater had burned down in the interim. Describe the apparition, if you please."

"A man of about sixty, although his hair and beard were still uniformly black. Dressed as a good bourgeois, slightly behind the times—as is only to be expected. His skin seemed a trifle sallow as well as wrinkled, but that might have been an effect of the reflected limelight."

"That could be anyone. Was there nothing more distinctive?"

"Yes. He had arthritis, probably in his neck, but definitely in his hands, I saw them quite clearly, in spite of the poor light, clutching the handle of his stick."

"Ah!" said Dupin. "That does sound like Thibodeaux. Describe the stick."

I struggled to remember, having paid no attention to that detail at the time. "It was wooden, I think, preserved by some kind of dark stain or varnish—dark brown, that is, not black. It was sturdy, and had a slightly curved handle set at an angle, not a pommel, so that it resembled an elongated lower-case letter 'r'."

"That's Thibodeaux's stick," Dupin confirmed. "He had arthritic ankles too—for him, a walking-stick was no mere affectation, but a necessity. What else?"

"There was something odd about his eyes, but I'm not sure exactly what...almost as if he were not the only one looking through them. He was watching the climax of the dance of the nuns when I first caught sight of him, but I don't know how long he had been there before I became aware of his presence. I might have missed the greater part of the apparition, in terms of its duration. When I did realize that he was there, he turned to look at me—or, more likely, at someone who was sitting in the chair where I was sitting—and he spoke."

"What did he say?"

"'Yesterday never dies, but such is the rhythm of time that one has to grasp its echoes on the wing'."

Dupin nodded his head. "Thibodeaux, without a doubt," he said. "His sentiment, his style. You did well, my friend— exceedingly well."

"With regard to the observation and reportage," I said, "I had a good teacher. With regard to the ability to see ghosts...that, I fear, might have been more a matter of infection."

He frowned. "Why do you say that?" Perhaps he had taken me literally, in view of the manner in which he had spent his evening.

"I never saw ghosts before I met you, Dupin," I said. "If consciousness is a refuge, as you're so fond of saying, I was secure within it until I became your friend. Now, it seems, I cannot go six months without some dread intrusion of my sense of reality. Once touched by the Crawling Chaos, it seems—even as a mere innocent bystander—one is tainted forever."

"I'm sorry," he said, again. This time, perhaps, he meant it.

"Don't be," I said. "It's a condition that requires company, if one is to endure it without going mad. Had you lost Madame Lacuzon tonight...but that's by the by. Who was the woman in the mask?"

"Not having seen her, I can't be sure," he said, scrupulously, "but given what she said to you, it was probably Marie Taglioni."

That name I recognized instantly, although I had never seen her dance. Marie Taglioni was, or had been, the most famous ballet dancer in the world: *La Sylphide* in person. She had retired now, though—to live as a recluse in Venice, if I was not mistaken as to what the newspapers had reported.

"No wonder Meyerbeer and Scribe dropped in to pay homage," I said. "But why was she there? Even if she did see the mysterious Thibodeaux's ghost, that can hardly have been the reason she came—and I cannot believe that she was eager to see a performance inferior to hundreds that she must have seen from the wings."

"Was it inferior?" Dupin could not help asking, even though he seemed to be impatient to be rid of me now that I had described the apparition in full. I had no intention of letting him get off so easily.

"Inferior to the previous one that I saw; I cannot speak for the one you saw in 1834, with Thibodeaux and Lucien Groix—who was also there tonight. Something strange happened that night, I assume."

"Slightly strange," Dupin admitted. "Strange enough to bring us all back, it seems—even poor Thibodeaux. Meyerbeer was there too you say?"

"And Scribe—not to mention the Comte de Saint-Germain."

"Saint-Germain! How on earth did he find out about it?"

"If by *it* you mean the ghost, I don't think he knew anything about that. I think he was there for quite a different reason, having obtained information from one of his spies—some street-urchin or member of the Society's menial staff—that Chapelain had gone to the theater, and barged into my box purely in order to look into his. I suspect that he was hoping to see Jana Valdemar, but she was absent until the interval, and he might not have seen her. Saint-Germain definitely knows that something is afoot now, though, because Groix came into the box while he was there, and although he gave nothing away, the mere fact of his extreme reticence put ideas into Saint-Germain's head. Now that his curiosity's aroused, he won't rest until he's figured it out."

Dupin shrugged. "He'll lose interest soon enough when he finds that there's no money to be made."

I wasn't sure that that was true, but I let it pass. "Groix seemed annoyed—more agitated that I have ever seen him before. I assumed at first that it was because we hadn't invited him to share the box. I would have let him, since you weren't there, but he went off in a huff. I think he might have watched from one of the upper galleries. Saint-Germain was up there too."

"I'm surprised that Lucien bothered, considering how busy he must be. In his situation, I think I'd be making preparations to flee to England or Italy, if and when it becomes politic. François Raspail doesn't want his blood, but there are plenty or Republican firebrands who do."

"Saint-German made the same observation. You've seen Raspail recently, then?"

"We met by chance last week and had a brief conversation over a glass of wine. We've known one another for a long time, as you know."

"And Groix knows that you've talked?"

"Obviously, since he's having Raspail followed—but I'm not in any danger of being named in Lucien's files or mistaken by Raspail himself as potential Revolutionary; they both know full well that I steer clear of politics...as clear as one can in times like these. Never mind that. Is that all?"

"No—Lucien wants you to go and see him tomorrow anyway, urgently."

Dupin frowned again. "If Amélie takes a turn for the worst...," he said, but then thought better of it. "But she'll be fine now," he added, presumably to boost his own morale. "She's asleep."

He seemed so confident of that that he did not turn round—but I could see past his shoulder by leaning slightly to the right, and I did so, reflexively.

"No, she's not," I said, taking that inference from the fact that her eyes were open—although I realized my mistake almost instantly.

Her eyes were open, but she was not awake, Indeed, it seemed to me that there might even have been a sense in which they were not her eyes, for the moment. Whoever or whatever appeared to using them was staring directly to me, and I had a strangely sickening sensation that it was not for the first time.

My own words echoed sardonically in the breached haven of my consciousness: *Once touched by the Crawling Chaos, it seems—even as a mere innocent bystander—one is tainted forever.*

When Thibodeaux's ghost had met my gaze, there had been something else therein. Now it seemed to be in Amélie Lacuzon's eyes: the eyes of the "old witch," who was, I suspected, a magnetizer as powerful as Chapelain or Saint-Germain, or perhaps a medium as powerful as Jana Valdemar.

Dupin had turned in response to my remark, and I assumed that he could see the open eyes as clearly as I could, but they still seemed to be staring at me. Automatically, he moved within the frame of the inner door so as to block my view—or perhaps to intercept the stare.

"Don't worry," he said, after a few seconds. "It's not uncommon for habitual somnambulists to open their eyes while they're asleep. I don't think she's actually going to try to move."

"I thought you preferred the term *somniloquist*," I said, feigning laconism.

"I prefer both terms to be used accurately," he said. "'Somnambulist' when someone moves in her sleep, 'somniloquist' when someone talks."

I didn't want to get into a pedantic discussion, although I could have argued that the concierge had not really moved, but only stared—ominously, it seemed to me.

By the time that Dupin had moved himself, however, sufficiently for me to obtain another glance at Madame Lacuzon's face, her eyes were closed again. She was, as Dupin had claimed, still asleep.

"It really would be best if you went home now, my friend,"

Dupin continued, "not just because of the threat of infection, assuming that whatever Amélie has *is* infectious, but because I'm very tired, although I mustn't go to sleep."

"But I've told you everything, and you haven't told me anything!" I protested. "Who is this Professor Thibodeaux? Why did you expect to see his ghost tonight? Why, come to that, did you go to the theater with him in 1834—and to see one of the 'devil operas' of which you're so scornful?"

Dupin was having none of it, though.

"I promise that I'll come to see you tomorrow, my friend," he assured me, "as soon as I'm sure that it's safe for me to leave Amélie alone—but probably not before noon. If anyone comes looking for me in the meantime, having failed to get any answer here, please make my apologies. When I see you, I'll gladly tell you everything—everything I know myself, that is—about Blaise Thibodeaux, the resonance of time, and why he once told me that he would do his very best to appear at the Opéra-Comique tonight, dead or alive."

I saw no point in raising further objections, in the circumstances, and gave in gracefully. "I'll tell Madame Bihan that her cousin is ill," I said. "I'm sure that she'll lend you all the assistance she can." Madame Bihan was my housekeeper, supplied on her cousin's recommendation.

"Thank you," Dupin said. "And I'm sorry, once again, for disappointing you this evening." I had never before heard him apologize three times in such a short span of time—and, even more remarkably, that was the second time that I actually believed his assertion.

I walked home without encountering any footpads, deep in thought—even though I had little real substance to fuel my ruminations.

I gave Madame Bihan the information about her cousin's illness, including Dupin's assertion that she seemed to be over the worst, and went to bed, hoping—in vain, as it turned out—that I would be able to sleep peacefully now that I had unburdened myself to Dupin.

CHAPTER FOUR: THE UNMASKED WOMAN

Perhaps I did sleep a little, but only fitfully, if so, and only between the hours of three and four o'clock, when my tiredness reached its inevitable extreme—a trough rather than a peak. By five, long before dawn, I was wide awake again, tossing and turning blearily. By the time I actually got out of bed at six-thirty, Madame Bihan had already set off to help Dupin care for her cousin, so it was her husband who made my breakfast.

That seemed an imposition and annoyance, so fractious was my mood, although I had insisted for some years after first renting the house that I did not need and would rather not have any servants, and would be perfectly capable of fending for myself, as a good American should.

The problem with servants, I thought, with Dupin's mysterious relationship with Madame Lacuzon in mind as well as my own trivial plight, *is that one falls into the habit of relying on them, and soon convinces oneself that one cannot possibly do without them.*

When I had restored my spirits with second-rate *pain-au-chocolat* and coffee, I went into the library—which always seemed more like a library than a smoking-room in the morning, when the air was still relatively fresh, at least until the first blasts of the winter wind forbade the opening of the windows. I did not intend to stay there—Bihan had lit the fire in the reception-room—but I wanted to search the books that Dupin stored there, his own meager quarters in the Rue Dunot no longer being able to accommodate his collection. I had a vague memory that I might have seen the name Thibodeaux there.

I had. Indeed, such was the reliability of my half-memory that I laid my hands on it almost immediately.

La Résonance du temps by Blaise Thibodeaux had been published by a perfectly respectable Parisian press; it was evidently not one of Dupin's fabulously rare "forbidden books." The copy was slightly battered, although it was only dated 1833, but that was because it had evidently been bought second-hand from one of the *bouquinistes* along the Seine. Thibodeaux had obviously not been such a close friend of Dupin's as to give him a complimentary copy—or perhaps he had been the kind of author who expects his friends to purchase brand new copies out of loyalty to his purse...a futile expectation in Dupin's case.

I carried the thick volume into the reception-room and sat down in my customary armchair on the side of the hearth next to the bay window, which was letting in a gray but nevertheless abundant light. The page count—well in excess of four hundred—and the small size of the typeface were hardly incentives to leisurely reading, but I assumed that the previous night's mystery would provide me with sufficient motive to keep turning the pages. Had the publisher been enthusiastic to offer the book to the public, I presumed, he would have set the text in two volumes, so the fact that it was uncomfortable crammed into one suggested that Thibodeaux had probably paid for it to be printed, and had been anxious to keep the cost down.

I had hardly opened the book when the doorbell rang. I closed it again and waited. Bihan, as usual, seemed to take so long to answer it that I began to wish that I had answered it myself.

Finally, the old man appeared on the threshold of the reception-room.

"There's a lady at the door, Monsieur, wearing a domino. She would not give me a card, but said that you would be willing to see her.

Marie Taglioni! I thought. *Marie Taglioni, here!* Given her curiosity outside the theater, however, I was not entirely surprised.

"Show her in," I said.

"Yes Monsieur. Madame Bihan will be out all day, Monsieur—may I go to the market in her stead?"

"Of course," I said, a trifle impatiently.

Bihan shuffled out, and shuffled back in again a minute late, escorting the lady in the domino. It was not Marie Taglioni. I reproached myself sternly for having jumped to the wrong conclusion, when I could just as easily have jumped to the right one.

She waited until Bihan had closed the door behind him before reaching up and taking off the hooded cape, mask and all.

Jana Valdemar was less than two years older than when I had seen her last, but she seemed to have aged at least five years. Oddly enough, maturity suited her—or would have done had she been entirely well. She did indeed seem a trifle indisposed, both physically and emotionally: pale, drawn, and a little sad. I knew one or two connoisseurs of art who considered that a touch of melancholy or consumption always added to a woman's charms rather than detracting from them, but I had never been of that opinion myself. She was still beautiful, but she no longer looked like a parody of a *femme fatale*; indeed, she seemed a trifle forlorn. She gave the impression that she might still have been able to play the *femme fatale* had she pulled herself together and made an effort, but at present she was not casting herself in such a role. Perhaps it was too early in the day. I guessed that she had slept even less than I had.

I reminded myself that she was a expert mesmerist, and that I might perhaps have cause to beware, especially given that she had planted a suggestion in my mind once before, which had not entirely ceased to plague my dreams even now.

"Mademoiselle Valdemar," I said, politely, trying to conceal my disappointment that she was not Marie Taglioni, although I did not doubt that she had taken note of my reaction. "Do sit down. How may I help you?"

She sat down. "Firstly," she said, "I wanted to thank you for pretending not to recognize me last night, and for warning me about Saint-Germain's presence in the auditorium. That was... chivalrous."

I was no longer in the theater, under the tyrannical rule of etiquette, but once a course has been taken, it is difficult to change tack.

"You're welcome," I said. "And secondly?"

"Secondly," she said, with a faint smile, "I was asked to come to see you by the...other lady in Dr. Chapelain's box."

I could not resist the temptation. "Madame Taglioni," I said.

"She is Madame in the theater," the younger woman said, refusing me any tacit reward of evident surprise for my powers of deduction, "but Mademoiselle in private life. Yes, Mademoiselle Taglioni asked me to come, to invite you to call on her today. She would like to see you again...and she is particularly keen to meet Monsieur Dupin." Her voice was slightly hesitant. I could imagine that the thought might make her apprehensive. I did not suppose that she was here by choice, but Marie Taglioni was presumably a woman used to giving out instructions, and having them obeyed, by her physicians and everyone else.

"I would be delighted," I said, "but I cannot speak for Monsieur Dupin. As you know, he was unable to get to the theater last night, although he dearly wanted to be there. I am not sure that he will be free today—certainly not this morning."

"The time is immaterial," Jana replied. "I would be very grateful if you could help me in this matter. Dr. Chapelain suggested that you might be willing to do so...in spite of our past history."

Since she had raised the subject, etiquette no longer forbade me to make any reference to it. "That's very kind of him, I'm sure," I said. "I have to admit, though, Mademoiselle Valdemar, that I'm not at all sure that you have any right to claim a favor from me, given what happened last time you introduced yourself into my house."

"I'm truly sorry about that," she, putting on a show of sincerity of which only an accomplished magnetizer—or, of course, a genuinely sincere person—would have been capable. "I have no excuse to offer for my behavior in that instance, and I take full responsibility for my actions. It is true that I had been under the sway of Monsieur Saint-Germain for some time—it was through him that I first made contact with Dr. Chapelain, as well as the Baron du Potet—but what I did when I tried to plant a suggestion in Monsieur Dupin's mind, and, as a corollary, in yours, was entirely my own idea. It was, I suppose, an aspect of my attempt to break free of Saint-Germain's influence. I wanted to go my own way; alas, I knew no other way to go, at the time, but to take a path parallel to his. I know better now."

Jana Valdemar had attempted, with the aid of one of her father's old acquaintances from New York, to establish herself as the sole possessor and dispenser of a fake elixir of life. Not content with recruiting the unwitting help of Honoré de Balzac, whose somewhat unfair reputation as a confirmed hypochondriac and insistent seeker of quack cures might have excited as much skepticism as credence, she had hatched a convoluted plan to involve Auguste Dupin, whose reputation as a hardheaded rationalist would have provided a much better advertisement. Her plan had, of course, misfired; Dupin had outsmarted her—and Saint-Germain, annoyed by his protégée's attempt to escape his control, had helped him turn the tables on her, somewhat to Dupin's annoyance.

So far as I knew, however, Saint-Germain had not been able to reassert his control, and Jana had fled from him. He had been searching for her ever since. Evidently, rumor had reached him that she was working with Chapelain again, and he had set someone to watch the physician's home. He must have gone to the Opéra-Comique last night expecting to find her there, probably intending to follow her to her present lodgings after the performance. Obviously, the much-vaunted seers of the Harmonic Society had been unable to locate her by less conventional means.

"What is it that you want me to do for you, exactly?" I asked.

"I would like you to smooth things over between Dr. Chapelain and Monsieur Dupin, if you can—but most of all, I would like you to persuade Monsieur Dupin to see Mademoiselle Taglioni, as soon as possible. She is very insistent. For what it may be worth, I believe that Monsieur Dupin will be very interested in what she has to say. There is a mystery involved."

"Which has something to do with the 1834 performance of *Robert le Diable* at the Comique, and Blaise Thibodeaux?" I queried.

"Of course," she said. She seemed to be on the point of saying something more, but did not. She was not sure whether it would be politic to raise the question of the ghost just yet. I thought that I ought to try to put her at her ease.

"I doubt that any 'smoothing over' will be necessary," I told her. "Chapelain and Dupin have always been on the best of terms, and I cannot imagine that Dupin will hold it against him that he's working with you again. He's not a man to bear grudges. As for Mademoiselle Taglioni, I'm certain that he will be interested in what she has to say, and that he will consider it a privilege to meet her, as soon as he is able to do so—my only reservation, I assure you, is that I cannot be sure when that will be."

She smiled, albeit wanly. "Thank you, Monsieur Reynolds," she said. "You really are very kind. Perhaps I should not have been intimidated by the thought of coming here, especially after what you said to me last night. After all, we do have something in common, do we not?"

"Do we?" I queried, genuinely puzzled.

"Yes," she said, trying unsuccessfully to maintain her smile. "On that night when Dupin beat me at my own game, you saw what I saw, didn't you? Dupin didn't see it, because he was watching me. Saint-Germain didn't see it, because he was outside, playing with the balloons that the two of them used as a trigger. Poor Falconer caught a glimpse of it, but immediately lost his head and shut his eyes, blasting away with that stupid pistol in the hope of keeping the Dweller with the Eyes of Fire at bay. But you didn't close your eyes. You saw what the trick with the balloons triggered, in all its awful glory, just as I did. You saw my phantom, my demon."

That seemed a roundabout way to introduce the topic of phantoms, but I was not unsympathetic to her desire for circumlocution. I felt, however, that I ought to correct her apparent misapprehension.

"I only saw it because you had put the suggestion in my mind," I observed.

She looked at me, but she looked away again almost immediately. She really did not seem trying to mesmerize me...either that, or she was playing an exceedingly subtle game. But why should she try to mesmerize me, given that I had agreed to help her, and had even shown myself to be "chivalrous" in her regard?

"That's not *entirely* true, Mr. Reynolds," she said, in a tone of conscientiously mild reproach. "Yes, I had planted the suggestion in your head while you were asleep, just as I had planted in Dupin's...and, of course, my own. But that suggestion only had the powerful effect that it did because it was reflected by something real. You have had experience enough by now, I think, to know how intricate the relationship is between suggestion and reality."

Chapelain had obviously told her something about our adventure with the *Cthulhu Encryption*. And why should he not? Dupin and I were not his patients, after all. I had thought that the greater part of the adventure had slipped Chapelain's mind, as extraordinary events often do flee into forgetfulness in the minds of all but a few extraordinary individuals—but I had no doubt, too, that he remembered it subconsciously, if not consciously, and that Jana Valdemar sometimes hypnotized him, just as he sometimes hypnotized her. The more intricate aspects of their relationship were not something I cared to think about too deeply.

"Does it really make a difference what I saw that night?" I asked, gruffly—although what was really on my mind was wondering what a difference my more recent ghost-sighting was going to make, when Dupin finally got around to explaining what was going on.

"It makes a difference to me," she said, softly. "You were the only witness to what *really* happened—the others have nothing but conjecture and inference on which to draw. I'm not asking for your sympathy, but I am asking for your understanding, and I really do believe that you're uniquely placed to understand."

She was still looking at me, without quite looking. She was not trying to hypnotize me—at least, so it seemed—but she was still trying to exert an influence upon me. And it was working; I really did feel that I wanted to understand, and to sympathize, even though I knew that Dupin might think me weak for doing so. I even wondered whether I ought to fight it, or at least attempt some sort of protest.

"Are you trying to seduce me, Mademoiselle Valdemar?" The words just slipped out. I probably blushed crimson.

She laughed, but rather bleakly. "What would be the point of that?" she asked. "Since Saint-Germain put that curse on you, you're one of the few men in the world that I would stand no chance of seducing, no matter what I did."

"What curse?" I said, utterly bewildered.

"The curse of *The Mad Trist*, of course. But that's not what concerns us now. My curse is a very different one, just as insidious, though not entirely without its advantages. Do you understand why I have been so determined not to let Saint-Germain find me, if I can avoid it?"

The turn that the conversation had taken was utterly unexpected. I tried to clear my thoughts and focus on the question she had asked.

"Yes, I think so," I said. She wasn't content with the mere affirmation. She wanted proof. "He was your first...partner," I continued. "You were presumably aware that you had medium-istic skills before you met him, but he was the one who helped to develop them. He forged a bond...a bond that, no matter how hard you try, you can't entirely break. You're avoiding him because you fear that he might be able to hypnotize you in spite of all your efforts to avoid it. You're afraid that he might be able to...take you under his influence again, even without your consent."

"What a delicate way you have of putting things, Mr. Reynolds," she said, with a slight sigh, attempting yet another faint smile, and not quite succeeding. "Yes, he was the first to magnetize me...and the first to rape me while I was magnetized. And even though he pimped me out thereafter to the Baron and Chapelain, in the hope of obtaining a kind of ascendancy over them, too, he retained the power of that violation. Yes, I fear that if he were able to hypnotize me again—and I do, indeed, fear that I might not be able to prevent him from doing so, by virtue of the residue of our former magnetic relationship—he would rape me again."

I was speechless.

"I've shocked you," she said. "But only by pronouncing the words, surely? You understood the situation, in spite of your circumlocutions. You know, do you not, that a person in a magnetic trance is a uniquely vulnerable position, all too easily manipulable? And you can see the logic of the situation in which the medium is a young woman and the mesmerist a man? Perhaps you think my use of the word 'rape' unjustified— and I dare say that others would agree with you and claim that nothing was or is ever done without consent—but do you really think that a medium in a trance is capable of consent?"

I was still virtually speechless, but I eventually managed to croak: "Chapelain...?"

"I have, as you can see, made an exception for Chapelain. With him, I am now...and perhaps always was, a willing... partner. Since it is a medium's vocation...well, suffice it to say that I have made my choice, and that I have every confidence that I can stick to it, resisting all temptation except one, if I am given the chance. Perhaps, if the circumstance arose, I could resist even that one...but I'm afraid, and certainly would not care to test the case yet. In time...but in time, of course, mediumistic abilities fade, as beauty fades. In five years, if things were to stay as they are, I might be solidly conjoined with Chapelain in alchemical marriage, if not in legal wedlock...but by then, I would be no further use to Saint-Germain, and he would not want me."

She sounded oddly desolate while making that speech—perhaps, I thought, because she could not think without a certain sadness about the prospect of Saint-Germain no longer wanting her, even though she did not want him to have her. She was rambling slightly, showing the effects of tiredness. I wished, belatedly, that I had offered to make a pot of tea—but the time had passed by now.

I felt that I could speak again, but I had no idea what to say. In the event, I did not have to improvise, because the doorbell rang.

"Who is it?" she asked, fearfully. Reflexively, she reached for her domino, although she could not have imagined that it would provide adequate protection against recognition by anyone she knew.

There was a certain angle through which I could look through the window and catch a glimpse of the person at the door, although it required a rather ungainly contortion. I looked.

"It's Saint-Germain," I told her.

I should have been amazed. Saint-Germain was not in the habit of calling on me, in spite of his insistence that we were friends, and I could not imagine why he should be doing so this morning.

"How does he know that I'm here?" she lamented.

"Perhaps he doesn't," I said. "Even if he does, I can send him away." I knew from past and recent experience, however, that Saint-Germain could be a difficult man to put off.

Jana Valdemar clutched at the straw, eagerly. "Perhaps he doesn't," she echoed. "Is there somewhere I might hide, until he's gone?"

"Upstairs," I said. "Bihan will come back eventually, but there's no reason for him to go up there, and even if he does, he won't give you away. You know the way, I believe."

She ignored the hint of sarcasm. "Thank you," she said, apparently sincerely. I didn't bother to point out, knowing that she could hardly miss the observation, that because the stairway had a one-hundred-and-eighty degree turn halfway up, she would be able to hear what Saint-Germain and I were saying if she were prepared to take the risk of sitting on the lowest step of the second half of the flight, out of sight behind the banisters.

I had no idea why I had abruptly entered into a tacit conspiracy with her, but I think it had far more to do with her mention of the word "rape" in connection with Saint-Germain than any shared experience in confrontation with the Dweller with the Eyes of Fire. In any case, had I not already taken her side, by warning her at the *Comique* that Saint-Germain was present?

I answered the door.

CHAPTER FIVE: THE ETHERIZED COMTE

Saint-Germain was past me in a trice, before I could even try to refuse him entry. He seemed more than usually agile. Indeed, as I followed him, he seemed positively jittery.

"Where's Dupin?" he demanded, on entering the empty reception-room. As he turned back to look at me, I was startled by the appearance of his eyes, which seemed unnaturally keen—not exactly diabolized, but nevertheless quite strange. They seemed a trifle crazed. He too, I decided, had not slept last night.

"Not here," I replied, testily.

"Then where is he, damn it? I banged on the dragon's door until my knuckles were raw, but the old witch wouldn't even answer me. Then I went up to Dupin's room regardless. It was locked, but he'd taken the key with him, so I peeped through the keyhole when my knock wasn't answered. He's not there. Don't tell me that he's gone to see Groix *already*!"

"I don't see that it's any of your business," I told him. "I really don't like the way that you keep barging in on me, and I'm certain that Dupin wouldn't like you going up to his room without permission from Madame Lacuzon, even if it is locked."

"This time," Saint-Germain stated, confidently, "he wouldn't object in the least. I have information for him—information he couldn't discover for himself, since he's so determined to cut his nose off to spite his face by refusing to join the Harmonic Society, thus depriving himself of access to its Archives. Indeed,

I've got more than information—I've got a mystery, and I've got the key to it. He can't resist a mystery; you know that as well as I do. He won't thank you for getting in the way, so tell me— where is he?" His speech had a strangely urgent quality, which was more than mere impatience; the words came out so rapidly that they were almost stumbling over one another.

He's drunk! I thought. Aloud, I simply said: "Why do you want to give him the information?"

"First of all, because he's the only man in Paris with intelligence enough to help me sort out what lies behind it, and secondly, because when I've told him what I have, wild horses won't stop him from going with me tonight to see whether anything comes of it. This stupid animosity of his has dragged on far too long. We ought to be friends, and I won't stop trying to make him see that until he realizes the fact. The Harmonic Society needs him—and he needs the Society, although he won't admit it."

"I can see why you think you need him," I said. "But it's no use—he's never going to help you in your money-grubbing schemes. It's completely contrary to his principles."

Saint-Germain stuck his Chinese bamboo cane in the umbrella-stand, perched his hat on top of it, took off his gloves and sat down—without being invited—in the armchair that Jana Valdemar had just deserted. He slumped back, and sighed, deeply and theatrically.

"It's not *about* that," he said. "You're missing the point completely—and you know as well as I do that his so-called principles are pure hypocrisy."

"I know no such thing!" I retorted, sharply.

"Oh, sit down," he said. "Since I can't find Dupin, I'll settle for you. Let's talk like two civilized human beings, and see if we can't settle these idiotic differences. I'll give you the information—the gist of it, at least—and let you decide whether you ought to pass it on to Dupin; but first, do you know why Dupin is so hostile toward me, when all I want to do is be friends with him? As fellow scholars, that is, not in pursuit of any money-making scheme."

I sat down, although it felt like conceding defeat. "I think the reason he has such an antipathy toward you." I said, trying to speak in a level fashion in the hope of sobering him up by example, "is that he believes that you're incapable of separating scholarship from money-making schemes. He's a *true* scholar."

"Oh yes," said Saint-Germain. He suddenly yawned, betraying his tiredness in spite of his agitation. The reflex seemed to take him by surprise too; he was too slow to cover his mouth, but he was quick to apologize: "Sorry, I've been up all night chasing tidbits of fact and legend. While I was excited at the prospect of communicating them to Dupin...but where were we? Oh yes. Dupin the true scholar: Dupin the true cynic, the follower of Diogenes, who believes that philosophers shouldn't seek worldly wealth. Very noble—but completely impractical. Even Diogenes couldn't live in a barrel for long. It's all very well scorning worldly wealth, but a man has to eat, and, if he lives in Paris and not in sunny Athens, to have some substitute for a roof over his head, and, if he lives nowadays and not in Diogenes' day, to pay for his books.

"Yes, it's true, the first time Dupin and I met, I tried to swindle him. In those days, I tried to swindle everyone. It was the way I made my living—but Dupin couldn't see the necessity, even of me living, let alone the swindling. Censorious prig. And now I have a nice town house, twice the size of yours and ten times the size of his little hovel in the Rue Dunot, with servants. I have a nice book collection of my own, as well as access to the Harmonic Society's Archives. I charge all kinds of people for various kinds of services, and I help myself to a proportion of the Society's funds in a fashion befitting its President—although, in fairness to myself, I ought to add that the Society's coffers have become considerably fuller since I became President. Dupin might call that swindling, but I don't...not any longer, anyway. I'm respectable now. It's business. More importantly, I'm a respectable scholar now, which is what I always wanted to be, which is what all the swindling was *for*."

"Good for you," I observed, dryly.

"Yes," he retorted. "It *is* good for me—and it could be good for Dupin too, if he weren't such a snob and a hypocrite. He looks down on me, but only because he knows, deep down, that he's no better. He takes such pride in not being a swindler or a beggar, but he still has to live, doesn't he? He still has to eat. And how does he do that? He sponges; he parasitizes—he parasitizes *you*, Monsieur Reynolds. He even came to live here for a while, didn't he, until he felt compelled to go back to his hovel, not because he was conscience-stricken, but because he couldn't bear to be separated any longer from his familiar spirit. How many times does he eat here every week, at your expense, Monsieur Reynolds? Have you ever seen him pay for so much as a cab fare?"

"He's my friend," I said, lamely.

"He's your friend!" Saint-Germain retorted. "Lucien Groix is his friend too—the other surviving victim of his parasitism. The Prefect of Police! Who would give him a position for the asking: Head of the Sûreté, if he wanted it; or, if that would be too much like getting his hands dirty, a position filing and cataloguing in the National Archives. But oh no—Auguste Dupin couldn't possibly get a *job*, because philosophers don't do *jobs*, because they're *true cynics* who need to maintain their asceticism and their independence. Except that it makes him *less* independent, not more, because it means that he has to rely on *you* to feed him and supply him with brandy, and accommodate his books, and pay his bloody *cab fares*!"

"Are you drunk, Saint-Germain?" I finally demanded, losing my patience.

He seemed surprised by the question. "I've been up all night working, and I had to keep myself awake," he told me, reproachfully. "I started out on black coffee, but halfway through the second cup I couldn't stand the taste anymore, so I started covering it up with cognac. That worked for a while, and then I switched to iced champagne. By first light, I needed a little extra, so I added a couple of drops of ether to the last glass—a trick one of the members taught me. Worked like a charm. I can keep going all day now that I'm past the dangerous hours—Thibodeaux was right about that, of course."

"I think you ought to make an effort to calm down," I told him.

"Don't be ridiculous. I'm perfectly calm. I'm making a sane and rational point. The point is that we all have to live—even people who've taken vows of poverty. It's all very well to decide not to take any active economic part in society, but that only leaves you dependent on the charity of others. It was the same for Diogenes, Buddha, Jesus, and Saint Rosalia. They were all too holier-than-thou to feed themselves, so somebody else had to do it. How else can you be a hermit, for God's sake?"

"Saint Rosalia?" I queried.

"Yes. Female hermit. Lived in a cave near Palermo. Probably not connected in any way with the Norman writer who borrowed her name, although she was Norman-descended, so they might have been distantly related. That's part of what I wanted to tell Dupin, if I'd been able to find him. The true story of Scribe's magic branch."

"Saint Rosalia has no business being mentioned in *Robert le Diable*," I told him, eager to prove my erudition. "Robert, Duke of Normandy, was dead before she was born. Different centuries."

His feverish eyes squinted at me. "You've been doing research too, haven't you? But I saw the opera too, and it's obviously set in a much later period than Robert the Great's, so the Robert in the play must really be some other Robert, even though people carelessly take the inference that he's supposed to be Robert the Great. Norman history is lousy with Roberts, even before you start adding in Hrolfs and Robins and Oberons and God only knows what—but all that's beside the point. Saint Rosalia is beside the point. What matters is Thibodeaux's legacy, and the timing of its employment."

When he mentioned the name Thibodeaux, my eyes automatically went to the book that was sitting on the arm of my chair. Striking like a viper, he took possession of it.

"Aha!" he said. "*La Résonance du temps!* We've got that too, although it was in the library rather than the cupboard—probably his own copy, deposited before he died. Would you believe that I'd never even heard of it until last night? I hadn't the slightest idea who Blaise Thibodeaux was, let alone that he'd been a member of the Society for thirty years. Doesn't that prove my point?"

"What point?" I asked, wondering whether I would be able to follow him better if I'd had a stiff brandy or a bottle of champagne to fuddle my head. I wasn't about to start sipping ether, though; according to Dupin, who had heard about the fad somehow, its stimulant effect was likely to be far too costly.

"The point that Dupin ought to join the Harmonic Society. We need to work together, to pool what we know. All the great loners who made fabulous discoveries in secret have been an almost total loss to humankind, because the greater part of their knowledge died with them—even if they wrote a prefatory book, like Thibodeaux. And don't try to tell me that their secrecy was purely a response to the threat of persecution by the Church. Of course that was a factor—a key factor—but that's why there have always been societies like ours, all the way back to the Pythagoreans. Yes, they were secret—they had to be, because of the danger of persecution—but at least they provided scope for passing dangerous knowledge on, for handing it down, for preserving it from extinction. I'll grant you, too, that they provided a golden opportunity for charlatans and poseurs—all the genuine societies have been polluted, and there are imitations that are fake from top to bottom—but even so, they've created the possibility of preservation and collaboration, and the loners who won't join in are refusing that possibility along with the charlatanry. It's too high a price to pay.

"Anyhow, the point is that Dupin should be working with us, not sitting on his high horse disapproving of us. There really are things that we know, and countless things buried in our Archives that we don't even know that we know, until we start digging. I can prove it to him, if he'll only consent to listen...and he will. He probably doesn't even know that we've got Blaise Thibodeaux's papers, given that he wasn't a member even before I came on the scene. They can't have been that close, given that this appears to be a used copy picked up on the bank of the Seine. Do you suppose that even Dupin has managed to read the damn thing? I have to admit that I've barely glanced at it myself, being too busy with the papers, but I saw enough to put me off trying to plow through it. I skipped all the statistics in the papers, of course. Couldn't stand all those numbers—they were making my head spin. Dangerous hours, eh? But I expect that Dupin has read it all, including the statistics—and he's probably the only man in the world who has. If I were a betting man, I'd wager that Dupin was actually *there* that night, back in 1834, along with Thibodeaux. Do you know who composed the music, by the way?"

Again, I was taken by surprise by the seemingly-arbitrary shifts in his drug-addled train of thought, in which I was difficulty seeing the underlying pattern. Automatically, however, I reacted to the specific question. "Meyerbeer," I said, reflexively.

"No, idiot," he said. "I mean the variant piece—the extended section replacing his version of the dance of the nuns. One of the members suggested Wagner, while I happened to hear the earlier argument, another Erich Zann, although Anton smiled at them both. Couldn't blame him—a naughty nuns' ballet is hardly Wagner's style, and Zann was dead by then...although rumor has it that his music didn't die with him, even though he was a loner...another one to prove my point. We can, I think, discard the possibility that it was the Devil himself, despite the rich legendry of the Devil's compositions. You and I and Thibodeaux all know—or *knew*, in Thibodeaux's case—that the Church's Devil is just a fig-leaf concealing the real forces working behind the scenes...behind Robert the Devil, Robin, or Oberon, if he wasn't just a figment of Thibodeaux's fascination with the self-signed Rosalia's house of women...I mean the Robert the Devil of legend, of course, not one in the opera, although it's the opera that features the magic branch. Am I making sense?"

"No," I told him, bluntly. It was the second time he'd mentioned an Oberon, and I wondered of he might mean Oberon Breisz, in pursuit of whom we'd made our odyssey to Brittany the previous year, but decided that he couldn't possibly, given the entirely different context.

"Sorry. Have to make sense, won't I, if I'm to get anywhere with Dupin—especially if you have to explain it for me. Where should I start? 1834? Thibodeaux's obsession? Rosalia of Palermo? No—the beginning. Always start at the beginning. Where was the beginning? The Pythagoreans, I suppose. You know about the Pythagoreans?"

"Of course," I said.

"You think you do. What do you know?"

"They're the ultimate precursors of both science and mysticism. Based on the observation that resonances between musical notes can be produced by strings of particular lengths that have a fixed numerical relationship to one another, they concluded that numbers were the key to understanding the universe, thus laying the foundations for mathematics and quantitative analysis. They also had theories of metempsychosis and the like, which linked them, via the neo-Pythagoreans and neo-Platonists, to Gnosticism and the entire tradition of occultism."

"Right. All true, but you're committing the typical modern error of putting the emphasis in the wrong place. The Pythagoreans' fascination with numbers never distracted them from the significance of the original phenomenon."

"Resonance," I said. It wasn't a difficult deduction, given the title of Thibodeaux's book.

"Exactly. The foundation, not merely of mathematical and physical phenomena, but of psychic and historical phenomena too. Reproduction at a distance by means of waves—sound waves in the context of musical harmony. But there are many other kinds of waves, as physicists are now beginning to realize: the light waves whose refraction causes mirages; the magnetic waves that induce electric currents; the waves of animal magnetism that produce and sometime confuse mesmeric phenomena; and—if Thibodeaux can be believed—temporal waves. Cycles, at any rate: daily, monthly, yearly—or horary, lunar, and calendrical, if you prefer Thibodeaux's jargon. And threes, sevens, and thirteens—dangerous numbers. Cycles that can reproduce images and other phenomena after an interval of time...provided that you have a string to pick up the wave as well as one to send it. Incredibly complicated—the man was obsessive, as I think I said; didn't know how to leave anything out. Anyway, to put it simply, things recur in time, more or less obviously in terms of days and years, not so obviously over longer periods. But they do recur, like distant echoes, under the right conditions."

"The apparitions of ghosts, you mean?" I suggested.

"That's one example," he agreed. "But ghosts are primarily visual phenomena, and what we're primarily concerned with in this instance is something more complicated, and more peculiar. The legend relates the magic branch of the opera to *in*visibility—except, of course, that Scribe got his information secondhand, and probably couldn't begin understand the account from which he borrowed that element, any more than he could understand the legend of Robert the Devil, and he had to put his own oar in to confuse things even further, as literary men always do. Anyway, the branch—which really is a branch, of sorts—is supposed to function like some kind of tuning fork, if I'm interpreting the situation correctly...although I'd really like to consult Dupin about that. It's not in Palermo, of course, and never was...."

I interrupted him. "You're getting ahead of yourself again," I pointed out.

"True," he admitted. "Mustn't forget the Vikings, must we? You know, of course, that the so-called Robert who was the founder of Normandy—not the one that Scribe was probably thinking of, but the first one—was actually called Hrolf, and that he was a Norseman who had been kicked out of Norway for practicing diabolism...and eventually became Christian in name, although he never really gave up the Old Religion?"

"I know that," I told him. "The word Norman is a contraction of Norseman, of course. The Norsemen ran riot throughout Europe for centuries, and the Normans continued the tradition. Robert's son—the son of Robert the Great, that is, not your Hrolf—went on to be William the Conqueror of England. Another, Robert Guiscard, captured various lands in Italy; his brother Roger was King of Sicily. There were other Roberts too, I think—at least one was involved in the crusades. And there were Richards too—later reprintings of the original *Robert le Diable* often juxtapose it with the legend of *Richard sans peur*, who was supposedly Robert the Great's son. The Italian branch of Hrolf's descendants led to the Palermo connection, and hence to Saint Rosalia...."

"My God, how you go on!" he said, with a theatrical groan—which seemed to me to be a blatant case of the pot calling the kettle black. "I give in—you know your history, even if it's mostly the wrong history. Forget the Rogers and the Richards and concentrate on the Roberts, Hrolfs, Robins, and Oberons. But we're really only concerned with Hrolf as the raider who ran riot up and down the Seine when he couldn't capture Paris in 911, and thus qualified himself for a bit part in more than one eccentric Norman romance. Thibodeaux, you see, searched the Archives and the Library long before I did, and much more assiduously, and he not only found the romance...."

He was only just warming up, and I was only just beginning to see the ghost of a connecting thread in his rambling. In the tapestry of myth and history that he was beginning to weave, patchwork-fashion, matters seemed finally to be on the brink of becoming interesting—and then the doorbell rang, again.

"Is that Dupin?" asked Saint-Germain eagerly.

Swallowing my dignity, I performed the necessary contortion.

"No," I replied. "It's Lucien Groix."

"Damn the man!" said Saint-German, angrily. "What does *he* want?"

"The same as you, I imagine," I said, dryly. "He's looking for Dupin."

CHAPTER SIX:
ALL HALLOWS

As I went to answer the door, I heard Saint-German muttering to himself, in a fashion that a man unaware of the fact that he had been up all night and had finished up sipping ether would have taken for clear evidence of insanity: "Always popping up where he's not wanted. Just because Lamartine's a member. I've told him we're above politics...."

It was news to me that Alphonse de Lamartine was a member of the Harmonic Society—but given that it was supposedly a secret society, there was no reason I should have known, and every reason why Saint-Germain should not have let it slip....

I opened the door. Like Saint-Germain, the Prefect did not wait for an invitation to come in. He barged passed me. Everyone seemed to be barging that morning—except, I conscientiously remembered, Jana Valdemar, who had been reasonably polite, except for the trick of having failed to send a card in, perhaps knowing that I would take the wrong inference from Bihan's observation that she was wearing a domino. On the whole, though, I preferred feminine wiliness to masculine coarseness. I had never been a typical American, even before I allowed Paris to civilize me properly.

Like the President of the Harmonic Society before him, the Prefect of Police strode straight into the reception-room—and stopped dead, reflexively raising his black-lacquered cane as if it were a sword, although he did not go so far as to put himself *en garde*.

"Oh, this is too much!" he said. "What in God's name is this clown doing here?"

"Looking for Dupin," I supplied, mildly.

"Don't tell me," said Saint-Germain, putting his hand to his forehead, theatrically, parodying occult concentration. "You've just come from the Rue Dunot, where you banged on the old dragon's door until your knuckles were raw, without getting an answer. Then you sneaked in anyway and went up to Dupin's room—but when you looked through the keyhole, you found that he wasn't in. Then...."

"Oh, shut up!" said the Prefect. I presumed that he had not been sipping ether, but he certainly gave every appearance of having been up all night, and having cultivated an exceedingly bad temper as a result. He controlled it, though, and turned back to me. "I'm sorry to intrude," he said, "but I really need to see Dupin."

"It's no trouble," I assured him, although the welter of confusion was driving me to sarcasm. "This is All Hallows, after all." It was such a weak pun that he probably wouldn't have seen it even if the English "Hallo" and "Hallow" hadn't been unfamiliar to him; to him, November the first was Toussaint.

He frowned, but he had no intention of being distracted. Saint-Germain, however, couldn't resist the temptation. "It's an English term," he put in, helpfully. "No one's quite sure when the day of the dead is actually supposed to fall, you see. The Irish and Scots think it was yesterday—All Hallows' Eve or Hallowe'en—but much of southern Europe thinks it's tomorrow—All Souls' Day in the sanitized calendar. Nobody's sure which of the three days actually corresponds to the old Celtic and Teutonic Samhain, where the idea of a recurrent day when the dead are permitted to return to Earth actually originated, but everyone knows that the Romans got it wrong by celebrating their Lemuria in May. Thibodeaux, of course, knew that it was a slightly movable feast—the day of the dead, that is—because the resonance has to be actively *produced*...."

Groix's face had been a veritable picture of splenetic annoyance until Saint-German pronounced the magic word—which was, of course, "Thibodeaux."

"What do *you* know about Thibodeaux?" he snapped, suddenly interested.

"Everything," said Saint-Germain, confidently—and took an obvious fiendish delight in adding: "But I can't tell *you*, because you're not a member of the Society, and I'm sworn to protect the secrecy of the Archives from infidels."

I suspect that Groix actually contemplated summoning a couple of agents, and having Saint-Germain arrested—and that the reason he didn't had more to do with the fact that he had left his usual bodyguard behind, the object of his visit being a personal matter, than any fear of making more enemies than he had already. Once again, he controlled himself, and returned to the real purpose of his visit, turning back to me.

"When will Dupin be back?" he demanded

"I'm afraid that I don't know, exactly," I said. "I did pass on your message, but he said that he won't be able to come to see you until this afternoon."

"*What!*" The exclamation came from Saint-Germain, not the Prefect. "You've *seen* him! So you *do* know where he is."

"As it happens, I do," I admitted, "But I'm not at liberty to say. All I can tell you is that he hopes to be free this afternoon. I'm certain that he'll answer your request then, Monsieur Groix—and for what it may be worth, given what you've just told me, Monsieur Saint-Germain, I believe that he'll be willing to speak to you too."

"What has he just told you?" Groix demanded.

"*He*'s not at liberty to tell you that either," Saint-Germain put in. "Not that it ought to interest you, at present, given that you have so many other things to occupy your time. Louis Blanc and Ledru-Rollin are outside your jurisdiction, I suppose, and Louis-Napoléon Bonaparte's nowhere to be found, as usual, but you could surely go and harass Raspail, or even Victor Hugo. It's not as if there were any shortage of would-be Revolutionaries in Paris at present."

"Shut up, damn it!" said Groix, even more intemperately than before. "This has nothing to do with Republican agitation—but I need to see Monsieur Dupin, urgently. If you can get a message to him, please do so, Mr. Reynolds. If not, tell him as soon as he makes contact with you."

"May I tell him what it's about?" I asked.

Groix looked at Saint-Germain and hesitated. His impatience got the better of him, though, and he replied: "Blaise Thibodeaux and the Unknown Woman of the Seine. He'll understand, I think."

I saw Saint-Germain's eyes widen, but he managed to hold his tongue for once. I had less reason to be surprised than he had by the reference to Thibodeaux, because I knew—as Saint-Germain presumably did not—that Lucien Groix had also been present at the mysterious performance of *Robert le Diable* at the Opéra-Comique on All Hallows' Eve 1834, but I could not imagine for the life of me what the notorious Unknown Woman of the Seine had to do with it.

"The Unknown Woman of the Seine," was a stock phrase used in the newspapers to describe female bodies fished out of the river—that being the most popular form of suicide among young Parisiennes, especially victims of inconvenient pregnancy—while identification was sought. The absence of suicide notes in such cases often made identification difficult, and there were usually half a dozen victims a year who never were identified. They, alas, were less than ten percent of the annual total.

It had already occurred to me that Lucien Groix might not have had the same reason as Dupin for wanting to attend the anniversary performance, even if he had been given a reason by the same man: Blaise Thibodeaux. I would have liked to ask him about that, but he was in no mood to hang around, now that he had seen Saint-Germain.

"I'll be in my study at the Prefecture," he stated, jamming his hat back on his head and making for the door. "Tell Dupin."

He was not to get away that easily. "I'll walk with you!" shouted Saint-Germain, bounding to his feet. "I'm going that way myself—and I might be able to tell you a *little* of what I know about Thibodeaux, provided that there's a *quid pro quo*. After all, we really shouldn't be enemies, you and I."

The Prefect of Police looked at the President of the Harmonic Society as if he were some kind of loathsome and poisonous insect, but he did not lash out with his boot or his walking-stick—or, for that matter, his tongue.

"I can't stop you," he muttered. I strongly suspected that what he really meant was that he would be grateful for any enlightenment that Saint-Germain might be able to give him about Thibodeaux and the Unknown Woman of the Seine.

I also strongly suspected that Saint-Germain would probably withhold anything he knew about that subject—if, in fact, he really knew anything at all—unless and until Lucien Groix explained why he was interested in such an esoteric subject at such a troubled time. And, to complete the set of three, I strongly suspected that there was only one man in the world to whom Groix would confide *that* information.

I consoled myself with the thought that Dupin would surely be able to listen to both of them soon enough, and that if anyone could make sense of the vast farrago of seeming nonsense, he was the man to do it.

"All Hallows," I muttered, as I watched them go off together, Groix trying halfheartedly to increase the distance between them and Saint-Germain scrupulously trying to reduce it, "but no saints."

Groix's black cane and Saint-Germain's bamboo now seemed to be performing an intricate dance, rather than threatening one another, as the two men walked in the direction of the Boulevard. I watched until they turned the corner, and then closed the door and went back to my armchair.

At least Saint-Germain had not walked off with Dupin's copy of Thibodeaux's book. I picked it up and sat down, but did not open it. There was no point. I was not alone yet.

Twenty seconds later Jana Valdemar came back in and resumed her seat, which was doubtless still warm from Saint-

Germain's slightly overheated presence.

"Thank you," she said. "I've never heard him go on like that before. I was under the impression that ether causes unconsciousness."

"Inhaled, it does," I said. I was not surprised that she knew something about the newly-discovered effects of ether, given that she was working with Chapelain, who had an intense interest in the physiology of mind-altering substances and in anesthesia. "Imbibed, however—just one or two drops in a glass of wine—it has a very different effect. It's an exceedingly dangerous stimulant, though. Do you have any idea what Saint-Germain was talking about?"

"Some of it," she said. "The rest, I think, might be very interesting—but he will tell Monsieur Dupin, who will surely be able to put the pieces together, if he consents to hear what Mademoiselle Taglioni has to say."

"Marie Taglioni was at the performance on All Hallows' Eve 1834 as well, wasn't she?" I said. "In fact, since she met Dupin in the Green Room, she must have been *in* it—dancing the lead in the nuns' ballet, I presume: the part she had played in the original 1831 performance."

Mademoiselle Valdemar hesitated, but presumably decided that there was nothing in the facts I had quoted that could possibly count as a violation of patient confidentiality, especially in view of the fact that she was here on Marie Taglioni's behalf. "Yes," she said.

"And that was why she was there last night," I said, not lending it the intonation of a question. "Just as Lucien Groix was, and Dupin wanted to be—all three of them because of something Blaise Thibodeaux told them. Except that he didn't tell them all the same thing. They were all on the lookout for something different. Dupin missed his ghost, but I saw it. What Groix was expecting, and whether he saw anything, I don't know. Mademoiselle Taglioni seems to have seen the ghost as well, and perhaps even recognized him—but it wasn't want she went there expecting or dreading to see, was it? The resonance of time is a trifle mercurial, it seems, in the rewards that it offers."

"Chapelain has a copy of Thibodeaux's book too," Jana said, seemingly filling in time while she pondered what Saint-Germain had said, trying hard to sort it out, "although he didn't manage to read it all the way through. According to Thibodeaux, as Saint-Germain said, the resonance is by no means purely mechanical. It has to be produced, and sometimes has to be amplified and augmented. The dating can't be exact, not just because the calendar doesn't have an exact number of days in it, but because the critical moment isn't a point, but a period of time. Toussaint—All Hallows, in your parlance—is only the mid-point. Hallowe'en and All Souls' are both part of...whatever you want to call it. Samhain, the day of the dead...the interval propitious for ancient things to return, if they have the will and the right assistance...."

"I'm sorry," I said, "but I'm not following you."

"You'd better try to read the book yourself," she said. "It's not easy, but you can probably pick up the gist. I expect that when Chapelain and Mademoiselle Taglioni have confided in Dupin, it will all become clearer. At least, I hope so. But what did you see, exactly? All I saw was someone in your box, who came in and went out during the dance of the nuns. I didn't know that Mademoiselle Taglioni thought it was a ghost until she stopped to talk to you after the performance, and even then, I wasn't sure—until you confirmed it just now."

I, of course, was not bound by any duty of confidentiality, nor did I have Saint-Germain's penchant for teasing. Even so, I was reluctant to disclose the details that particular fact to anyone but Dupin. I hadn't said a word to my other visitors, and I could see no reason to make an exception for Jana Valdemar, although I'd already let the crucial word slip out.

She persisted in the face of my hesitation. "You saw a ghost, you said?" she prompted. "What kind of ghost?" As a medium, she was presumably familiar with several kinds.

I didn't want to issue a dishonest denial. After a further

moment of hesitation, I caved in. "Yes, I did see a ghost," I confirmed. "As to what kind...I don't know how to classify it."

"It was definitely a man, though—not a woman?" she asked.

Given that she had seen it, however obliquely, she ought to have been certain of that. I was interested to note that that she wasn't. "It was definitely the apparition of a man," I confirmed. "I never met him, but I have every reason to believe that it was the ghost of Blaise Thibodeaux. Except that...."

"Except?" she prompted, when the pause had dragged on for three or four seconds.

"There was something in his eyes...."

"Oh!" she said—but did not elaborate. After a brief pause she added: "I wish that I could tell you more, Mr. Reynolds—but you'll hear it. I'm sure, directly from Mademoiselle Taglioni, when Dupin can arrange to meet her. He *will* be back this afternoon, will he not?"

"I believe so," I said, wishing that I could be more certain myself. "I have every reason to expect...."

This time, I did not leave the sentence incomplete on purpose. I was interrupted by the banging of the front door. It was not like Bihan to make such a racket, but I deduced that he must have his hands full with the purchases from the market.

For once, though, my well-educated deductive skills had failed me. It was not Bihan; it was Auguste Dupin, who very rarely bothered to knock—and had no reason to do so, given the number of times I had urged him to treat the house as his own.

He came in, moved by a spirit of urgency considerably more dignified than Saint-Germain's or the Prefect's—but he suppressed his eagerness instantly on catching sight of Jana Valdemar. Unlike Groix, he did not raise his stick as if it were a sword, but he planted its tip solidly on the floor, as if marking a barrier.

"I'm sorry, my friend," he murmured. "I had not realized that you had a visitor, or I would have rung the bell." He bowed to the medium, but very stiffly and without greeting her by name. Then he put the cane in the umbrella stand, and carefully removed his hat and gloves.

"You just missed the Prefect," I said getting up to greet him formally. "He's still very anxious to see you—about Thibodeaux and the Unknown Woman of the Seine, he said. He said you'd understand."

Dupin frowned, and suppressed any comment he might otherwise have made. He sat down, in the armchair that I always thought of as his own. "I'm terribly sorry, old friend," he said, "but you couldn't possibly supply me with a buttered croissant and a cup of chocolate, could you? I've been up all night, as you know, and haven't had an opportunity to get breakfast." The strain of his nursing effort did seem to have taken a toll on him; had I not known the circumstances, I would have been quite alarmed by his apparent distress, although he was doing his best to maintain his customary poise.

"Certainly," I said.

The request gave me the opportunity to ask, belatedly, whether I could get anything for Mademoiselle Valdemar, but she declined. She had other things on her mind than breakfast or beverages. "You just missed the Comte de Saint-Germain, too," she told Dupin, as I drew away.

I cocked my ears as I made the necessary preparations in the kitchen, eager not to miss a word. "He's just as eager to see you as Monsieur Groix," the young woman continued, "and I'm here myself on behalf of Mademoiselle Taglioni, who asked me to request that you call on her at Dr. Chapelain's house, as soon as you're free."

"Indeed?" said Dupin. "That would be a privilege—but I'm not quite at my best right now, and with all these competing requests...Saint-Germain was here, you say?"

"He appears to have access to Professor Thibodeaux's papers, held in the Harmonic Society's Archives. He says that he has a mystery, and the key to it."

"He told you that, did he?" Dupin queried. He was obviously exceedingly tired, but I didn't doubt that his mind was still sharp.

"He told Monsieur Reynolds," the medium admitted. "I was hiding on the stairs. I didn't want the Comte to see me—but I found what he was saying very interesting. He mentioned Robert the Devil, an eccentric Norman Romance, and an object corresponding to the opera's magic branch. He might have been about to connect them all up, but he was interrupted by Monsieur Groix's arrival. I've forgiven you, by the way, Monsieur Dupin, for nearly striking me dead. I issued a challenge; you met it. It was only fair."

After a brief pause for thought, Dupin seized the covert inference. "But you have not forgiven Saint-Germain?" he said.

"No," she said. "You answered a challenge; he betrayed me. Even if I had no other grievances against him, I could never forgive him that. Why the Unknown Woman of the Seine? I can understand the Prefect's citation of Thibodeaux, in the circumstances, but not that."

Dupin was not a man to be caught off guard by tactics of that sort. "I can't be sure," he said evasively.

She tried a different tack. "Saint-Germain obviously saw something at the opera last night that sent him scurrying off to research the legend of Robert the Devil—that's what led *him* to Thibodeaux. But you knew him—and so did the Prefect. The Prefect was there *because* of him."

"Thibodeaux and I were acquainted," Dupin admitted. "Lucien knew him better that did, and so did Francois Raspail. Raspail put him on to me, I think, although there really wasn't much help I could offer him—which is why our acquaintance remained slight, until he invited me to the theater to see *Robert le Diable*. I was reluctant, but he insisted. Until then, I hadn't bothered to read his book...in fact, I didn't actually get around to it until after his death, and even then...."

"You didn't manage to finish it."

"No," Dupin admitted. "I confess that I wouldn't even have bothered to buy the second volume, if he'd ever managed to complete it...although I might have dipped into it if a copy had come my way, in order to read what more he had to say about

Robert the Devil."

"The play or the legend?"

"Either—both."

She contrived a laugh. "It's a silly legend, isn't it?" she said—a trifle coquettishly, to judge by the tone of her voice—"and an even sillier opera. Except, perhaps, for the nuns' ballet. Have you seen both versions, or only the one that was tried, and failed so spectacularly, in 1834?"

"Only the 1834 performance," Dupin confirmed. "But you must have been a mere child then, Mademoiselle. If you've seen the opera, it must have been much more recently than that."

"Indeed," she agreed. "But it *is* silly, is it not? The episode of the magic branch most of all. The idea of the nuns buried in a convent rising from their graves and dancing in remembrance of a past of vile debauchery? Scurrilous anti-clerical gibes aside, nuns are essentially virtuous women, wouldn't you agree, Monsieur Dupin?"

I came back in with the tray then, containing a generous cup of chocolate, two croissants, with cheese as well as butter, and a glass of brandy. "It's neat, I'm afraid," I said, referring to the brandy. "I have none of Raspail's Elixir to hand." Although marketed as a hygienic compound, for its antiseptic properties, he and I both knew that Raspail's Elixir was fourth-fifths brandy—but he did not seem to appreciate the joke.

"Thank you," he said, stiffly. While he began buttering the croissants, slowly and methodically, he redirected his attention to the young woman.

"I have no insult to level against the virtue of nuns," he said, speaking slowly, as if it required an unaccustomed effort to keep his voice steady and his train of thought orderly. "Indeed, I think very highly of their devotion to various charitable duties, especially caring for the sick, in which capacity they probably do more good than most physicians. One of the things I admire most about them is their spirit of forgiveness. They do not hold a person's past against them, but only her future. For that reason, I suspect that nunneries have always been, as they sometimes are today, the only possible refuge for prostitutes who are to longer able, for reasons of health or conscience, to continue in their profession. The idea that nuns might be familiar with debauchery is therefore not absurd. I suspect, however, that such women would not look back on that debauchery with any fondness, and might well have less difficulty with vows of future chastity than sisters who have not had their experience—so I agree that it is highly unlikely that an entire company of dead nuns would remember a history of enthusiastic erotic indulgence. In that regard, the version of the opera that I saw in 1834 was, indeed, a travesty—and would have been, even had so many things not gone wrong during the performance. I have not had the opportunity to compare that version with the original; I was compelled to miss last night's performance by factors beyond my control."

Jana Valdemar had doubtless read a subtext in Dupin's remarks about forgiveness, just as I had, but she made no allusion to it.

"I missed the first two acts myself, because of a slight indisposition," she said, "but I doubt that you would have found it any less silly. Do you think, then, that the existence of nunneries has cut down significantly on the number of dead women fished out of the Seine?"

"Perhaps," Dupin answered. "My understanding is, however that when sympathy is invited for the Unknown Woman of the Seine, by newspapers, poets, or novelists, it is because she has supposedly preferred suicide to entry into a career of prostitution, having run out of other options by conceiving an unwelcome child, whose eventual birth would mark her, in the eyes of the world, as a harlot fit for nothing else."

Dupin was eating the laboriously-buttered croissant now, but he was still doing everything slowly and methodically, even though he must have been hungry. He appeared to be treading very warily indeed in the conversation, but that might well have been an effect of the exhaustion that he was trying so hard to master—or, at least, to hide.

Mademoiselle Valdemar was evidently aware of that too, and

decided to come to the point without further procrastination.

"As I said, Monsieur Dupin, I came here to invite Monsieur Reynolds and yourself to visit Mademoiselle Taglioni. Will you be able to do that? Today, if possible?"

Dupin nodded his head vaguely. "I will certainly try," he said, "but I really ought to see Lucien Groix first; we are old friends, and he is entitled to my first consideration when I am faced with multiple requests. I must go to the Prefecture as soon as I can, and cannot tell how long I shall be there. I would not like to keep Mademoiselle Taglioni waiting in expectation of an afternoon visit that might be delayed, so perhaps it would be best to make a firm appointment at Dr. Chapelain's consulting-room this evening? Would six o'clock be convenient?"

"Perfectly," she agreed. She stood up. "Shall I see you then, Mr. Reynolds?" she said to me.

"I wouldn't miss it for the world," I assured her.

She collected her domino without further ado, bade both of us a formal farewell, and left.

CHAPTER SEVEN: THE RESONANCE OF TIME

Bihan arrived back just as I was about to close the front door, with shopping-baskets suspended from each of his arms, as anticipated. I stood aside to let him pass, and then went back into the reception-room. I paused before sitting down to study Dupin. He had relaxed slightly now that Jana Valdemar had gone, and seemed to have slumped in his chair. He was still chewing slowly and sipping his chocolate very moderately indeed. I had known him stay awake all night many times, and had never seen him as depleted by the experience as he was now. Obviously, the strain of his anxiety for Madame Lacuzon had taken a great deal out of him—unless he, too, was falling sick.

I could not help wondering whether he might already have caught what it was that had afflicted Amélie Lacuzon, and that all his precautions following Raspail's hygienic prescriptions might have been a matter of closing the door after the parasite had already wormed its way in. I wondered whether he would be able to keep his appointments with Chapelain, Marie Taglioni, and Jana Valdemar.

"How is Madame Lacuzon?" I asked, mildly, once I had taken my seat again.

"She'll live," Dupin said, but felt forced to add, in a slightly dispirited voice: "This time."

"She's very old, I imagine."

"Yes, she is, alas. I used to think of her as invulnerable, but no one is, in reality."

"I'm sorry that you missed all the excitement—and I'm sorry, too, that you found Jana Valdemar here. I felt that I ought to hear what she had to say, though."

"I haven't missed *all* the excitement, it seems," he observed, but was quick to add: "And there's no need to apologize about Mademoiselle Valdemar. She has forgiven me, she says—although I'm not entirely sure that I had any need of forgiveness—and I am prepared to let bygones be bygones, if she is helping Chapelain in his good work. Better that than remaining under Saint-Germain's sway."

"He seems equally desperate for you to forgive him—he claims to be a reformed character, although it was difficult to believe him while he was drunk on coffee, brandy, champagne, and ether."

"Ether! The poor fool! He'll kill himself."

"Would that be such a bad thing?" I asked, curiously.

Dupin looked at me sharply. "I don't like the man," he said, "but that's not the same as wishing him dead. When he came to me for help, in fear for his life, I didn't refuse him, did I?"

"No," I admitted. "He'll catch up with you soon enough, I don't doubt. He's been working all night, it seems, ferreting out information from the Society's archives. He started delving into the legend of Robert the Devil, and that somehow led him to Thibodeaux. You knew that Thibodeaux was a member of the Harmonic Society, I assume?"

"It never came up in conversation, but it would not have surprised me in the least, given his fascinations. Although he qualified as a schoolteacher in his youth, and still sometimes used the title of Professor, he came into some money in his early thirties, and devoted his entire life thereafter to the dogged pursuit of his chimeras—exactly the kind of amateur that the Harmonic Society attracted in those days. He already knew the Marquis of Puséygur, and his fascination with resonance would immediately have struck a chord with many of the Society's stalwarts."

The pun, I assumed, was unintended. "But not with you?" I queried.

"Rather faintly, I admit. We had certain overlapping interests—he was very curious about *Les Harmonies de l'enfer*, and interrogated me constantly about its various theses."

"Like Erich Zann," I observed. "Did he know Zann too?"

"I doubt it. Why do you ask?"

"Saint-Germain mentioned that someone in the Society suggested that Zann might have composed the music for the 1834 version of the dance of the nuns."

"Ridiculous. Zann was dead—and I heard the music in question. I have no idea who did compose that fiasco, but it certainly wasn't Erich Zann."

"Or the Devil?"

"Or the Devil—or any of his minions."

I changed tack. "Given that you and Thibodeaux had overlapping interests," I said, "why didn't he 'strike a chord' with you?"

"Because he had no mental discipline. He was interested in everything, and he had a theory of everything—the kind of theory into which everything will fit, because nothing can be excluded. He might have done some useful work, if only he had narrowed his focus. If he had only limited himself to the data he obtained from the Observatoire, or the Palais de Justice, or the hospitals, and subjected it to rigorous mathematical analysis without a preconceived idea as to what he would find, he might well have discovered some real patterns of real significance. Dragging in history, mysticism, folklore, and literature only confused the issue irreparably. I tried to persuade him of that. Of course, there are recurrent patterns in folklore, legend, and literature, not only because storytellers, poets, playwrights, and novelists copy, revise, and elaborate one another's ideas relentlessly, but because the very nature of esthetic experience demands the simulation of resonance—the resonance of the past in such works as Meyerbeer's opera is consciously manufactured and carefully contrived. It is of no significance with respect to hypothetical radiations diffusing through time."

"That seems obvious enough," I admitted.

"Not to Blaise Thibodeaux. He accused me of putting the cart before the horse. Of course, esthetic experience demands recurrence and resonance, he said, because it is recurrence and resonance determined by diffusions from the past that produce, define, and shape esthetic experience. Of course storytellers and the descendants repeat and copy the same themes, he said, but they select certain themes for repetition and reconstruction *because* of their significance in terms of the resonance of time. And when he couldn't find sufficient repetition or resonance, or couldn't fit their periodicity to his magical numbers, he simply bent the evidence to fit. It wasn't enough for him that there are a dozen different versions of the legend of Robert the Devil in French; he had to equate the French Robert with the English Robin, as in Robin Goodfellow, and then to move back into French by claiming that the author of *Huon de Bordeaux* had derived the name of Oberon the Fay from the English Robin rather than, or as well as, some obscure figure in Greek myth. When I pointed out to him that that would make Oberon and Puck in *A Midsummer Night's Dream* two versions of the same character, he simply said that yes, it would, and that Shakespeare was a true genius. The man was infuriating, from a logical viewpoint."

"But you went to the theater with him in 1834—to see *Robert le Diable.*"

"Yes, I did—because there are certain ideas that are infectious in spite of, or perhaps because of, their apparent craziness. What's more, I would have gone again last night, to see whether his prediction checked out, if Amélie hadn't needed me so desperately. I even made certain that I would have an objective witness with me. And now, it seems, the man was even more infuriating than I thought, because he really *did* manage to reproduce his image at a distance of thirteen years, and the sound of his voice too—and reproduce it, not by the power of suggestion, but for the eyes of the aforementioned objective witness. That really *is* remarkable, and it poses a challenge to potential explanation; but it doesn't prove that there are fairies at the bottom of the garden, no matter what Thibodeaux thought—or what Saint-Germain thinks, now that he's spent the night reading the notes Thibodeaux made for the uncompleted second volume of his supposed masterwork."

The breakfast seemed to have warmed him up and woken him up; he seemed a great deal livelier now than when he had first come in. I was reassured that he would be able to keep his six o'clock appointment after all.

"I was entitled to be skeptical, you know," Dupin added, with uncharacteristic defensiveness. "About his overgenerous interpretations of the supposed patterns of the past, and about his projections too—especially given that he was only able or willing to issue predictions for a distant point in future, which he wouldn't survive to see. 1847 seemed distant in 1834, and his arthritis was already crippling him. He died a broken man in more ways than one, I fear—but if his ghost is still capable of paying attention, I honestly hope that it can take the satisfaction from last night's materialization to which it's entitled. I really wish I'd seen it—but I'm glad that you did, since I couldn't. Lucien should have stayed in the box when he realized that I couldn't be there. That way we'd have two witnesses."

"We have, I think," I told him. "Marie Taglioni saw it too, and I suspect that she recognized Thibodeaux, in spite of the distance and the poor lighting. That's why she's so keen to see us."

"Ah!" he said, nodding his head in apparent satisfaction. I was certain, then, that he wouldn't miss the appointment, if it were humanly possible for him to keep it.

"The Prefect wasn't there to see the ghost, in any case," I remarked. "He was looking for something else—the fulfillment of a different prediction, probably. And Thibodeaux must have given Marie Taglioni reason to expect something too—something other than the ghost, I presume."

Dupin nodded sagely, but his silence signified that he was

as yet unable or unwilling to draw any conclusion about the specific reasons for the presence of the Prefect and the dancer.

"This has something to do with Samhain and the number thirteen, doesn't it?" I queried, hoping at least to prompt him into speculation.

All that Dupin would say, however, was: "Thibodeaux certainly thought so."

I tried again: "Saint-Germain and Mademoiselle Valdemar both said something about the resonance having to be *produced*—Saint-German likened the mysterious magical branch to a tuning-fork."

"Again, that's exactly what Thibodeaux thought," was all that the logician would concede.

"But I didn't *produce* anything, did I?" I said. "You might have, but you weren't there. So why did I did I see a ghost? Did Mademoiselle Taglioni produce it? And why was Groix looking for *his* ghost in the upper gallery, rather than on the banks of the Seine?"

"You're getting ahead of yourself, my friend," Dupin said. "Not only can I not answer those questions, but I'm far from sure that they're the right questions to ask. We need to know what everyone else knows before we can even begin to formulate hypotheses. I really must go to see Lucien, since he was anxious enough to come banging on Amélie's door in Saint-Germain's wake, so urgently that I almost let him in. Before I go, though, did Saint-Germain say anything of interest? Mademoiselle Valdemar's account was exceedingly vague."

"That wasn't her fault," I admitted. "He was *very* drunk, and exceedingly vague himself. As Mademoiselle Valdemar said, he mentioned Robert the Devil, including the Robert/Robin/Oberon connection that you just mentioned, adding the Viking Hrolf to the list, and referred to some unspecified Norman romance, from which the story of the magic branch was supposed taken. He said that the branch isn't in Palermo, though, and never was. He rambled on about Pythagoreans too, and their interest in resonance...but that didn't seem to me to be relevant to anything but the intellectual ancestry of Thibodeaux's theory. I've got his book, by the way." I pointed to the volume lying on my chair.

Dupin nodded, approvingly. "I noticed," he said. "By all means take a look at it, although you surely won't have the time or the inclination to read it all—and it's only the first half of the story, in any case. The poor fellow died before he'd even started on the sequel. He survived the 1832 cholera epidemic, but his arthritis had weakened him so much by 1839 that the disease caught up with him belatedly—or some other similar infection. Raspail tried but couldn't save him. At any rate, I'll know more when I've talked to Lucien, and Marie Taglioni. Another minor mystery is the question of why Mademoiselle Taglioni has consulted Chapelain. What is her illness, I wonder?"

He was beginning to relapse into weariness again, and even stating to ramble slightly, although he had had nothing to keep him alert through the "dangerous hours" of the night but the stink of human wastes, camphor, and phenol. While he was speaking, he had stood up, obviously intending to depart, but he was still clutching the tray, as at a loss as to what to do next. I had to retrieve his hat and stick, of which he had momentarily lost track, from the umbrella stand.

"As you say," I said, knowing that I ought not to try to delay him now that he was on his feet, "we'll find out in due course. Shall I meet you at Chapelain's, if you don't manage to get back here first?"

"Yes," he said. "Six o'clock." He finally put down the tray, carefully, and took the hat and cane. Then he hesitated over saying something else. He decided against it, but seemed conflicted.

"What is it?" I asked him.

"Don't allow yourself to be charmed by Jana Valdemar," he advised, trying not to speak sharply. "Charming men is what she does, and she appears to be very accomplished in the art. If she's ensnared Chapelain...."

Again he hesitated, and this time, I didn't want to press him. I didn't bother to tell him that the medium had represented herself and her situation in a very different way, in which she was the ensnared rather than the ensnarer. He would have been skeptical, and perhaps rightly so.

"You don't have to worry about me," I said, in jest. "It seems that I'm immune to womanly charms since I read that book Saint-Germain gave me for you—the one with the curse on it."

"You don't believe that, do you?" he said, frowning.

"No," I confirmed.

I was confident, then: in November 1847, the curse of *The Mad Trist*—if there really was one—had not fully worked out yet. There were not quite enough dire events on record at that time to establish the existence of a significant pattern of sinister resonance.

When I was finally alone again, I went to give some instructions to Bihan—including an instruction that he was not to disturb me unless it was a matter of extreme importance—and then I returned to Blaise Thibodeaux's book, which I began to read attentively.

At least, I tried.

Before attempting to summarize the contents of *La Résonance du temps*, I ought to say in my defense that it really is a very dense and difficult text, evidently the distillation of a life's work by a man who had become so familiarized with his own ideas that he did not fully appreciate the difficulties and necessities of explaining them carefully to his readers. Presumably, it all made sense to him, but I have to confess that it never quite made sense to me, even in the early phases of the argument, which attempted to marshal relatively ordinary and familiar facts, and in the medium phases, which collated a bewildering array of statistics.

The ultimate foundation of Thibodeaux' argument seemed to be the simple observation that life is repetitive and cyclical, perpetually reproducing the same patterns, in part because it is subject to the changes necessitated by the Earth's rotation on its axis and around the sun: the day's alternation of light and darkness, and the year's cycle of the seasons. Because of certain complicating factors—the slight irregularity of the Earth's orbit, the periodicity of the Moon's orbit around the Earth, and other as-yet-undetected variables, these cycles are slightly confused, and the interaction of variables can make certain phenomena seem almost random—the periodicity of solar eclipses, for instance—even though they are produced by immutable laws, and hence strictly calculable once the relevant data has been collected and analyzed.

Thibodeaux was not the first person, by any means, to attempt to link psychological and historical events to these kinds of astronomical cycles. He was dismissive of the supposed conclusions of astrology, because he thought its analytical theory defective; but he was not unsympathetic to its impulse of enquiry, and was grateful for the encouragement it had lent to astronomical observation—in particular, to the obsessive collection of detailed astronomical data. He was complimentary to the Pythagoreans in much the same way, praising their realization of the significance of resonance and its connection with mathematics; but he regretted their failure to accumulate the statistical data that would have allowed them to detect and measure temporal patterns, and their failure properly to connect their theory of musical resonance with their theory of metempsychosis.

From the very beginning, it seemed to me, Thibodeaux had been interested in the idea of an afterlife, of recurrent manifestations of human beings after death, not continuously but periodically—but that idea seemed to have remained a kind of metaphorical magnetic pole guiding his work, while he had committed himself to gathering other data to shore up his fundamental thesis. Although there had long been a lamentable lack of reliable statistical data relating to other phenomena than the astronomical, from which patterns might have been induced long ago, he believed that folk wisdom might nevertheless have been able to gain a rough appreciation of certain significant periods, preserved in their notion of the significance attachable to certain numbers. The numbers that interested him most were three, seven, and thirteen, the first two being frequently associated by folklore with patterns of recurrence and the last being widely regarded—in Western culture, at least—as an "unlucky number."

Armed with this supposed hint, Thibodeaux had gone in search of patterns of all kinds, in all kinds of events, searching in particular for intervals of three, seven, and thirteen. In the argument set out in his book, this initially led him into more abstruse areas of astronomical observation; in addition to the obvious instances of comets and meteor showers, he had become particularly fascinated by sunspots, whose manifestation he had tried to fit to a thirteen-year-cycle. In subsequent chapters, however, he began to make use of other kinds of historical persistent data. He had evidently mined records of births, marriages, and deaths as extensively as he could, and records of epidemics of disease. With regard to death, he had taken a particular interest in the periodicity of suicide—and one of his key examples was the record of drownings in the Seine.

I guessed easily enough that Lucien Groix had assisted him in collecting the latter data, in the days when he was still a magistrate, with ready access to records held in the Palais de Justice as well as the Prefecture. There was also a chapter on murders, again using examples mostly drawn from Paris. The input of François Raspail was also clearly evident, not so much in the raw data about epidemics, but in their linkage to a theory of infection. Thibodeaux had not only attempted to use Raspail's germ theory of disease to help him account for patterns in the geographical spread of diseases, but had recruited a version of it that seemed to me to be merely metaphorical to account for the communication of mental disturbances that Raspail surely would not have classified as parasitic contagions. In the latter respect, he had made a concerted attempt to shore up traditional account of the linkage between mental disturbance and the full moon, not merely to map a supposed pattern of recurrence, but also to compliment the supposed insight of the relevant folklore.

I must admit that I skimmed over many of these chapters,

which were far too densely packed with figures to make comfortable reading. It did not help that Thiboeaux had a slightly florid style of writing, which might have been admirably suited to writing mock-Norman chivalric romances, but was not at all suited to a supposedly scientific treatise, sometimes obscuring meaning when it was attempting to clarify it.

From suicide, crime, disease, and madness, Thibodeaux moved on inexorably to historical cycles, paying particular attention to social disturbances: wars, invasions, and revolutions. As usual, he focused very much on France, because that was the data he had had found it easiest to collect and collate—Hrolf the Viking made his first appearance in one of those chapters, in the context of sieges of Paris—but he did not neglect the history of the Roman Empire and the supposedly historical accounts of ancient Egypt that had been produced in such profusion since Napoléon's historic campaign

He then made a beginning on the collection and collation of information about folk beliefs related to periodicity, paying particular attention to supposedly-periodic phantom manifestations, and also made a start on attempting to identify "resonance phenomena" in the arts and music. Perhaps inevitably, given the period in which he had written his text, he made an attempt to accommodate the rise of Romanticism within a recurrent evolutionary pattern and, more specifically, the recent boom in what Dupin referred to contemptuously as "devil operas." The timing of his endeavor rendered it unsurprising that he should have taken a particular interest in *Robert le Diable*, the most popular of all the products of the fad, first produced—belatedly, and in a form different from that originally envisaged—in 1831, two years before the publication of his own book.

Thibodeaux mentioned the play's links to ancient myth and legend, implying that there were other temporal patterns lurking therein, and sinister implications. Here again, there was mention of Hrolf, and also of the supposed equivalence of the name Robert to Robin, and hence, allegedly, to the Oberon of *Huon*. Quite abruptly, however, the argument was broken off and left in suspense, the author saying that the subject-matter was too profuse, and that he would discuss it in much greater detail in a sequel to his present volume. The remaining chapters of the book were mostly devoted to increasingly abstruse theoretical inductions supposedly drawn from the data that he had so far presented.

These later chapters seemed to me to be particularly bizarre, and even more indigestible than the welter of statistics. Again, I began to skip and scan, while remaining perpetually uncertain as to whether I was catching the author's meaning—or whether, indeed, there was any real meaning there to be caught. The material was full of jargon, some of it borrowed and some of it improvised, and I simply could not understand what it was trying to say most of the time. Toward the end, though, when the author began to map out the supposed "wider implications" of his supposed theoretical inductions, the text became easier to follow again.

I took a particular interest in a dense chapter on what Thibodeaux called "esoteric calendrics," which attempted to interpret the attribution of particular significance to days of the year over and above those following naturally from the cycle of the seasons. Although he had taken an interest in many days attributed by the Church to particular saints, and the legends thus connected with them, Thibodeaux had evidently paid particular attention to apparent transfers of meaning from earlier calendars, and had formed a particular obsession— perhaps not unnaturally—with the idea of the "day of the dead": a period of the year seen as particularly propitious for the dead to remanifest themselves in the world, usually as phantoms, but also sometimes by means of physical reincarnation. He seemed to think that he had proven the reality of reincarnation somewhere along the way, although, if he really had produced any such proof, I had missed it. His thesis also seemed eccentric, in that it was less concerned with alleged human recurrence than with the recurrence of entities of some other kind, whose nature he was unable or unwilling to spell out, although he promised to return to the theme in is next book. After that, he moved on to a conclusion of sorts.

After years of toiling through various records and annals, and finding only fragmentary or uncertain patterns of cyclical recurrence, a more scrupulous logician might have come to consider his initial thesis defective; but Thibodeaux had done what almost all scholars do in that situation, and had simply introduced modifying factors, which he represented as important discoveries and revelations. His conclusion, such as it was, sought to stress the significance of these supposed discoveries and revelations. The most important was his assertion that many resonant phenomena could not simply occur of their own accord, but required some kind of careful "pretuning" on the part of the "resonance receiver." The converse was also the case: recurrences could also be inhibited by appropriate effort and preparation.

In order to support the latter point, Thibodeaux borrowed an analogy from the most basic psychological cycle of all: the diurnal cycle; or, in his jargon, "the horary cycle." The most basic feature of that cycle, he argued, was sleep. There is, he noted, an inbuilt physiological tendency for humans to sleep once a day, at night, and thus an innate tendency to feel tired, the psychological effect in question intensifying as sleep is delayed, reaching a crisis point during the "dangerous hours" of the early morning. Although the time in question can only be approximately defined, it is nevertheless a real and regular phenomenon. However—and this was the key to his argument—people can, in fact, resist the determination of the cycle. They are able to stay awake all night if they are very determined, and there are various things that they can do to help themselves in that quest, just as there are obvious things that they can do to invite and promote sleep, in order to cooperate with and secure the natural rhythm.

Thibodeaux argued in his conclusion that the same principle applied to all psychological and historical cycles; the underlying patterns of resonance are not completely definitive; the manifestation or non-manifestation of the resonant phenomena are partly dependent on the willingness or unwillingness of the people involved to fall in with the pattern, or actively to oppose or comply with it. He offered further "evidence" with respect to the potential modifiability of other human cycles, including the female menstrual cycle—even suggesting at one point that we might soon discover a drug capable of altering or suppressing that cycle altogether. He also argued that natural cycles were subject to similar modification, where means permitted, and that agricultural endeavor and animal husbandry both offered examples of modifications introduced into natural life-cycles by selective breeding over many generations.

He seemed to me, in sum, to be a man yearning to prove his point with the aid of any argument that came to hand—and also to become, himself, a *producer* of resonance, a sensitive string capable of capturing the echoes of the past on the wing.

Given that he had appeared in the Opéra-Comique thirteen years after his actual visit, and some years after his death, he had apparently succeeded in that.

The earlier chapters of the book I was holding had, of course, only summarized the supposed results of his statistical analyses; without including the raw data, it was very difficult to tell whether any of his conclusions really were calculable therefrom, or whether he was manufacturing patterns by mathematical artifice, but he certainly considered his basic thesis to have been proven. In his mind, there was no longer any shadow of a doubt that there was an important phenomenon of "temporal resonance," which was as important, in its way, in accounting for the recurrence of various kinds of events as the astronomic determinism of the Earth's rotation and orbit. Frankly, I could not work out exactly how he had "proved" that thesis—perhaps because he had accepted it before he had even started, and had simply slotted everything else in with it—and I could not accept it on the basis of what I had been able to distil from the book... and yet, I was tempted by it, all the more so because I had the extra evidence available to me of having seen his ghost, and knew that its appearance had been predicted, to no less a skeptic than Auguste Dupin.

Had I not been in a slightly vulnerable state of mind, Thibodeaux's book would probably have seemed to me to be an elaborate exercise in finding imaginary connections based on mere coincidence. For Thibodeaux, however, there had obviously been no such thing as coincidence; his obsession with resonance, and with the potential enhancement or subversion of resonance, had driven the very possibility of *mere* coincidence out of his world-view and out of his mind. For him, everything was meaningful, folklore substituting for real evidence when none of the latter existed—and why should it not, I asked myself, if *everything* in human experience, including sleep and dreams, had to be fitted into the same framework of eternal recurrence...or, at least, eternal *potential* recurrence? As Dupin had said, certain ideas can be tempting, even when they seem to be manifestly crazy.

Having laid the book down, I attempted to collect my thoughts, and sum up the very marginal clarification that my cursory reading seemed to have brought to my understanding of the present mystery.

In the book, the success of *Robert le Diable* and the potential significance of its plot were only mentioned briefly, as one example among many, supposedly sustaining a case with which most readers would have lost sympathy at least a hundred pages earlier. That entire aspect of the text was a series of sly hints, not a developed thesis. In life, however, I now knew, Thibodeaux had taken the example further. He had gone to see the performance of the opera on All Hallows' Eve 1834 because he had expected, or at least hoped, to see or produce something unusual there—and he *had* seen or produced something unusual. On the basis of that apparent confirmation of his conviction, he had apparently issued predictions to at least three individuals: the two he had persuaded to accompany him to the performance, and one of the performers. Presumably, he had predicted that the opera would be staged again thirteen years later, on All

Hallows' Eve 1847—and the fulfillment of that prediction alone had been sufficiently remarkable to cause all three individuals to be present, in expectation, fear, or hope of some supplementary prediction being fulfilled.

The prediction that Thibodeaux had made to Dupin—or the promise—had been that he would be manifest himself, as a phantom. Given that Dupin was a notorious skeptic, with definite ideas about the nature of "ghosts" and the conditions under which they might be seen, that had been a bold move. Lucien Groix had been a magistrate at the time, occupied in examining various kinds of cases, and had obviously provided Thibodeaux with some of his statistical data—including, no doubt, statistics relating to suicides; hence Groix's probably-sarcastic reference to the Unknown Woman of the Seine. That did not necessarily mean, though, that he had told Groix that he would see the ghost of a drowned woman. Whatever Thibodeaux *had* suggested, though, it had been enough to prompt Groix to attend the performance, and whatever the Prefect had actually seen, the combination had obviously been sufficient to excite him considerably.

As for Marie Taglioni, the greatest ballet dancer in the world—*La Sylphide* herself—Thibodeaux had presumably suggested to her that she should look for an apparition on the stage; more specifically, a real apparition to supplement the fictitious apparition of the phantom nuns. Had he, perhaps, suggested that she might see an image of herself, refracted through time, dancing the part instead of, or in addition to, the ballerina actually playing the role of the abbess?

Such speculations only served to increase my eagerness to hear from Dupin what Lucien Groix had had to tell him, and to hear from Marie Taglioni's own lips what she had to say—but the eagerness in question was slightly tempered by a growing anxiety.

It might only have been the power of suggestion, enhanced by Saint-Germain's drunken ramblings and Jana Valdemar's equivocal conduct, but the admittedly-slight references to the legendry of Robert the Devil, and his possible association with the mischievous Robin Goodfellow and Oberon in the Fay *Huon de Bordeaux* had put an idea into my head, which I could not entirely shake off.

Put simply—although the idea was by no means simple, let alone the implications it dragged behind it—I was no longer convinced, in spite of appearances, that the ghost I had seen in the theater really had been the ghost of Blaise Thibodeaux. Obviously, it had mimicked his appearance, right down to his arthritis and his walking-stick, but had its eyes given it away? Was it possible that what I had actually seen was an apparition of Robert the Devil?—not the repentant sinner of the evidently-Christianized versions of the tale, but a defiantly unrepentant spirit, more akin to Hrolf the Viking, or a malicious fairy king, that had featured in even earlier versions?

I remembered, of course, in formulating that possibility, that I had seen the revelatory gaze for a second time, in Madame Lacuzon's bedroom, looking through *her* eyes while she was temporarily unable to use them or protect them. And no matter how ridiculous some of Thibodeaux's ideas about the occult significance of the number three might be, from a purely logical point of view, I felt morally certain that I would see those bizarre eyes, and their almost-invisible owner, again.

All Hallows was not yet over—and All Souls' Day was yet to come.

CHAPTER EIGHT:
LA SYLPHIDE

Dupin did not return to my house that afternoon. I had no doubt that Saint-Germain had caught up with him, probably having waited for him outside the Prefecture, knowing that he would respond to Lucien Groix's summons. However, I trusted in Dupin's ability to shake the importunate impostor off before the time came for him to visit Chapelain.

Given that I had had very little sleep the night before—although I had at least gone to bed and had probably dozed off for a while, unlike Dupin or Saint-Germain—I would have appreciated the opportunity to take a short nap before going to Chapelain's myself. It had taken me so long to get through *La Résonance du temps*, however, even skipping over the less interesting and more challenging parts, that by the time I laid it down I only had time to wash and change into a suit fit for visiting, and then to go in search of a fiacre.

As the cab drew away and turned into the Boulevard Saint-Germain, I could not help wondering whether Dupin would take one of his own, with no alternative but to pay the fare, or whether he would walk. The probability, I thought, favored the pedestrian option.

I should have had plenty of time to reach my destination before six o'clock began chiming on all the clocks in Paris—inevitably reflecting their slight differences of opinion with a discordant racket rather than a perfect harmony—but we had to turn left into the Boulevard Saint-Michel, which was, as always, a favorite site for impromptu gatherings of students. Although there were doubtless better and angrier orators at the quasi-legal meetings of the Campagne des Banquets, the students of the Sorbonne always made up in verve what they lacked in polish, and their meetings were always likelier to descend into brawls if Monsieur Groix's agents tried to intervene.

Although the meeting in progress that afternoon was still far from qualifying as an all-out riot, the crowd was dense and agitated, and there was simply no way of getting through to the bridge by that route. The cab-driver was obliged to turn left again and seek a different route onto the *quais* and across the Seine. He was a skilled man who knew his trade, but the bells began to chime while he was still a few hundred meters short of his objective, and had died away completely by the time I rang Chapelain's bell.

The physician answered the door himself, and took my hat, stick, and gloves before ushering me into a drawing-room, where everyone else was already assembled. I half expected Jana Valdemar to leap up and greet me, but she remained in her seat, seemingly possessed by melancholy again, while Chapelain—who still seemed a trifle surly himself—introduced me to Marie Taglioni, now unmasked and dressed in a very expensive and elegant evening gown.

By contrast with her host and his medium, who seemed to have had a slight contretemps, Mademoiselle Taglioni seemed reasonably optimistic, although she too was showing distinct symptoms of tiredness. Dupin, whose chair was occupying one corner of a rectangle, with Chapelain's chair at the nearer angle and the two women further away, was still heroically fighting his own weariness, and seemed to be winning the battle, buoyed up by his participation into the gradually-unfolding mystery.

While Chapelain pulled up an extra armchair for me, positioning it between his own chair and Jana Valdemar's, I bowed to Mademoiselle Taglioni, more deeply than is my wont; she was, after all, a living legend, having revolutionized the entire art of ballet in *La Sylphide*—not, as vulgar parlance had it, merely by shortening her skirt, but by means of the *en pointe* work that the shorter skirt had allowed her to demonstrate more explicitly. Her father Filippo, of course, deserved much of the credit, not so much for his choreography *per se* as for his ingenuity in making *en pointe* work so relevant to the theme of the ballet. He had translated the essential magicality of ballet into an imaginative context and storyline far more ingeniously appropriate than the dance of the nuns in *Robert*, which had first been produced a year before *La Sylphide*. Loosely based on Charles Nodier's *Trilby*, in which a mischievous sprite falls in love with a farmer's wife. Filippo's version had reversed the sexes, making Marie the sprite, or sylphide.

I was yearning to ask Dupin what he had learned from Groix and Saint-Germain, but I knew that I had to be patient. He would doubtless communicate the other pieces of the puzzle to me in due course—and perhaps to Chapelain and Marie Taglioni too—but for the time being, he was enthusiastic to hear what the dancer had to say: the reason why she had, in effect, summoned us into her presence

First, however, we had to listen to Chapelain.

He was not usually a bore—anything but, in fact—but today he was not himself at all. He ran through the litany of apologies first, seeming more flustered by having to offer pretexts for Jana Valdemar's presence than was necessary, given that she had already forewarned us and obtained our consent. He seemed equally embarrassed by the necessity of explaining that, even with the help of the finest medium in France, his attempts to get to the bottom of Mademoiselle Taglioni's problem had not been successful. Finally, he went through the expectable but tedious ritual of admitting us into the circle of confidentiality surrounding the case, with more than usual emphasis on the necessity of protecting the dancer's privacy. As if to support that emphasis, he filled our wine-glasses personally, taking care to emphasize that he had sent both his servants away, so that no disturbance would be possible.

Then, finally Marie Taglioni was given the floor. She was

still beautiful, although she was now in her forties, and although it was hardly surprising that she had retired from dancing, she still seemed very athletic in her build and exceedingly graceful in the movements of her arms, which she used expressively to support her story. I got the impression that she was always, to some extent, "on stage."

I expected her, especially after Chapelain's awkward preamble, to come straight to the point and interrogate us about the ghost she had glimpsed, but she was more scrupulous than that, and more methodical. She thanked us warmly for responding to her invitation, and told us that Chapelain had forgotten to mention that a cold collation had been set up in the dining-room, in order that we would not go hungry. Dupin stirred slightly in response to that news.

Then she began to tell her story.

"You know, of course," she said, "that I was the first person to play the abbess in Monsieur Meyerbeer's opera. I suppose that I ought to be grateful for that, as the immense success of the opera, and that scene in particular, helped enormously to bring my own career to its peak. I must confess, however, that I never liked the opera or the role. I was initially very reluctant to return to it three years later, when the Opéra-Comique revived the opera, but I was persuaded to do so by the new director, Monsieur Guiscard, who assured me that the music and choreography that he had commissioned to replace Meyerbeer's would be far more suited to the new techniques that I had developed in the interim, since *La Sylphide*.

"Technically, in fact, my father's new choreography was a genuine challenge, and his desire to experiment was the principal reason why I agreed to take on the role. Perhaps I was overconfident of my own abilities, for the dance did not go well on either of the first two nights; the performance on the eve of Toussaint was, as Monsieur Dupin might remember, the third. I was convinced that I would render it perfectly that night—and I knew that I had to, because news had already reached us that Monsieur Meyerbeer was furious when he had heard the news of the changes to his score, and was returning to Paris to insist on the restoration of the opera to its original state. Monsieur Guiscard had, of course, insisted that he would resist any threats, and had even expressed the hope that when Monsieur Meyerbeer actually saw the new version, he would drop his opposition. That was, I fear, lunacy rather than mere optimism.

"At any rate, the whole performance was a disaster; it seemed cursed. The orchestra was out of tune, especially the lead violin, the singers were off key, and by the time the third act began, I had entirely lost my confidence. Perhaps it was because of that loss of confidence that the ballet went badly too, or perhaps, as Monsieur Thibodeaux subsequently suggested to me, there was some strange resonance from the past interfering with the performance—I thought at the time that he was merely trying to be kind, but I realized subsequently that he meant it literally. At any rate, it was a fiasco, worse than on the previous nights. The only person in the Theater who was delighted was Monsieur Meyerbeer; his score was immediately restored for subsequent performances, and I handed the role over to another dancer.

"Although I thought at the time that Professor Thibodeaux was merely trying to comfort me for my failure, like all the egregious hangers-on in every Green Room I have ever set foot in, he did say one thing that struck me. He said that if I wanted to see my role danced the way that fate and my father intended it to be danced, I should be sure to present myself at the theater on the thirteenth anniversary of the performance. I didn't take the remark seriously at the time, but I remembered it in the course of my consultation with Dr. Chapelain, when I read in a newspaper that the Opéra-Comique did indeed intend to perform another new version of *Robert* on the night in question—but I must confess to feeling some relief when Monsieur Meyerbeer assured me before the curtain went up that he had insisted in the most strenuous terms on his own score being honored...as, of course, it was."

"The Toussaint performance of 1834 was my last performance of any sort in Paris for some time; I wanted to put it behind me—to forget it, if I could; but that proved far more difficult than I expected. It preyed on my mind. I initially expected, of course, that it was the kind of wound that time would heal, and that the sensations with which it had left me would fade away. They did not. At first, they did not affect my dancing, but only my sleep. As time went by, however, their grip seemed to increase rather than diminish, and they not only began to affect my dancing, but actually to interfere with it—or so it seemed. I battled with that perceived affliction for years on end, determined to extend my career as far as possible, for my father's sake if not my own, but in the end, it got the better of me. I was forced to give up.

"Perhaps I am now too old to dance leading roles in any case, but I feel that I still have a great deal that I might do, if I were capable, even if only in educating and training a new generation of dancers, or following in my father's footsteps as a choreographer. I do not feel that I can do that while I am still haunted—and I do mean *haunted*, for that is what it feels like— by whatever happened to me that night. I have been told by other physicians, of course, that the problem is purely psycho- logical—a kind of mild madness, I suppose—and have tried to follow a number of absurd prescriptions supposedly capable of dealing with the problem in that way. Nothing worked, and even Dr. Chapelain, with Mademoiselle Valdemar's assistance, has been unable to get to the bottom of the problem. It is, they have assured me, both complex and deeply puzzling, and although it runs contrary to his instincts, Dr. Chapelain has even begun to wonder whether it is a case of authentic haunting.

"Naturally, I was reluctant to accept that possibility, in spite of my subjective impression—until last night, when I saw Professor Thibodeaux's ghost appear in one of the vacant seats in Monsieur Reynolds' box. I was certain of what I saw, even before Monsieur Reynolds confirmed it, even though Dr. Chapelain had tried to persuade me that it was a mere halluci- nation. Obviously, I did not see the part of the abbess danced as I had tried to dance it in 1834—but nevertheless, I believe that I saw what I was really intended to see—what Professor Thibodeaux intended me to see. Whether Professor Thibodeaux was responsible for the affliction that I began to suffer that night, I do not know; I make no accusations. I am now convinced, however, that there is a connection between what happened to me and whatever Professor Thibodeaux did that night in order to prepare for his remanifestation—his reincarnation, one might almost say—last night.

"If that is so, it shifts my problem from the realm of the alienist to that of...well, I might have said the metaphysician, but Dr. Chapelain tells me that you prefer to be represented as a logician, Monsieur Dupin, and that pleases me even more. If there is any hope of obtaining a rational explanation of what has happened to me, I would be exceedingly glad to hear it, for rational explanations give rise to solutions, while alienists' attempts at analysis, however well-intentioned or plausible, often do not. I know, Monsieur Dupin, that you have seen Monsieur Groix and Monsieur Saint-Germain, both of whom were at the theater last night, as well as Monsieur Reynolds, so I assume that you are now in possession of the full facts of the matter. Will you kindly tell me, therefore, whether there is a rational explanation for all of this?"

"I certainly hope that I can be of service to you, Mademoiselle," Dupin said, politely. "Logic, however, can only process information, and only produces reliable results when the information is reliable. I now have a great deal more than I had yesterday, it's true—and would have even more if Monsieur de Saint-German were not so churlishly determined to tease me by withholding the items that he deems to be key—but I cannot be certain, even in the light of the evidence of Professor Thibodeaux's reappearance, that his thesis regarding the resonance of time is really reliable.

"One thing of which I am sure, however, is that we have only seen the first installment of his intended demonstration. Whatever Thibodeaux hoped to produce by way of a resonant reproduction of long ago, it is something far more spectacular than a momentary apparition in a theater box. This scheme has been at least thirteen years in the hatching, and we have only seen the prelude. We are, I think, playing out the preliminary acts, but will not reach the denouement for several hours yet. I am sorry to have to ask you to be patient, and also to have to ask for your cooperation in tonight's adventure, but I suspect that might be the only way that you can hope to obtain the solution you desire."

"What *adventure*?" demanded the dancer, bluntly, speaking for us all.

"In Thibodeaux's theory," Dupin said, "the most plangent resonance of the past has to be actively produced. If he were still alive, doubtless he would produce it himself. Since he is not, Saint-Germain will have to do it for him. The Comte has kindly invited us to watch—and I fear that we have no alternative, if we want to understand this business."

"All of us?" Chapelain questioned.

"Seven of us, in all," Dupin said, with a slight sigh. "Himself, of course, the five of us—and Lucien Groix."

"But what is it that he wants us to do?" Marie Taglioni demanded. "And what does he think is going to happen?"

"He won't tell me. All that he would tell me is that we shall have to go to Fontainebleau to do it—the forest, not the town—and that he wants to set off before eleven o'clock, in order to get there at the appropriate time. It's infuriating, I know—all the more so as he was the only one of us whose presence at the Opéra-Comique last night was purely coincidental."

"According to what I've been reading today," I put in, "there's no such thing as coincidence. Everything is resonance, in Thibodeaux's worldview."

"A fair point," Dupin conceded. "At any rate, that is the situation. If we want to know what Thibodeaux's plan was, we shall have to follow the man who has the instructions—and, apparently, the magic branch. It might all be nonsense, of course, and we might all have another sleepless night for nothing—but the ghost did appear last night. We have two unimpeachable witnesses to that fact. It was certainly no mere hallucination—indeed, it had a materiality that I find both surprising and, I must admit, slightly disturbing."

"Do you think there might be some danger in carrying this plan through?" Chapelain asked. He had shared one of our adventures before.

"Perhaps," said Dupin. "Perhaps there might also be danger in refusing. I cannot tell, as yet, exactly what resonance Thibodeaux contrived to lay groundwork for thirteen years ago, but his ghost was no mere mirage. It seems to be something capable of action, and perhaps of intelligence. We must not forget that Thibodeaux's scheme permits resonant patterns not merely to be echoed, but to be amplified and augmented. Strictly speaking, it might not be Thibodeaux's plan that we are dealing with here."

"Whose, then?" Marie Taglioni asked sharply. She was entitled to her sharpness, I thought—she was more heavily invested in this than anyone, given that it had been tormenting her for thirteen years rather than a mere twenty-four hours.

I knew the answer, of course; I think we all did, but I was as eager as anyone to hear exactly how Dupin would phrase it.

"The entity," he said, carefully, "that is, in Thibodeaux's view, echoed in a whole series of folkloristic and literary references: Robert the Devil, in the legend first recorded by the *Chronicle de Normandie* and Étienne de Bourbon, Robin Goodfellow in English folklore, Oberon the Fay in *Huon de Bordeaux*. Unsurprisingly, Thibodeaux seems to have preferred Oberon, as the most distinguished appellation."

"The Fairy King?"

"In Huon, merely a king blessed with fairy gifts, but in Shakespeare, yes, the King of Faerie—although Thibodeaux was rightly unconvinced that whatever entities lie behind fairy mythology actually possess the institution of monarchy."

"But this invocation of Oberon the Fay is all absurd, is it not?" said Chapelain. "Surely, whatever Thibodeaux succeeded in doing thirteen years ago, and however he conceived it, we can only have to deal with the projection of his own ideas and desires—the resonance, as it were, of his own obsession?"

"Possibly," was as far as Dupin was prepared to go on that issue.

Again, it was Marie Taglioni what wanted to take a pragmatic line. "But whatever it is that Thibodeaux produced or reproduced, your opinion, Monsieur Dupin, is that we ought to do as Monsieur de Saint-Germain asks, and attend his supposed demonstration—his conjuration of the past?"

"I would not presume to give instructions to anyone else," Dupin said, "but for myself, yes, in view of what he has told me, I feel obliged to do as he asks. At the least, there is a chance of taking part in an interesting experiment. I am willing, in spite of the fact that I do not like Saint-German, and that I shall have to offer a *quid pro quo* in order take part."

I did not have to ask what *quid pro quo* Saint-Germain was demanding.

There was a momentary pause. No one immediately volunteered to go with Dupin on Saint-Germain's excursion to Fontainebleau—but no one refused either.

Eventually, Marie Taglioni said: "Can you tell me what connection all this—Thibodeaux's ghost, Saint-Germain's magic branch, and the mysterious archetype of the Fairy King—has to do with the distress I have been suffering these last thirteen years?"

Dupin was, of course, far too polite to say "perhaps nothing," even if that was what he thought, or suspected.

"That is one matter," he said, "on which I do not have sufficient information to license a plausible hypothesis."

"In that case," said the dancer, decisively, "we had better give you all the information that we have. If it is agreeable to you, I shall give you as much as I can before we take time out to eat something. Afterwards, perhaps, Dr. Chapelain and Mademoiselle Valdemar can add their insights."

Dupin immediately nodded, and said: "Of course." The doctor and his medium seemed more hesitant, and actually exchanged a quizzical glance—the first, I thought, since I had come into the room—before making vague signs of consent.

Marie Taglioni did not press them—but only, I suspect, because she was supremely confident that if she wanted them to speak, they would speak.

"Very well," she resumed. "I have already said that eventually, when my vague discomforts reached a certain stage, I began to think that I was haunted—not necessarily by a person, and certainly not one to whom I could put a name, and quite possibly by a phantom of my own imagination....but nevertheless, that is the way in which I came to conceive the phenomenon.

"If I did not give it a name, I did eventually begin to personalize it, at least to the extent of attributing a sex to it...to *her*. I might have been ashamed to mention this if you had not introduced the subject, but she did seem to me, from the moment I began to personalize my affliction, to be a spirit of some sort—a *sylphide*, perhaps, although a wilder one than the delicate creature I portrayed in the ballet of that name.

"What can I tell you about her? Well, if she ever was a person, or an individual of any sort, then she was surely a dancer; if she never was a person, then she is a creature whose very nature involves dancing...which would, I suppose, be entirely expectable if, like Dr. Chapelain, you consider her to be merely a projection of my own personality, an aspect of myself with which I had begun, unaccountably, to quarrel.

"When I took on the role of the abbess that night in 1834, it seemed to me that I took it on in a more intimate fashion than I had ever taken on a role before, or have ever done since. Indeed, it seems to me now, in retrospect, that the role took on a life of its own that night, and was only employing me as an instrument, in order to be danced—but that it only served to confuse my feet, and I danced badly.

"You must not think, however, that I imagine that I am being possessed by an actual abbess with a history of debauchery. When I say that the role was using me, I do not mean the role as imagined by Messieurs Scribe, Delavigne, and Meyerbeer, nor by the composer who provided Father with the alternative version, in order that he might extend and reorganize the steps. The spectral abbess was mere artifice—but within the artifice there was, so to speak, an *echo* of something more distant. A resonance, Monsieur Thibodeaux called it, when I tried to explain to him, in the Green Room afterwards, what had gone wrong. I was still dazed, or I would not have said anything at all, and what I told him was a good deal vaguer than what I have just told you, but he seemed very sympathetic and understanding."

Almost as if he had been expecting to hear it, I thought—but I said nothing aloud. Dupin was conducting the performance.

"Do you happen to know who composed and choreographed the substitute music?" Dupin asked.

"Yes, of course—but the composer did not want the fact broadcast at the time, because he did not want to offend Monsieur Meyerbeer, with whom he had a slightly uneasy relationship of rivalry. I don't suppose it matters any longer, but I'd be obliged nevertheless if you did not pass the information on. It was Hector Berlioz."

I wanted to ask whether Berlioz had redeployed the music in question in any of his own compositions—specifically, the *Damnation*—but it did not seem sufficiently important to warrant an interruption. I presumed that Dupin had merely wanted final confirmation of the falsity of the suggestion that Zann, or any other diabolically-inspired composer, had been involved. For all his fascination with occult themes, Hector Berlioz was certainly no diabolist.

"And your father was the sole choreographer?" Dupin prompted.

"As usual," Mademoiselle Taglioni said, "Working in close association, of course with Monsieur Berlioz, Monsieur Guiscard, and me. It was a challenge, but one that interested us all. My father and I were, if you remember, in the process of trying to redefine and extend the limits of ballet. It was an exciting time for us...and that was probably why we overreached my talent, or the capacity of the art."

Dupin was nodding, slowly, but I had long since learned to read such gestures on his part, and I could tell that he had was still direly uncertain as to what kind of interpretation to put on what Mademoiselle Taglioni was saying. His nods were the nods of a master of deduction who was still unable to see the wood for the trees. Perhaps, if he had not been so tired, he would have been quicker in his calculation.

She, presumably, had taken enough heart from what Chapelain had told her about Thibodeaux's theories, further endorsed by what Dupin had just said about Robert the Devil, alias Oberon the Fay, to believe—perhaps even to hope—that she really had been invaded by some kind of unruly spirit that might yet be expelled; but for the moment, at least, I thought Chapelain's opinion that it was merely a aspect of her own personality far more plausible.

"Has the haunting been constant or sporadic?" Dupin asked.

"Sporadic, I suppose—but I must say, in qualifying that observation, that I never really felt that my haunter was *absent*, merely quiet. It is most often, or most obviously, present when I am dancing, but even that is not consistent; its force seems to wax and wane. It also seems to be exceptionally evident in my dreams. I sometimes wake up in the early hours—usually between three and four o'clock—sweating copiously, with my heart hammering, as if I had been dancing madly in a dream, but without actually moving. Oddly enough, however, I can never remember the choreography of the dream-dance."

"I realize that you might not have been able to take note of this, Mademoiselle," Dupin persisted, "but is there a seasonal aspect to its manifestations? Is it, for instance, more insistent at this time of year?"

"I believe that it is—but I had always attributed that to my own sensitivity. People do tend to be sensitive about anniversaries, do they not?"

"Indeed," said Dupin. "Forgive me if the question seems

indelicate, but did you, perchance, wake up between three and four o'clock this morning in the condition you just described?"

"No," she said—defying my expectations, at least until she added: "But that is perhaps because I did not sleep a wink last night, in spite of my relief that I felt no exceptional symptoms during last night's opera—not even in the third act. Is that good news, do you think?"

"We may certainly hope so," Dupin answered—which was perhaps his most delicate way of saying *probably not*. "Have you attempted to dance the steps of the nuns' ballet since that night?" he asked.

"Of course I have," she said. "Only the original version in public, of course, but I have certainly attempted the other in private, in the vain hope of appeasing my haunter—and my father, who still feels the bruises of the failure. Perhaps that was unwise."

"Perfectly understandable," Dupin opined, "and less likely to have done any harm than stubborn avoidance might have done, whatever the true explanation of the apparent haunting might be."

Mademoiselle Taglioni did not seem to approve of the stubborn uncertainty of my friend's doubts. "Do you have any better idea, now, of what is happening to me, Monsieur Dupin?" she demanded, showing a hint of asperity for the first time.

"Not yet," he replied, candidly, "but with Monsieur Thibodeaux's aid, I think I might soon be able to formulate a hypothesis."

"Monsieur Thibodeaux is dead," she pointed out.

"True," Dupin agreed, "but he left behind a book summarizing his life's work, and, dead or not, he was present at last night's performance. When I accompanied him to the 1834 performance, at his request, he told me that he would be able to prove his thesis to me if I did so. I admit that I was disappointed, because I thought he meant that I would see some manifestation of the past on that occasion, but I did not...or did not realize what I was seeing, if I did, and could not interpret it in that way.

After the performance, however, when he dragged me down to the Green Room—where I was briefly introduced to you, as you have been kind enough to remember—he told me that I ought to make every effort to be in the Salle Favart again, in the same seat, in exactly thirteen years' time. He said that he would see me there, and that I would then have my proof of the virtue of his method. In the interim, he died, and the original Salle Favart burned down, and had it not been for one singular factor, I might not even have given the matter another thought...but when the company announced its intention of performing the same opera that it had staged thirteen years before, I thought, just as you did, that it might be interesting to conduct the experiment.

"Had I known what Thibodeaux had told Lucien, I would have been more determined, but at that time, I only knew that Lucien had been supplying Thibodeaux with statistical information from records of murders and suicides. I even made a joke about it, regarding the famous Unknown Woman of the Seine, which obviously stuck in Lucien's mind—but he never mentioned Thibodeaux's prediction to me in all this time. I think I can understand why, now."

Tantalizingly, he paused.

I would have been unable to stay silent then, but Chapelain beat me to it.

"What prediction?" he demanded, a trifle churlishly.

"Thibodeaux had already told him, before the performance, that the bodies of three young women would be recovered from the Seine during the seventy-two hours from the beginning of Toussaint Eve to the end of All Souls' Day, and that one of them would have been present at the performance. He invited Lucien to look around the audience, in order that he might recognize that particular corpse when it was displayed in the Morgue—but that was a tease, for it was an impossible task.

"After the performance, he told Lucien that the pattern would be repeated, exactly, in thirteen years' time. He also told my friend that Paris would be on the brink on Revolution at that time, and that his own life would be in deadly danger: that he too would hurl himself into the Seine before the seventy-two hours had expired, if he was not exceedingly careful. He advised him that he ought to practice swimming against a current in the meantime. Even when the prediction of the three deaths turned out to be correct, Lucien refused to take the affair seriously—but he too decided, albeit belatedly, to go to the anniversary performance. He found out early this morning that one of the two suicide-victims so far recovered from the Seine in the relevant period had, indeed, been present at the performance, in the very gallery from which he was watching."

Groix's agitation was easy to understand now. Doubtless it had only been increased by wandering around the theater, gazing at the crowd, wondering whether one of the hundreds of woman present might be on a slab in the Morgue the following day—and probably wondering whether, however crazy the idea was, he might save himself from the danger of drowning if he could only identify the potential suicide and dissuade her from that ultimate desperation, thus breaking Thibodeaux's ominous pattern. No wonder he had got no sleep, and had been so desperate to seek Dupin's advice

"And has Monsieur Groix practiced swimming against a current?" asked Jana Valdemar, with a hint of malice in her voice.

"I doubt it, in a literal sense," Dupin replied. "But he has risen to the position of Prefect of Police, and in metaphorical terms, he has been swimming against a powerful current ever since."

"Do you really think that Monsieur Thibodeaux was speaking metaphorically?" the dancer asked.

"Probably not," Dupin conceded. "But Blaise Thibodeaux was always so desperate to find a coincidence that could be squeezed to fit one of his pattern, that he was invariably willing to stretch a point. Given the peculiar and strangely exact nature of the predictions he made that night, however, he must have made some significant breakthrough in his research after publishing his book, of which he never breathed a word. Unless...."

"Might I ask a question of Mademoiselle Taglioni?" Jana Valdemar put in.

Chapelain seemed surprised. "We have not yet told Monsieur Dupin the results of our magnetic investigations," he pointed out—only just resisting, it seemed to me, the temptation to add some further critical comment.

"In a moment," she said. "First, we must conclude Mademoiselle Taglioni's testimony. I'm sorry that I have not asked you to ask the question before, Mademoiselle, but this has all been very mysterious, and it simply had not occurred to me before. May I?"

"Of course," said the dancer and Dupin, simultaneously.

"I understand, perhaps better than anyone else," the medium said, choosing her words carefully, "how very disturbing this experience has been for you, and why you have become desperate in your attempt to be cured of it: to be rid of the affliction that you characterized, a few minutes ago, as a sylphide. If I might ask you, however, to set aside your own distress momentarily, however, and consider the sylphide *in itself*, as it were, have you ever had the sensation that it was actively trying to harm you?"

It was obviously a question that had not occurred to Mademoiselle Taglioni either. She had to pause in order to think about it. Finally, she said: "No, I haven't; but that, surely, is because my thinking about it as an active agent—a sylphide, or whatever other label one might apply—is just an artifice, a metaphor. One does not consider that a disease—even one as deadly as cholera—is *actively* trying to harm the person it kills. That would be a very primitive superstition, would it not? Nevertheless, the harm is done."

I saw Dupin's head come upright then, as if a thought had just struck him, and had caused a spark of light to glint in all the dark confusion. "Would it be reasonable to infer from your choice of analogy, Mademoiselle Taglioni," he said, "that you have the impression—literally or metaphorically—that you were somehow *infected* on that night thirteen years ago?"

"I have always considered it to be an affliction—a disease of sorts," she replied, as if that were obvious. "Why else would I have consulted a physician?"

"Forgive me, Mademoiselle," said Dupin, "but that is not quite what I said. The term I used was *infection*."

I was not sure whether the dancer could see a meaningful distinction in that pedantry, but I knew what Dupin, as a follower of Raspail, meant by it. He was asking Mademoiselle Taglioni whether she felt that she had been invaded by some kind of invisible parasite.

"I suppose so," she conceded. "Why—do you think that I really have been infected by some physical entity?"

"Thibodeaux might," was Dupin's only answer to that; he was still reserving his judgment.

It was to me that he turned then. "When Mademoiselle Valdemar came to see you this morning," he asked, bluntly, "did you give her details of what you saw in the theater last night?"

I must have blushed crimson. I actually stammered in replying. "I...er...well, I did mention it. I saw no harm...."

"I'm not accusing you of anything, my friend, and there was, indeed, no harm done. Perhaps, for the benefit of the doctor and Mademoiselle Taglioni, you would repeat your account again—taking great care, this time, to be exact. We were in such haste last night, and I was so distracted, that perhaps we did not give the circumstance the attention it warranted."

I collected myself, and disciplined my tongue. Even so, I was uncertain as to how far I ought to go in my account, given that my last private thought about the sighting now seemed a trifle absurd...perhaps too absurd to repeat in the presence of Auguste Dupin and the afflicted ballet dancer.

"It was during the third act," I said. "I was watching the dance of the nuns when something—I don't know what—caused me to turn my head to the right. In the nearer of the two empty chairs, a man seemed to be sitting, although there had been no one there last time I glanced in that direction, and I am sure that I would have heard if anyone had entered through the door. He was conventionally dressed, in the kind of outfit that any man would put on to go to the theater in 1834 or 1847 alike. He was about sixty years old. His hair and a beard were still black, but he was arthritic, and was propping himself up on his walking-stick. I knew immediately that he—perhaps I ought to say *it*—was a ghost. It gave such a strong impression of being...how can I put this?...*displaced*, but not so much in space as in time. At first, he was looking at the stage, and seemed puzzled...perhaps not surprisingly, if it had been expecting to see the old Salle Favart rather than the new one. Then it turned to look at me, and said: 'Yesterday never dies, but such is the rhythm of time that one has to grasp its echoes on the wing.' It seemed meaningless at the time, but I had not yet read Thibodeaux's book...."

"Are you *sure* that the ghost was Thibodeaux?" Dupin interjected, his voice like the crack of a whip.

"Of course not," I said, defensively. "I'd never heard of Thibodeaux when I saw it. It was only later that I began to put two and two together and use the methods of deduction that...." I faltered, and stopped; then I collected myself again, and continued: "At the time, I had no idea whose ghost it might be. Later, logic told me one thing, but...when it looked at me, you see, there was something about its eyes....as if they were looking at me from a vaster depth of time than his outward appearance suggested...and then...well, it suddenly seemed to me, after I thought I'd seen the stare replicated, that whatever I had been looking at, the person, or thing, that had been looking at me was Robert the Devil." I hastened to add: "Not the character in the opera, or Robert the Great of Normandy, or Hrolf the Viking, or the Devil's son in the Christianized legend, but something older, and stranger...."

Dupin's head was as steady as a rock. "Where and when," he asked, coldly, "did you think that you saw the stare a second time?"

Again the stammer gripped me. "Well...um...it was probably my imagination. A flicker of memory...an after-effect...or just a coincidence....the effect of her illness...but...you were *there*,

Dupin. When Madame...."

Impatience got the better of him, and he did not wait for any more stumbling pauses. "When Madame Lacuzon opened her eyes in her sleep," he said, softly. "You thought that you saw Robert the Devil—or an older and stranger equivalent thereof— looking through her eyes?"

"I didn't think that *then*," I hastened to insist. "Later, though... this afternoon, when you'd gone and I'd read...you'll have to forgive me, Dupin—I'm not sure that I'm thinking straight. I didn't get much sleep last night, you see...."

He cut me off with an imperious wave of his hand. "There's nothing to forgive, my friend. In all this confusion, anyone might make a mistake...or see something without realizing its importance—and even a clown like Saint-Germain might accidentally put his finger on the key to a profound mystery. But Mademoiselle Taglioni reminded us, a little while ago, that we ought to remember to eat. We have a long night ahead of us, I fear. Might we go to table?"

Although it was Chapelain's house that we were in, it was to Marie Taglioni that he looked for permission.

And with a grace befitting a queen, she said: "Of course."

CHAPTER NINE:
MAGNETIC INSPIRATION

Having filled his plate himself, Dupin attacked the cold buffet with grim determination, presumably having missed lunch. The others were more circumspect, as I was myself.

Slightly embarrassed by our final exchange in the drawing room, I sat down beside him and said, in a rather tentative fashion: "I tried to read Blaise Thibodeaux's book."

"But you found it hard going—something impossible to accomplish," Dupin suggested, between mouthfuls of cold ham.

"Yes," I admitted.

"There are forbidden books and there are forbidding books," he said, as if trying to comfort me. "Some texts remain unread because they are so difficult to find, others hide in plain view, unread because they are unreadable. Alas, that does not necessarily mean that there is nothing in them."

"You think there's something in Thibodeaux, then?"

"I do now," he admitted. "Far less than he thought, I don't doubt—but something."

"Do you think that what I saw last night really was this... Oberon thing? That it somehow followed me to your house, and briefly invaded Madame Lacuzon?"

"To the first question, probably. To the second—or at least the second part of it—probably not."

"But I did see it in her eyes!" I protested, faintly.

"I did not," he said. "Perhaps I was too slow in turning round. Or perhaps...you were mistaken."

I was slightly insulted by that, but I understood his skepticism. "I rather wish I'd been mistaken about everything, especially the ghost," I said. *That would have saved me a nocturnal journey to the forest of Fontainebleau, at least*, I thought.

"That is, indeed the core of the mystery," he agreed. "Perhaps, if you had not gone to Chapelain's box...but even then.... When Saint-Germain and Lucien came to yours, did you shake hands with either of them?"

"No," I said, mystified by the question.

"And nothing passed between you?"

"Certainly not," I said, slightly repelled by the thought—but then I had to correct myself. "Actually, yes. Saint-Germain demanded that I lend him my opera-glasses. He peered into Chapelain's box, and then returned them. Why?"

"Your opera-glasses," he repeated, thoughtfully. "Which you doubtless set to your eyes to watch the nuns' ballet, immediately before you saw Thibodeaux's ghost. Yes, that does have a certain ironic resonance." Then he seemed to quiver, as if a frisson had run through him. "But I'm falling into the same trap as Thibodeaux, inventing connections and echoes where nothing probably exists but mere coincidence. I'm even forgetting to eat."

As I watched him feeding himself, mechanically and rapidly, it seemed to me that what he had actually forgotten was the fact that he *was* eating, relentlessly nourishing himself while being somehow unaware of the fact. But consciousness, as he was so fond of remarking, is a refuge, whose very function is to exclude inconvenient awareness—and it is a refuge in which we huddle and shiver when illness threatens.

Like theaters, meals have their own etiquette, no matter how casual they may seem. Chapelain left the ladies chatting together and came to sit down with us, on Dupin's left.

"I'm sorry about all this," he said, to both of us.

"No apology is necessary," Dupin assured him. I endorsed the opinion with a nod of the head.

"I should never have shown her Thibodeaux's book," the

physician said, regretfully. "As soon as she saw the advertisement for the revival, I should have realized that it would only fuel her fantasy. It won't take much, now, to convince her that she's being haunted by Titania—nothing less than a Fairy Queen will do for her, of course, although she was content with a sylphide while she was still convinced that it was all in her imagination. At least it's not a midsummer night."

"No," I observed. "It's the day of the dead—much jollier."

Chapelain looked at me then, and changed the subject. "What did Jana tell you this morning?" he asked.

"That Mademoiselle Taglioni was only Madame in the theater—and that she wanted to see me," I replied.

"Is that all?"

"We were continually interrupted," I told him. "Saint-Germain, Groix, Dupin...the poor young woman hardly had time to finish a sentence." It seemed a sufficiently clever evasion to me, but Chapelain seemed to be in a mood to persist. I excused myself and went to the buffet.

Immediately, Marie Taglioni abandoned Jana Valdemar and buttonholed me. I thought that she might talk about ballet, or at least about fairies, but in fact she simply took up where Chapelain had left off, albeit more delicately. "I apologize for sending Mademoiselle Valdemar to see you this morning," she said. "I did not realize that you and she had quarreled in the past, and that it might cause embarrassment to both of you. Is that why you would not get into the carriage last night?"

"Our differences have been settled, Mademoiselle," I told her. "Mademoiselle Valdemar had nothing to do with my not wanting to accept a lift from you. I had, as you pointed out yourself, seen a ghost. I needed time to think, and, as I pointed out, I would have taken you out of your way."

She returned to ground that was a trifle less sensitive—for me, at least. "Chapelain still thinks I'm a hysteric," she said. "A typical *prima ballerina*. But Monsieur Dupin believes me, does he not?"

"Monsieur Dupin never rushes to judgment," I told her. "He

always keeps an open mind."

"How very diplomatic of you," she observed. "But you and I saw the ghost, did we not? We *know* that something strange is going on."

Do we? I thought. *Or did Saint-Germain merely put a spell on my opera-glasses?* It was such a bizarre idea that I almost smiled, and had to catch myself up in order to focus on the response that Marie Taglioni was demanding of me. I could not help remembering the similar appeal that Jana Valdemar had made earlier, with respect to another exotic vision—one of the many things she had said that I had no intention of confiding to Chapelain.

"Yes," I said, boldly. "We do."

"But this Saint-Germain fellow is not a reliable man?"

"Very well put, Mademoiselle. He's clever, and he's a talented magnetizer, but one thing he certainly is not is reliable."

"You don't believe that he has some kind of magic branch?"

"I imagine that he believes it—and that Thibodeaux believed it before him, with all the intensity of desire that an awareness of impending death sometimes brings. Perhaps the object in question was never anything more than Thibodeaux's lucky charm, invested with power purely by his own intensity...but it does seem to have worked, thirteen years ago, in stirring up echoes today."

"One echo," Mademoiselle Taglioni pointed out, scrupulously. "Of three predictions made only one seems to have come true."

I suppressed the temptation to say: *so far.* It would have seemed like ill-wishing poor Lucien Groix, who surely had enough troubles already, but was certainly not a man to throw himself in the river in despair. I merely nodded assent.

"Still," she said, "it might be amusing, might it not—this nocturnal voyage?"

It was a point of view worth considering. "It might," I agreed. "If nothing at all happens at the end of it, it might be worth the trip, just to see the expression of anguish on Saint-Germain's face."

She looked me in the face carefully, exuding charm as only a true artiste could. "But that's not your preferred outcome, is it?" she said.

"I never liked amusement much," I told her. "There was a time when I didn't like excitement either...but it's addictive. Once you've had glimpses of other worlds, this one always seems a trifle drab."

"And you really think that Thibodeaux's magic branch might give us a glimpse of another world?"

"If my experiences of the last few years are a reliable guide," I told her, philosophically, "it's not unlikely. Dupin is a veritable magnet for the extraordinary—and he always comes through unscathed." *Unlike me*, I refrained from adding.

"He seems a trifle scathed tonight," the dancer observed, "but then, so do we all."

That too was true. I wanted to say a brief word to Jana Valdemar, whose melancholy was showing no sign of improvement, and might well have been getting worse, but I did not have the opportunity. As soon as she turned away from me, Marie Taglioni—a *prima donna* if ever there was one—began marshaling her guests for a further session in the drawing-room-*cum*-interrogation-chamber. We all obeyed meekly— even Dupin, who could probably have eaten another mouthful or two, if given the opportunity.

It was Chapelain's turn to contribute information. Usually, he was succinct, even witty, but whatever had got into him tonight was definitely weighing him down.

"When Mademoiselle Taglioni first consulted me," he began, "my plan was to treat her myself, by direct hypnosis. I explained to her that hers was probably not the kind of illness that would yield to any kind of chemical treatment, because its primary seat is in the mind rather than the body—although, with all due respect to Descartes, one ought not to be to extreme in drawing such a distinction. I told her that many illnesses of that kind could be cured by a person's own powers of self-healing, with the guidance of expert suggestion.

"Unfortunately, Mademoiselle Taglioni proved to be one of those individuals who is very difficult to render suggestible. I do not like the term 'somnambulistic sleep,' and am far from certain that speaking in terms of 'trances' is any better; but there is nevertheless a certain psychological state of relaxation that needs to be attained if the power of suggestion is to be fully implemented. Experience has taught me that it is much easier for some people to attain that state than others, and that there are a few individuals who seem incapable of it. The latter are often dedicated artists—painters, poets, or performers—whose cultivation of their art has extended to the point of vocation, perhaps even obsession. I do not mean any insult by the latter word, for it is of such exceptional concentration that genius is born.

"There is a sense in which great poets and musicians are always composing, even in their sleep, and great painters and dancers always painting and dancing, even when they do not have a brush in their hand or are shaping *entrechats*. They cannot let go—not because it is physically impossible, but because their personalities have become so bound up in their art that to do so would seem akin to tearing themselves apart. Even an artist who desperately wants to be cured of his ailments— and, indeed, is mortally imperiled by them—sometimes finds it impossible to surrender to the attentions of a mesmerist. Mademoiselle Valdemar obtained some marginal and tempo-rary success with Honoré de Balzac, as you know, Monsieur Dupin, but was driven in the end to attempt desperate measures in the hope of curing him...and failed. I believe that you also tried yourself, with equally temporary and limited success."

Dupin did not nod his head, but the slightly chagrined expres-sion on his lips suggested that the oblique shot had hit the mark.

"At any rate," Chapelain said, "I was unable, in spite of all my efforts, to bring Mademoiselle Taglioni anything more than slight and temporary relief. Her affliction, in the context of her personality, was too powerful in its resistance—all the more so, I thought, because she had come to characterize it, over time, as a possessive spirit whose very nature was that of dance. Consciously, she wanted to be rid of it, but at some subconscious level, she felt it intrinsic to her own nature...or so, at lest, I thought.

"With Mademoiselle Taglioni's permission, I asked Mademoiselle Valdemar for her help. I hoped that she might succeed where I had failed, as a magnetizer—female patients sometimes find it easier to relax under the influence of female magnetizers. When that did not work, I suggested that we try an indirect method. I explained to Mademoiselle Taglioni that a magnetizer as sensitive as Jana...Mademoiselle Valdemar...can often gain considerable insight into another person's condition and plight when magnetized in her presence. It is a matter of sympathetic identification; although male magnetizers generally reproduce common masculine psychological traits of assertiveness and domination, females generally reproduce the feminine traits we call intuition: emotional understanding and tacit communication. With Mademoiselle Valdemar's mediumistic talents, I suggested, we might be able to get a clearer picture, at least metaphorically, of Mademoiselle Taglioni's affliction, and thus render it easier to address.

"I say 'metaphorically,' of course, because the state of enhanced suggestibility into which a medium can be deeply plunged, by the combination of her own efforts and those of her guide, is a dreamlike state, in which sympathetic suggestions do not always express themselves clearly or literally, often taking on symbolic form. In more superstitious times, of course, afflictions of the kind with which we are dealing here were invariably conceived in terms of demonic possession, with the active involvement of minions of the Devil, just as mediums were seen as witches, and themselves conceived, in the eyes of the Church, as instruments of the Devil. We are now living in an era of science, or attempting to, and trying hard to see things more objectively and rationally, but the inherited vocabulary is hard to escape, at least as metaphor. I warned Mademoiselle

Taglioni, therefore, that we must not take what Mademoiselle Valdemar said during our sessions, while deeply hypnotized, as a literal account of what was happening to her, but merely as a metaphorical account that might be useful to both of us.

"There was, however, no talk of demonic possession in what Mademoiselle Valdemar reported in response to my interrogation, and I must confess that I found it deeply puzzling. It is often the case that mediums retain no memory of what they experience in such conditions, but Mademoiselle Valdemar has always been exceptional in that regard, and I think it would be better if she told you in her own words what she felt when I asked her to identify herself mentally with Mademoiselle Taglioni, to explain her suffering, and to advise us as to how it might be alleviated."

All eyes turned to the young medium.

"Firstly," Jana Valdemar said, "You must remember that it has always been as difficult for me to understand what it is that I do—what it is that I am—as it has been for others. When Dr. Chapelain says that the old vocabulary is hard to escape, he is offering a typical understatement. It has always been hard for me to see myself as anything other than a witch, and my experience of my first...mentor did not make it any easier, given that he believes in a straightforward continuity between witchcraft and mediumship, within the context of the evolution of a tradition of arcane knowledge that has extended into modern times from the primary inspiration of philosophers who raised up such figureheads as Pythagoras and Hermes Trismegistus. It was not until I began working more exclusively with Dr. Chapelain that I began to understand that might be different ways of seeing things—and actively to try, with all my heart, to find those different ways, and see things differently.

"Sa...my first mentor believes that some individuals are effectively immortal, often living exceptionally long lives and surviving death by means of serial reincarnation, albeit sometimes confused by partial forgetfulness. Unlike the Buddhists and Hindus, he does not believe that reincarnation is the prerogative of all souls, but that it is a rare privilege. He persuaded me that I was such a privileged individual, perhaps the reincarnation, if only I could bring he memory to the surface, of one of the great witches of old...Circe, perhaps, or Medea...and I began, for a while, to imagine myself in those terms. Now, I do not. Now, I am trying to penetrate that mist of illusions to see the reality that lies beyond...and it is in that context that I attempted to obtain a sympathetic insight into Mademoiselle Taglioni's... affliction. I honestly do not know whether there is any reality in what I perceived, save for that which I projected into it by my own efforts and uncertainties, although what I overheard this morning, garbled as it as, gave me a little more confidence.

"I can sympathize with what Monsieur Reynolds said just now about his impression that the apparition he saw had been displaced in time, not simply in terms of one or a few human lifetimes, but from a much remoter past, because I had a very similar impression when I first attempted to visualize Mademoiselle Taglioni's...I do not know what word to use, but I am convinced that it is not a demon, and I do not want to envisage it as an elementary spirit either. I will simply call it... her...if I may, the *other*.

"The *other*, it seemed to me, is very ancient—perhaps so immeasurably old as to qualify as eternal, but she has not always had a presence in the world; her manifestation has been intermittent...and, I ought to say right away, irregular...or, at least, of a regularity continually disrupted and subverted by other factors. I have gradually come to believe—and the answer to the question I asked a little while ago has confirmed it in my mind—that the other feels trapped in her present situation, as a component of Mademoiselle Taglioni's personality. From her viewpoint, if she is sufficiently self-conscious to have a viewpoint, the fact that Mademoiselle Taglioni is not merely a dancer, but a dancer of genius, is a hindrance rather than a boon. In a more pliant host, she might have found it far easier to express herself, to *be* herself; but in much the same way that Mademoiselle Taglioni is resistant to Dr. Chapelain's hypnotic powers—perhaps in exactly the same way—she is resistant to her...I will borrow Mademoiselle Taglioni's own analogy of disease, and call her an *infection*.

"To put it baldly, in a fashion that is admittedly an oversimplification, it seems to me, on the basis of my intuition, that Mademoiselle Taglioni is in conflict with an ancient entity that invaded her on the eve of Toussaint 1834, which wants to dance in a manner opposed to her own determination. I say 'wants,' but I am not at all certain that it is a conscious desire rather than an animal instinct or a psychological compulsion akin to a monomania or obsession.

"I think that the other might be easier to conceptualize and deal with if she did have conscious desires that she could express within Mademoiselle Taglioni's thoughts, rather than being driven by some impulse that she is incapable of understanding herself. If that were so, I might have been able to obtain a clearer idea of what else it is she 'wants,' and *why* she is so determined to dance in her own way. There is another factor involved—of that I'm sure. It would probably be overstating the case to say that she has a mission to fulfill, but there is certainly some attraction to which she is subject, some objective toward which she is orientated. I could only sense it vaguely, at first, because it was innately vague itself, but it has recently become more definite, a least in temporal terms.

"I do not believe, as Mademoiselle Taglioni suggested, that the reason she was not tormented last night was because she did no go to sleep. I suspect that it was because the other has finally found her proper orientation, and has, as it were, sighted her objective. I do not mean that the affliction is nearing its end, necessarily—but I do believe that it it in now on the brink of its crisis. Within twenty-four hours, I believe—thirty at the most— the other *will* dance, if Mademoiselle Taglioni will allow it, and she feels that she *must* dance...although I cannot tell whether the imperative is entirely subjective, or whether something more is at stake than her own satisfaction. I am inclined, however to suspect the latter.

"Dr. Chapelain was correct to say that demons have been excluded from my intuitions thus far, but after hearing everything that I have heard today, I can no longer exclude whatever it is that Thibodeaux and many others have called Robert the Devil, with the qualification that its actuality is far older and stranger than the Christian conceptualization of it. I am sure, on the basis of last night's events and what Saint-Germain said this morning, that there is an intimate connection between Robert the Devil and Mademoiselle Taglioni's other. They are, I think, infections of the same kind, parasitic—at least for the moment—on human bodies and human minds. They mean no harm...but that does not necessarily mean that they will not prove harmful, perhaps fatal, if we cannot deal with them."

There was a momentary silence when she had said that, because no one realized, at first, that she had concluded what she had to say. Chapelain was scowling. Obviously, he did not approve of his colleague's diagnosis—and felt somewhat betrayed, having called on her for help in what he had good reason to deem the mot important case of his career thus far.

I felt obliged to break the silence. "If this entity that you do not care to describe as a demon has been parasitic upon Mademoiselle Taglioni since 1834," I said, "where is the one we have been calling Robert the Devil?"

"I don't know," said Jana, gesturing with one hand in a manner infinitely less elegant than Marie Taglioni. "It was presumably parasitic upon Thibodeaux thirteen years ago, but where it has been since Thibodeaux died, I cannot tell. It has, I suppose, infected someone else, if it really is behind this business, actively and cleverly. Monsieur Dupin has told us what he learned from the Prefect of Police, but has not yet told us what he learned from Saint-Germain, and why he thinks that Saint-Germain holds the key to the problem. Presumably, if some kind of exorcism is required, Saint-Germain has the necessary bell, book, and candle—or their pagan equivalent, the magic branch."

"What is this famous magic branch?" Chapelain queried, a

trifle contemptuously. "I know the opera version, of course, but whatever Saint-Germain has can't possibly make people invisible, and it can't have anything to do with the historical Saint Rosalia, or Palermo."

"I've never heard of Saint Rosalia," Mademoiselle Taglioni confessed. "I had always thought that the name of the convent cited in the opera was an invention. I never heard of an order of nuns with that title."

"Saint Rosalia existed," Dupin put in, "at least as a legend of the Church, if not in the flesh. She is the patron saint of Palermo, where the opera is set, and where one might expect to find a convent of Saint Rosalia, if one had ever been founded— although, as Mademoiselle Valdemar observed earlier today, it is difficult to believe that, if one did exist, it was exclusively populated by nuns regretful of a past of hectic debauchery. Saint Rosalia is said to have been a hermit, who retired to live in a cave, and died in an epidemic of the plague while helping to tend the sick. According to Saint-Germain, however, the name was taken in vain by the author of a Norman romance far less well-known than the tale of Huon de Bordeaux, and that usurpation confused Eugène Scribe when he heard a second-hand account of the romance in question.

"What is relevant to us now, however, is that Saint-Germain told me this afternoon—taunted me with the suggestion, in fact—that the object represented in the opera by the magic branch is currently in his possession, having remained is the Society's custody after Thibodeaux's death. Not only is he convinced that he knows what it is, he also believes that he knows what needs to be done with it, in order to complete the resonance that Thibodeaux—or Robert the Devil—initiated in 1834. He also believes that something important will result from the resonance, although he would not tell me what—I think he wants to reserve all of that for some theatrical flourish just before we reach our destination."

"And you believe him?" Marie Taglioni prompted.

"I would like to say, as is my habit, that it is not a matter for belief—but I am not so sure of that. It might well be that what those of us who are involved in this choose to believe, or are able to believe, will strongly influence the shape that the resonant event takes. I am at least prepared to accept, as a basis for procedure, that Thibodeaux's Oberon le Fay might indeed be able do what he intends to do, provided that we help him—and that we should, if we hope to be free of our infections."

"But I am the only one here who is, as you put it, *infected*," Mademoiselle Taglioni objected.

"Perhaps," said Dupin, "but probably not. I cannot help suspecting that both Lucien and I were infected thirteen years ago, albeit by quieter parasites than yours; and that Saint-Germain has certainly been infected in the interim, although I am not sure how, since he claims that he never set eyes on Thibodeaux's notes or the branch before last night. I will reserve judgment on Chapelain, Mademoiselle Valdemar, and Monsieur Reynolds, but if Thibodeaux were here, in the flesh or in spirit, he would surely have concluded by now that all three of you were infected last night, before or during the performance of the opera."

There was a stunned silence, eventually broken by Jana Valdemar, who laughed—but there was no humor at all in her laughter.

"He's right," she said. "I should have seen it before, but I was blinded by other things. He's right—I see it now. We're all infected, and we must all go to our fateful rendezvous. But what is the *qui pro quo* that Saint-Germain is demanding of you, Monsieur Dupin, before he will admit us to his cure?"

"He is very determined to obtain my membership in his society," Dupin aid, with a sigh "and I suppose that I ought to grant his wish, if it will help us in the present circumstance, given that it is a trivial price, and there is nothing to prevent my paying it but a slightly absurd pride. Saint-Germain gave me a long lecture on the sin of pride and the foolishness of intellectual isolation this afternoon, which struck me as a rather Luciferian performance, but it had some truth in it. If we are to employ his magic branch, however, perhaps we ought to make haste, for I'm exceedingly tired, and All Souls' Day is wearing on."

"You can't leave things there, Dupin," I said. "You haven't explained anything at all. What are these parasites that are supposedly infecting Mademoiselle Taglioni and God only knows how many others?"

"We have no word to describe them accurately," Dupin said, "any more than we have any but the most tentative words, as yet, to describe Raspail's hypothetical agents of disease. All we have are terms that have been used in the context of various kinds of conceptual error: devil, sylphide, fairy, elf, goblin, lutin, korrigan...there has never been any shortage of empty labels."

"But you think it's just a sort of *disease*?"

"That notion too might be an artifact of our perception, one idea echoing another. In the case of Mademoiselle Taglioni's *other*, however, it has indeed manifested itself as a series of symptoms, as a chronic illness. In mine, until last night, it lay dormant, quite imperceptible...but I am beginning to perceive it now, unless it is an ironic symptom of incipient delirium. The same, I think, is true of Lucien and Saint-Germain, although I doubt that either of them is consciously aware, as yet, of anything but a slight bad temper—but Mademoiselle Valdemar seems to understand."

"Mademoiselle Valdemar seems...," the lady in question echoed, very faintly, speaking to herself

"But what about Thibodeaux?" I wanted to know. "Was he killed by his...other, do you think?"

"No—he was definitely killed by another infection entirely, having been severely weakened by his worsening arthritis. I suspect that his...other...Robert the Devil...Oberon the Fay... would have saved him, if it could, even though it no longer needed him."

"But what I saw last night *was* Robert the Devil, not Thibodeaux?" I persisted.

"No," said Dupin. "You saw *and heard* Blaise Thibodeaux's

ghost. You only caught the merest glimpse of Robert the Devil, looking through his eyes—just as you apparently caught another glimpse later, which I'm obliged to admit that I missed, in Amélie's eyes. Invisibility has its limits, of course. Sight is a physical process, requiring a physical interaction with light; an invisible entity is blind unless it can somehow borrow another individual's eyes. The fact that you saw Thibodeaux, even though you had no inkling whatsoever of the likelihood of his presence, suggests that he had a material presence of some sort, however faint and temporary, which Robert the Devil was able to use."

I thought about that for a few moments—as everyone else was doubtless doing, and probably making no more headway than I was. Then I said: "But that implies that he...it...*followed* me, from the theater to the Rue Dunot."

"Yes it does," Dupin admitted.

"But if it was able to follow me that far," I said, "as an invisible, and presumably disembodied, presence, how do I know that it isn't following me still—that it isn't in this room, right now?"

"You don't," said Dupin, simply.

Everyone looked around the corners of the room—and then they looked at one another, searching for some hidden presence in their eyes. I found none, and took the comforting inference that if some kind of exotic entity were present, at least it could not see us...but the comfort vanished when I wondered whether it might be using borrowed ears, imperceptibly, to listen to our discussion.

A frisson of alarm went through me, but I suppressed it firmly, refusing to allow it to turn into a visible shudder.

"But if there are such invisible entities, recurring through time," Chapelain said, "what do they want?"

"If we were to judge by the Christian conception of them," Dupin replied mildly, "they want to tempt us to damnation. Even the mythology of Faerie suggests that no good usually comes of traffic with fays—but you are absolutely right, my friend, to say that we ought to try to think in scientific terms, in spite of the handicap of obsolete vocabularies. Whatever we are dealing with, it is not a *literal* devil, or a literal fay."

"Maybe not," I said, "but that's no guarantee that trafficking with them *isn't* dangerous." I had been possessed once before by a not-quite-literal devil; it had not been a pleasant experience, and had definitely been dangerous.

"Of course not," Dupin agreed. "But we no longer have any choice as to whether to traffic with them; the only question remaining is what kind of bargain we can conclude—and in order to take an active role, we need the magic branch, which is in Saint-Germain's possession, as well as the instructions for its use."

"Left to him by Thibodeaux," I said, "or by Oberon."

"Indeed. Perhaps, if I had treated Thibodeaux more generously, he might have left them with me, but I dare say that he always considered that they would be better left in the custody of the Harmonic Society, where his ideas always struck a chord."

This time, I thought, the pun had to be intentional, but it was no mere stroke of whimsy or wit.

"All this is bewildering in its absurdity," Mademoiselle Taglioni put in, "and I'm sure that Monsieur Dupin, at least, is deriving some esthetic pleasure from that, but I hope you'll forgive me for reminding you, Monsieur Dupin, that I invited you here in the hope of finding some solution to my own predicament. Given everything that you now think you know and half-understand, Monsieur Dupin, do you think that this magic branch can actually cure me—that it can drew the other out of me, when Monsieur de Saint-Germain casts his spell?"

"I hope so," Dupin said, a trifle wearily. "I wish that the instrument in question were in my hands, but it is not, and Saint-Germain will not hand it over. Whatever can be done, therefore, will be done by him...or by his *other*. We are already agreed, are we not, to follow him?"

No one said no.

"Then I suggest we go," Dupin said. "It's a long way to

Fontainebleau, if that is really where we are going, especially by lamplight—and the weather is dull."

Dupin stood up as he completed his sentence. I naturally stood up with him—and so did everyone else, including Jana Valdemar.

"Is it really necessary for us all to go to the Harmonic Society right away?" I asked, thinking solicitously of Jana Valdemar. "Surely we can come back to collect the ladies once you and I have concluded our diabolical bargain—and if you come with us, Doctor, Saint-Germain is likely to raise his price and demand that you join his organization too."

"As Monsieur Dupin points out," Chapelain answered, "it's a trivial price to pay. Membership need not imply involvement."

The reaction of the two ladies was less predictable, although I ought perhaps to have realized that Marie Taglioni would be a feminist as well as an egoist. "I have no intention of being left behind like some shrinking violet," she stated. "I brought you here, and I shall stay with you until the affair is settled."

"I can't keep avoiding Saint-Germain forever," Jana observed. "If I have to face him eventually, I think it might be better to do so in company like this. I'm already a member of the Harmonic Society, so he can't use that condition against me."

It occurred to me that the Comte might easily be able to think of other conditions to demand of her, if he was of a mind to, but I held my tongue on that score, and simply said: "We can't all fit into one cab, and I didn't see any carriages waiting outside when we arrived. Chapelain's is presumably not hitched up."

"Then we shall take two fiacres," said Marie Taglioni, decisively. "You may keep the doctor and Miss Valdemar company, Monsieur Reynolds, while I travel with Monsieur Dupin."

It was definitely not the arrangement that I would have chosen—indeed, I doubt that I could have contrived a less satisfactory arrangement—but the dancer was as imperious as ever, and plainly took the view that, since she was paying Chapelain's fees, she was fully entitled to issue orders to all his consultants.

Dupin raised no objection, however, and that was the manner

in which we organized ourselves, once we had hailed two fiacres
and set off in quest of the magic branch.

CHAPTER TEN:
LA SOCIÉTÉ
HARMONIQUE DE PARIS

I had never visited the premises of the Harmonic Society before, and did not even know where they were located, although I was not unduly surprised to find them discreetly set back from the Rue Vivienne, within a stone's throw of the Bourse. The concierge regarded us with some suspicion, and hesitated even after Dupin had given his name and the old woman had acknowledged with a cursory nod that she had been told to expect him, presumably because she had not been expecting such a numerous and various company. She was probably as old as Madame Lacuzon, and almost as ugly, but she was obviously not quite so fearsome, for she eventually decided to let us in, without even seeking further authority

From the street, the town-house in which the organization's headquarters were located seemed deliberately nondescript, but once we had been admitted, had crossed the inner courtyard, and passed through the ancient oaken door into the vestibule, it took on a more sumptuous appearance. The high-ceilinged vestibule was decorated with intricately-woven wall-hangings of oriental origin, and the carpet was undoubtedly Persian. We were met there by a flunkey, who showed to visible sign of fluster at our number, and immediately undertook to show us to "the master's study."

The corridor beyond the vestibule was elaborately decorated with ornate lamps, paintings of various kinds—but no formal portraits—and glass-fronted display cases, some merely containing old books, but others housing various objects in silver, wood, ivory, and various fabrics. The corridors were not deserted—indeed, I guessed that the Society was the kind of institution that might be busier by night than by day, especially in winter.

We passed a smoking-room where half a dozen people—all aged men—were engaged in deep conversation and the furious consumption of tobacco. I half-expected to see the Baron du Potet there, in fervent political argument with Alphonse de Lamartine, but there was no one I recognized, and the few members who spared us a glance gave not the slightest flicker of recognition on sighting Dupin, Chapelain, or even the unmasked Marie Taglioni.

By 1847 there were harmonic societies in a dozen European cities and at least two in the United States, but this one, I knew, was the original, and the model for all the rest, which had not only numbered Anton Mesmer and the Marquis de Puységur among its members, but the pseudonymous Comte de Cagliostro and Antoine Lavoisier. I could not help a slight sense of awe as I walked silently along its padded floors. Even our ascent of the marble staircase was soundless, so thickly padded was its carpet.

Saint-Germain's study—or, to be strictly correct, the Presidential Study, currently occupied by the pseudonymous Comte de Saint-Germain—was surrounded by alternating bookshelves and wood paneling. Here there were portraits, presumably of past presidents, none of whom I recognized by sight, although I'm sure that I would have recognized many of their names. There was a huge marble fireplace, by no means in the best possible taste, whose mantelpiece bore two fully-equipped candelabras. There were two other lanterns mounted on sconces behind Saint-Germain's sturdy desk, which gave the appearance of having been hewn in ebony—and the desk, I imagined, was slightly less likely than the man himself to be a fake. There was a cluttered umbrella stand behind the desk, and an impressively ornate inkstand on top of it.

Saint-Germain seemed genuinely delighted to see us—as well he might be. He also seemed to be sober, although there were dark circles around his eyes, and he looked like a man direly in need of a good night's sleep—although I had to admit that he probably thought the same of Dupin and me.

It was, however, to Jana Valdemar that he went first when he surged around the desk to greet us.

"Jana, my darling!" he said. "You don't know how I've been longing to see you! And who is your beautiful companion? Do introduce us, Chapelain, won't you?"

I assumed that he knew perfectly well who Marie Taglioni was, even though he had not recognized her in the domino the previous evening, but he was putting on a show. This was his stage, and he was firmly in command of it, even in the presence of a *prima donna*.

"Mademoiselle Marie Taglioni," said Chapelain, a trifle stiffly. "The Comte de Saint-German, President of the Société Harmonique de Paris. I believe you know everyone else, Saint-Germain."

"Indeed, indeed," said Saint-Germain. "I knew that I could rely on Monsieur Dupin and Monsieur Reynolds, but to see the rest of you is a real pleasure, as well as a slight relief, although I was prepared to call upon members of the Society to make up the number if need be. This is what I have always dreamed of, you know—that we might all come together, as one big happy family. But you have not brought dear Lucien! We are only six, as yet, and must to be seven—which is, after all, the magic number. No matter—we can pick him up at the Prefecture on the way. Oh, I foresee a bright future for us all, now! You have no idea how direly the Society needs an injection of new, young blood. The Baron will be so pleased—and I hope you told Monsieur Groix, Dupin, that should he need sanctuary when Louis-Philippe falls, he need only come to our door."

"Won't Lamartine object?" I could not help querying.

Saint-Germain was in too good a mood to be upset, though. "We're above politics here," he said. "As you know full well, all of you, there is a higher community of minds than the one that devotes itself to bickering in the Chambre. Monsieur de Lamartine is a devout Republican, it's true, but our Royalist majority—most of whom are Bourbonists rather than Orléanists, admittedly—and our Bonapartist minority do not hold that against him within these walls. Here, we are all seekers after truth, and democratic to boot. Yves, who showed you to my office just now, is one of our oldest members, and Anton the coachman, who will drive us to Fontainebleau tonight, has also been a member longer than I have myself. They have full access to the library, and I don't believe that there's a servant in the house who isn't an amateur scholar of some sort, in his leisure hours. That's why they're so loyal to us, and would never dream of giving information to Monsieur Groix's assiduous spies, about Monsieur de Lamartine or anyone else. We shall welcome François Raspail too—who will surely want to join us when he hears that Monsieur le Chevalier Auguste Dupin is in our midst—and Victor Hugo will surely follow him. This is the beginning of a glorious era, my friends."

"Do you actually want my signature on a document, Saint-Germain," said Dupin, seemingly exasperated by the flow of the charlatan's eloquence, "or will my word be sufficient?"

"Your word!" Saint Germain exclaimed. "Of course it will be sufficient, Monsieur Dupin. Your word is worth a thousand signatures. Let us be clear though—since you have all come together, I assume that Dr. Chapelain's word is included in the bargain, and Monsieur Reynolds' word too?"

"Why would you want me as a member?" I demanded.

"And why should I be excluded?" demanded Marie Taglioni, pugnaciously.

"My dear lady," Saint-Germain was quick to say, flatly ignoring me, "the thought of excluding you had never crossed my mind—but I would not dream of demanding a formal promise from someone of your standing; whereas, if you'll forgive me for mentioning it, there has, in the past, been a certain reluctance on the part of these two gentlemen to yield to my...blandishments. I felt it necessary to clarify the situation in their regard."

"If it will hurry matters along," said Chapelain, "I'll join."

Everyone looked at me. "Well, certainly," I agreed, "Although I can't imagine...."

Nobody was interested in what I couldn't imagine. I couldn't blame them. No matter how hard I tried....

Their gazes had shifted away as rapidly as they had fixed upon me.

"All this is on condition, of course," Jana Valdemar put in, laconically, "that your information proves to be sound, Monsieur Falleroux. If we do not locate the...branch, or it proves ineffective, the bargain is unsealed."

Saint-Germain put on a show of seeming hurt, although I was not sure whether it was caused by the clarification of the conditions of our trade, or the fact that she had addressed him by his real name.

"You, of all people, should not seek to insult me, Jana," he murmured, although the reasoning behind the remark was arcane to me. He was swift to add, however: "Understood, of course! The Society's finest coach is waiting in the rear courtyard, fully harnessed, with two of the finest post-horses in the city. Fortunately, it has room for eight to travel in comfort, and we shall only be seven, once we have collected the Prefect *en route*. You'll find it a good deal more comfortable than a fully-laden diligence, although Anton is busy packing the luggage compartment with all that we might need to secure our comfort in the dark of the forest and the dead of night. There's plenty of room for everyone and everything—sometimes, an inclination to ostentation does not come amiss."

"Are you not going to show us the mysterious branch first, Monsieur de Saint-Germain?" Marie Taglioni put in, her voice suddenly crackling with skepticism.

"Why no, my dear Sylphide," Saint-Germain replied. "The

very essence of the branch's magic is its invisibility. I'll reveal it when the time is ripe—but you would not want to deprive me of my *coup-de-théâtre*, would you? Dupin would, of course, but he's a logician. You are an artiste, and must surely understand." He seemed to be getting completely carried away.

"According to Monsieur Dupin the logician," Mademoiselle Taglioni said. "We're all suffering from some kind of fever, caused not by an invisible branch but an invisible worm. In Dr. Chapelain's drawing room, I could not quite believe that—but you, Monsieur de Saint-Germain, do indeed seem to be feverish in the extreme."

As if to deny the accusation, Saint-Germain, who had been fluttering around his enormous desk like a damsel-fly, sat down again and assumed a pose of contrived sobriety.

"Monsieur Dupin has always been a man in denial," he said. "He never would take Thibodeaux seriously. A lifetime's work, the distillation of thirty years of assiduous labor...but to Monsieur Dupin, it was all fancy and fairy tales. If Monsieur Dupin were struck like a gargantuan bell, and made to vibrate with force enough to torment flesh, he would call it a shiver, and if he were a wine-glass that had shattered at a singer's perfect note, he would conclude that he had merely been dropped from a height. But we are all friends and colleagues now, all embarked on the journey of the intellect in the same craft. Very well, I admit it—Monsieur Dupin is correct. I am suffering from a fever, a delirium, and a strong dose of Raspail's Republican Elixir would doubtless bring me down to Earth. The magic branch is an illusion; the forest of Brocéliande does not exist, and if it ever did, it was always as inaccessible from Fontainebleau as from Palermo. Were I to take you there, nothing would happen, for there are no echoes of the past to be caught on the wing. Indeed, there is no past; the present is silent, a veritable grave-yard of dreams. We are not such stuff as dreams are made on after all, but mere lumpen flesh, mere dull statistics, pattern-less and meaningless. Why are we even here? Let us simply go home to our beds, and sleep...for we all need sleep, do we not?"

He fell silent—and even his silence seemed weirdly eloquent.

Again, we looked at one another, searching one another's gazes for a glimpse of something strange.

"You're mocking me, Monsieur de Saint-Germain," Dupin said, when no one else spoke, "and doubtless you feel entitled to do so. Blaise Thibodeaux certainly would, since he appeared, as he said that he would, even though I was not there to see him; but you're quite wrong, as you know full well. I was the one who persuaded Mademoiselle Taglioni to come here tonight; I was the one who held out the hope that this excursion of ours might produce a beneficent result. I confess that I don't know what result it will produce, or how, or why, but I am prepared to accept, for the time being, that you really do have a device that will facilitate some phenomenon of resonance, provided that we are there to lend the assistance of our bodies and minds. We are in your hands...and we really do want to go with you to... Brocéliande. Lead on.

Saint-Germain sprang to his feet again. "So says the logician!" he proclaimed.

He really did have the upper hand, and he was enjoying it immensely. He had custody of Thibodeaux's "resonance-receiver," and his faith in it seemed absolute. He was confident in the extreme that his magic branch could do *something*, and that he could deliver on his promise. Was his confidence justified? I reserved judgment on that. He was evidently certain that his search of the Archives—the search that his visit to the opera had unexpectedly precipitated—had borne exceedingly luscious fruit. I had, however, read about the fruit that grows on the shores of the Dead Sea in the Holy Land, where Sodom and Gomorrah were destroyed, which seems luscious to the eye, but has nothing inside but desiccated pulp that tastes of ashes.

Dupin's capitulation seemed just as false to me as Saint-Germain's ecstasy.

And yet, I reminded myself, Thibodeaux's ghost *had* appeared, in company with its barely-visible *other*, and I could not believe that it was merely a phantom of some infection, communicated to my eyes by the opera-glasses that Saint-Germain had touched.

Whether Mademoiselle Taglioni was convinced or not, she did not want to waste any more time in argument or empty posturing. She abandoned her demand to see the branch before we departed.

"Lead on, Monsieur le Président," she said, decisively—and gestured with her regal arm, as if to indicate that the final decision had been taken, and was now irrevocable. Saint-Germain picked up his hat, his gloves and his stick, and waltzed into the corridor as if dancing on air.

Marie Taglioni waited until we were strung out in the corridor to turn to Dupin and say, in a hushed tone: "Will the Prefect really consent to come with us, do you think? Surely *he* will not accept to be blackmailed into becoming a member of he Harmonic Society?"

"I don't expect that he will pay his subscription, any more than I shall," Dupin opined, sarcastically, "but he is an honorary member of so many societies already, that another will make no difference." A thought had obviously struck him in that connection, however, because he accelerated his pace considerably in order to catch up with Saint-Germain. "The location to which you're taking us is on the bank of the Seine, I assume?"

Saint-Germain hesitated, but he said: "You're a sly one, Dupin. You always know more than you let on, don't you? How did you know that there's a river in the tale, in which...? But no matter. In a manner of speaking, yes—if Fontainebleau will stand in for Brocéliande, then the Seine will definitely stand in for its stately river—but the names have no significance, except to allow us to tell the stories...never quite the same stories, and never quite the same names." He was still walking rapidly, and Dupin was having difficulty keeping up with him. So was I, but I wanted to hear what they were saying. The Comte turned as he walked then, to look back at me. "Be careful to take notes, if you can, Monsieur Reynolds. You are the recorder of the party, are you not? It will be a long journey, but we shall doubtless while away the time by telling one another stories, like all the pentamerists, heptamerists, and decamerists of old."

"We'd do better to sleep," I said, "if the jolts in the road will allow it."

"The jolts might," Saint-Germain said, "but the magic branch will not." And he flourished the stick that he had picked up from the umbrella-stand behind his desk—which was not his usual Chinese bamboo cane.

I had not noticed before, but I recognized it now: it was Blaise Thibodeaux's walking-stick. It was also, I realized, the magic branch. It had to be. As soon as my attention was called to it, that became obvious. I had, after all, seen it only twenty-four hours ago, in the arthritic hands of Thibodeaux's ghost, while he watched the dance of the nuns, and doubtless found some echo therein of something far more ancient.

I was practically running, in order to keep up with the fake Comte.

"That's it, isn't it?" I gasped. "The stick—the magic branch."

"Full marks for observation, Monsieur Reynolds," Saint-Germain retorted, his arrogance wavering ever so slightly. "Or may I call you Sam? We're all friends now, are we not? We're not about to start quarreling over a piece of poorly-stained wood, are we? A piece of wood that only I know how to deploy, in order for it to draw the hosts of Faerie from the depths of time, and perhaps restore their empire?"

Dupin must have heard the exchange, but said nothing. Instead, he dropped back as quickly as he had moved forward, grabbing me by the arms in order to hold me back too, and he whispered in my ear: "Can you swim, Reynolds?"

"Of course I can," I said. "Can't you?" The question had never come up before, in all the years of our acquaintance.

"No," he admitted—and said no more, while we made our way in Saint-Germain's wake, through the final stage of the not-quite-labyrinthine corridors of the house to the rear courtyard, where a carriage stood ready and waiting. It was even larger than the one in which I had been privileged to ride when Dupin and I had accompanied him and the crazy Italian to the Baron du Potet's garden party. It did indeed look infinitely more salubrious than a public diligence.

I realized that I had seen the vehicle before, trundling through the streets of Paris, at least half a dozen times. It was unique and unmistakable—but I had never known to whom it belonged. I had noticed it, as a curiosity, and had then forgotten it, as one forgets so many things glimpsed, but not truly apprehended, because they are in their natural context.

"The journey will take a long time, I fear," Saint-Germain said, as we climbed aboard breathlessly, one by one, the coachman having turned down the step and stationed himself beside it in order to lend the ladies a supportive hand. "The detour to the Prefecture won't add much to it, mercifully." I presumed that he could have given us a more precise estimate of our time of arrival, but had refrained from so doing in order to conserve what mystery he could, now that we had identified his magic wand. It did not matter in the least how long the journey might be, since we were now fully committed to traveling in his company; but some instinct drove him nevertheless to keep some information up his sleeve, in order to maintain us in a state of slight uncertainty. The was one of the many reasons why he was such an unreliable man

The journey to the Prefecture did not take long, and we did not have to wait for more than three minutes for Lucien Groix, once a messenger had set off for his study. As soon as Dupin's summons reached him, he must have raced down the stairs.

As he climbed in, presumably having paid little or no heed to the nature of the carriage, he paused on the threshold, evidently taken aback by the sight of such a large party—and he was by no means delighted to see Saint-Germain among the company. He only hesitated for a moment, though, and took the space that Dupin had cleared for him, between himself and Chapelain. Jana Valdemar was sitting to Chapelain's left, and Saint-Germain had taken the seat directly opposite hers; I was sitting in the other window-seat, opposite Dupin; Marie Taglioni was between myself and Saint-Germain, possessed of all the extra elbow-room that a queen or a *prima donna* might desire.

"The magic number seven!" Saint-Germain exclaimed, as the carriage pulled away again. "We are the seven heroes of...well, perhaps not Christendom, but surely something like. Seven demon-hunters, or fairy-catchers."

"Let's hope that that we are only seven," I muttered, no intending to be overheard—but Saint-Germain evidently had keen ears.

"Have you lost faith in your arithmetic, my friend?" he asked, sarcastically.

"No," I said, curtly.

"I believe that Mr. Reynolds is apprehensive that the invisible spirit of Robert the Devil might be accompanying us," said Marie Taglioni serenely, "but if that is reckoned to make us eight, I suspect that our true number might be nine. Who knows—perhaps there is a crowd of unquiet spirits assembled around and within us, and we are even more than thirteen...a veritable legion?"

Saint-Germain pulled out his watch, and consulted it by the light of the bull's-eye lantern on his side of the compartment. "Toussaint has a while to go yet," he said. "It's not until All Souls' that the dead are supposed to complete their return journey to the world of men. We still have time in hand before the witching hour, let alone the dangerous hours. Once we get beyond the lights of the city, mind, it'll be as black as Chinese ink out there. November cloud is hiding the moon and stars tonight. The Society's coachman is a veritable master, though, and the horses are accustomed to following a road with only a lantern on a long pole to guide them. The roads are in good condition, thankfully—the Autumn has been mild and dry thus far. We shall be able to listen to one another's stories in relative comfort. We are each going to tell one, I hope?"

"I hope not," said Dupin, not quite matching my curtness.

"Oh, come on, Dupin," said Saint-Germain. "Don't be surly. You can't really have expected me simply to hand the information over to you this afternoon and then curl up in my armchair and go to sleep. The branch is mine by right, you know—the Society's, at least. I'm the one entitled to use it. And you know that I'm always ready for a *quid pro quo*. I'm sure that you know things I don't know, just as I know things you don't. Wouldn't it be better, as well as more polite, for us to amuse one another while we make our way through the Stygian gloom to the Enchanted Forest, so that we'll all be better forearmed when we get there?"

"I have no intention of telling my story again," said Marie Taglioni. "I've told it once, and that's enough."

"I'm with Dupin," said the Prefect of Police. "I'm too tired for idle banter. I haven't slept for forty-eight hours, and I'm certainly not idiot enough to take ether as a means of waking myself up."

"I haven't touched a drop today!" Saint-Germain protested. "I'll need a clear head if I'm going to work miracles, won't I?"

For myself, I wasn't averse to the idea of conversation, although I had no story to tell, as yet. I wanted to hear Saint-Germain's account of what he had found in the Archives, and I wanted to hear Dupin's comments on it. Because of Mademoiselle Taglioni's commands, I had not had a chance to exchange ideas with Dupin on the way to the Rue Vivienne, and there seemed to be a useful opportunity now, given that we would not reach the edge of the forest of Fontainebleau for quite some time. I felt that I was still lost in the wood of confusion, and direly in need of a story that would help me through it rather than leading me—as Marie Taglioni's story had—deeper into its undergrowth.

Saint-Germain was certainly not going to be condemned to travel in silence. "Very well," he said. "If you don't want to indulge in 'idle banter,' Monsieur Groix, you'll surely have no objection to earnest philosophical discussion, given that there are two first-rate scholars here—meaning no disrespect to you, Dr. Chapelain. Would you prefer to start with Pythagoras or skip straight to Thibodeaux's theories of temporal resonance?"

From what as I could see in his face, Lucien Groix's preference was definitely for the latter, but he was not about to say so,
lest it seemed like conceding the point to his adversary. He had
probably guessed that his secret anxiety, based on Thibodeaux's
prediction, was no longer secret from anyone except Saint-
Germain, but he did not want Saint-Germain to be let in on it
too.

Dupin would not make an explicit choice either, so it was left
to Saint-Germain to carry on trying to cut through the curtain
of resentment drawn by his cavalier conduct and vulgar exuberance.

"The common understanding of the Pythagorean doctrine
of metempsychosis," he said, exercising his own preference,
"equates it with simple notions of the translocation of unitary
and coherent souls—a view that persisted all the way to dear
Descartes, with his quaint idea of the mental substance of the
soul lodged in the pineal gland, pulling the levers of the body-
machine until it was time to move on to pastures new. Even Plato
endorsed some such idea, vaguely, in the formal curriculum of
the Academy. The inner circle of the Pythagorean Harmonic
Society knew better, of course, and drew much more elegantly
on the idea of resonance to account for the partial and confused
phenomena of what the vulgar call reincarnation. Anticipating
Thibodeaux by two thousand seven hundred years, they realized that only the most powerful souls could establish temporal
chords capable of being reproduced perfectly, and in their
entirety, by sympathetically-tuned instruments in the future.
Even that could only involve a *kind* of rebirth—achieved not by
occupying some embryo as yet devoid of a soul, but rather by
blending and fusing with a mind already in development, but
incomplete, yearning for an adequate fulfillment.

"Take, for instance, myself—for this is, after all, my story.
My darling Jana thought to hurt me just now, by calling me
Falleroux, just as Monsieur Groix did last night—but why
should I take offence? I was, indeed Laurent Falleroux when I
was a child, and I see no reason to be ashamed of the fact, just

as I have been other children in the past, with other names with which their parents had baptized them—but that was never my *true* identity. I was always the Comte de Saint-Germain, even though that was not a name ever conferred upon me by baptism, always destined to find my place, repeatedly, in the metaphorical Boulevard Saint-Germain: the proud aristocracy of the greatest city in the world. Laurent Falleroux was never more than a string of a particular length and tension—metaphorically speaking—awaiting completion by a wave traveling through time from the past, which would set me vibrating urgently when the time was ripe, and make me who and what I truly am.

"That was, and is, a wonderful thing. The process was not competed in a day, and was, indeed, only truly completed a little while ago. Monsieur Reynolds was present at the time, as it happens, although I doubt that he was aware of the consummation, having been disturbed by a vibration of his own, which was not in harmony with his own soul, and cursed him with a temporary discord. He is, I fear, a mere individual, incapable of bringing any of the echoes of the past radiating through him into any kind of mental coherence—but that is ever the lot of the *common* man.

"Monsieur Dupin is, I think, a much more interesting case. I cannot believe that he is *entirely* unaware that he is one of the immortals, but he does seem strangely and stubbornly determined to deny it. Perhaps Dupin really was his baptismal name, although I beg leave to doubt it, and perhaps his body really is only as old as he seems, although I doubt that too—but I am certain that he has borne other names, and lived other lives, in the past, at regular or irregular intervals. He will not confirm it, of course, but you have known him longer than any of us, Monsieur Groix. What do you think of our dear friend? Can you really believe that he is only human? Can you believe that he is not the stuff of which immortals are made?"

The Prefect had been staring out of the windows of the bizarre vehicle, but not in order to look at anything. There was nothing to be seen, because we had passed beyond the lights of the city with such remarkable rapidity that I was almost disposed to wonder whether the carriage had taken off, and was now flying through the air. He had been staring into the darkness in order not to look at Saint-Germain—or, indeed, anyone else in the vehicle. When summoned, however, he responded.

"You're being ridiculous, Saint-Germain," Groix said. "All that's poppycock, and you're a common-or-garden poseur." He said it uneasily, though—like a man who had believed that Blaise Thibodeaux's ideas were *poppycock*, until that faith had been rudely shaken.

"What about you, Reynolds?" Saint-Germain asked. "Do you really believe that Dupin is less than superhuman?"

"It's not a matter for belief," I stated, never quite having realized before just how useful Dupin's favorite assertion was. "Monsieur Dupin is my friend. I accept him for what he is. If he were to tell me that he is superhuman, or immortal, I would accept it, although he is the only man in the world from whom I would accept such an assertion. In fact, he has never made any such statement, and has, on the contrary, claimed on many an occasion to be only human. I have, therefore, no reason for any other conviction than his true humanity."

"Spoken like a true acolyte," Saint-Germain said. "You, Chapelain?"

"I'd rather not involve myself in your game, Saint-Germain," the physician said. "Monsieur Dupin in my friend, and talking about him like this would be unfair to him, even if he were not present."

I wished, belatedly that I had thought of saying that.

"I'll play," said Jana Valdemar, suddenly. "I don't know Monsieur Dupin at all, of course—but I agree with the doctor that you're exploiting your current ascendancy by trying to mistreat him, and that it would be better, if we're going to debate such matters at all, to do it in the abstract. Thibodeaux I don't know either, but I think I do know something about harmony and resonance...more now, at any rate, than when my education was in your hands."

"Oh, of course, you're *in love*," said Saint-Germain disdainfully. "But that's hardy a topic for serious discussion, and would surely be embarrassing for poor Chapelain."

I was startled by the indelicacy of the remark, even coming from Saint-Germain—but I remembered that he had been the one who had borrowed my opera-glasses in order to search Chatelain's box for a glimpse of her, and that he had been direly disappointed to find that she was not there. He was jealous, and jealousy can be an aggravating ache.

"Then I shall restrict myself to logical ratiocination," Mademoiselle Valdemar retorted, coldly, "which is a language that we all understand, and of which we all approve. I cannot compete with Monsieur Dupin in that field, of course, but I hope that he might forgive me my naivety.

"Let us suppose, as a basis for argument, that you and the Pythagoreans are correct about the capacity that human souls have to establish resonances in time, given a properly-tuned receiver of some kind. Let us also accept, as a virtual axiom, that the phenomenon of coherent and elaborate reproduction must be rare, and somewhat fugitive, given that we are not permanently surrounded by a cacophony of that kind. Perhaps that does open up the possibility of the kind of reincarnation that you describe, of which you have cited yourself as a prime, if unconvincing, example—but let us also consider some of the other, perhaps equally interesting, possibilities.

"Are you correct in your assumption that the chief determining factor of the phenomenon is the power of the initial transmission? Yes, I think you must be; there must be some discrimination at source, and I cannot think of any other word to describe it but *power*—a power that must be renewable and reproducible in the chain of echoes as they extend through time, because it cannot be sufficient merely to provoke an accidental response in future receivers; they too need to be developed as powerful transmitters if the sequence is to continue over long periods of time before fading away...or meeting a more abrupt fate.

"Perhaps, though, we ought to be careful about conflating—as you just did—the notion of the kind of power necessary to function as a powerful transmitter of temporal resonance with the power of the human will. Perhaps it is a natural conflation for a man, especially one besotted with assertion and domination; but as a poor, weak woman I cannot help wondering whether one might conceive such power in other terms—perhaps, for example, pure animal instinct, devoid of intelligence...or maternal instinct, possessed of a very particular focused intelligence. But we need not be exclusive, need we—much as you would doubtless like to be? In purely logical terms, there might be more than one kind of power capable of self-replication over time...three, or seven, or any other number seemingly possessed of more than merely descriptive power."

Saint-Germain frowned. "Demonic power, you mean?" he said—although I had not taken that inference from what she had said...not exclusively, at any rate.

"Obsolete terminology of that sort does more harm than good," she said. "Let us reject out of hand the notion that Robert the Devil really is the Devil that he was imagined to be by Christian commentators when the legend was first written down—which is to say, the son of a fallen angel, a hereditary follower of Satan. But let us reserve judgment, too, on whether he was even a Robert—which is, of course, the French equivalent of a whole host of names in other languages, including the Norse Hrolf and the English Robin, the latter also being the name of a kind of sprite, malicious and mercurial without necessarily being evil...but not, I think, Oberon. That etymologically-unjustifiable connection was surely a phantom of Monsieur Thibodeaux's imagination.

"All of that is obsolete terminology too, of course—but the idea of fays is perhaps a trifle more apt than the idea of fallen angels. Accounts of the activities and habits of the fairy folk were once commonplace, of course, including the legendry of changelings. We inherited one rich set of folktales from the Norman invaders of the Kingdom of the Franks, who became such an important force in the realm of France—but those tales, and their literary embellishments, undoubtedly overlaid and confused an older set, more closely akin to the legendry of Brittany, whose most important sprites are korrigans."

"Whose primary feature," Marie Taglioni suddenly put in—although, as a Swedish-Italian, she could only have known it as a stray item of supposedly-useless information, "is that they *dance*."

"And they are certainly not alone in that," I observed, "for folklore is replete with images of entities that dance...and whose dancing sometimes warps time...." My voice trailed off, however, not because I could not have continued to elaborate the train of thought, but because it had been interrupted by a flash of memory: the remembrance of the eyes of the phantom of the Opéra-Comique, and the difficulty I had had in evaluating the particular quality of their malice. Korrigans and the like, I knew, had a great reputation as tricksters—and a horrible thought suddenly crossed my mind.

In the meantime, however, Jana Valdemar had fixed her eyes on Dupin. "Do you like my story, Monsieur Dupin?" she said. "Have I atoned adequately for my sins?"

"I have already told you that I have forgiven you for your past errors," Dupin reminded her.

"The forgiveness of a chivalrous man is easy to obtain," she said, "and the forgiveness of an unchivalrous man only a little more difficult"—she glanced at Saint-Germain then—"but that was not what I asked."

Dupin frowned. "It is not for me to measure atonement...," he said. He would certainly have added something more, but at that moment Saint-Germain banged loudly on the partition separating the compartment of the coach from the driver's seat, and the interruption made us all jump in our seats.

"Anton!" he shouted, loudly enough to make us all wince. "Lanterns!"

I looked out of the window then. It really was exceedingly dark outside—but no longer *completely* dark.

CHAPTER ELEVEN:
THE FOREST OF
FONTAINEBLEAU

The carriage came smoothly to a halt, and I heard the coachman climb down from his perch and move to the rear of the vehicle, where Saint-Germain had assured us that everything we might need for our excursion had been packed.

The coach's lanterns had, in fact, burned very low and needed replacement. The thunderous noise of Saint-Germain's command had inevitably drawn my attention back to the walking-stick that the fake Comte had used, and I studied it carefully, trying to see it not as a ugly and ill-stained piece of wood whose only function was to lend support to arthritic ankles, but as Blaise Thibodeaux's talisman: a crutch for his ailing beliefs as well as his stiffening limbs.

It was possibly, I knew, that there was nothing in this infectious fantasy but Thibodeaux's own dreams: that his idiosyncratic Robert-the-Devil-*cum*-Oberon-the-Fay was merely a product of his unhinged imagination, and that the only product of 1834 that was resonating in 1847 was the urgency of the professor's delusions. But what did that matter, since they undoubtedly *were* echoing, and that they consisted in themselves of a nest of far more distant delusory echoes, having no other possible form to take?

As he laid the stick down again, Saint-Germain took his watch out of his pocket and flicked the case open. "Midnight," he declared, as the lantern outside his portiere flicked. He giggled as he added: "The witching hour."

"Have we reached our destination?" Marie Taglioni asked.

"Not yet, I fear," the Comte replied. "We have a way to go yet. The dangerous hours are the hours of resonance; midnight is merely the hour of transition: from one day to the next, if not one world to the next."

"But I can see lights," said Lucien Groix, peering past Dupin into the darkness that fell outside like a black curtain as soon as the coachman had removed the external lantern on that side from its hook. Dupin and I looked too. I had been correct in judging the night not completely dark. There were, indeed, faint lights in the distance, which illuminated nothing, and seemed quite eerie. They were definitely not fireflies, but for a moment, I could not imagine what they might be.

"We must be on the outskirts of Melun," Chapelain declared. "They're night-lights in houses."

"I doubt it," Dupin demurred. "Surely we have not been traveling long enough to reach Melun. Some village or hamlet perhaps, accessible by a side-road."

"Let's leave the logicians to argue the point," Saint-Germain said, laconically. "Logically, of course, they cannot be the hopeful foxfires of Faerie, gathering in order to follow us to out appointment with destiny. They can only be tiny candle-flames, kept burning by people who are afraid to go to sleep in the dark, for fear of...well, anything at all. Utterly useless, of course, but somehow comforting—the memory of light, rather than true illumination. Dupin's right, though: we're not so very far from Paris, although we're already moving into the limits of the ancient forest of Fontainebleau...and thus the borders of Brocéliande. People hereabouts still harbor ancient fears, as well as modern ones."

"Given that we're steadily nearing our destination," Dupin said, "and that it's certainly too late for any of us to have a change of heart, will you consent to tell us now what you found in Thibodeaux's papers?"

Saint-German opened the carriage door before replying and leapt down to the ground, but immediately turned to offer his hand to Jana Valdemar. "Of course," he called back to Dupin. "Have I not been advocating that we tell one another stories to while away the remainder of the journey? I don't mind doing more than my share—but I expect a *quid pro quo*. When I've told you what I found among Thibodeaux's papers in the Society's Archives, you must tell us what you know. But first, we ought to stretch our legs—we have a way to go yet, and Anton will have to water the horses as well as renewing the lanterns."

Jana Valdemar accepted Saint-Germain's hand in order to get from the carriage, but immediately drew away from him thereafter. He did not attempt to go after her, but helped Marie Taglioni down.

In the meantime, I opened the other door and leapt down myself. I offered my hand to Dupin, who took it, and then helped Lucien Groix get out. Chapelain had followed the ladies on the far side.

I immediately drew Dupin to one side and whispered in is ear "I suspect that we're being duped, Dupin. This excursion might not be what it seems. We are being manipulated—by Thibodeaux, if not by Robert the Devil, or whatever entity lurks behind that name. The whole purpose of this haunting was to gather us here, so that we might *produce* the resonant phenomenon that Thibodeaux planned."

"We already know that," said Dupin, tiredly.

"Yes—but have you considered that it might be a *trap*?"

"What kind of trap?"

"How do I know? But you must admit that we've been lured, perhaps by a baited hook."

"It's possible—but as Mademoiselle Taglioni said, I have no sense that whatever is luring us wishes us *harm*. Have you?"

How could I tell? But I looked around anxiously, staring into the darkness, and wondering whether those distant gleams might be predatory eyes.

"If it is a trap," I said, "then you must be one of its prime targets. Pierre, Jana, and myself might only be making up the magic number, while Saint-German is an instrument, but you, Lucien, and Marie Taglioni must surely be the focus of the endeavor."

"Of course," he replied, calmly. "We are completing a pattern. I cannot see the whole of it as yet, but its intricacy is...amazing. Thibodeaux was quite mad, of course, toward the end, but that, I think, is what has enabled him to reach out from beyond the grave."

"But it really might be a *trap*," I said, insistently. "What Thibodeaux said to you all thirteen years ago was intended to bring you here like this. I'm a supernumerary, but you and Lucien were intended to come. Even then, Thibodeaux had been invaded and possessed...or infected by *something*. We really might be in danger—Lucien in particular. Prophecies can be self-fulfilling, as you're fond of pointing out."

"Of course they can," he said. "Why do you think I'm here, except to play my part? Don't you think I'd rather be in bed? I wish that Saint-Germain would stop playing games, though, and tell us exactly what his magic wand is supposed to do, and how, and *why*. It's possible that he's still uncertain himself, but we wouldn't be here if he didn't have information that might allow us to work it out."

"You realized that he wasn't drunk as soon as you saw him, didn't you?" I hazarded. "You realized that he'd been...infected?"

"I realized that his drunkenness had assumed a particular and peculiar form, By the way, I think that you ought to keep an eye on Mademoiselle Valdemar, as Chapelain seems direly distracted. She made one mistake, though, in her little speech."

"What mistake?" I asked, utterly confused yet again by all the abrupt changes in conversational direction that seemed to be whirling us around, preventing us from settling on any coherent train of thought and sending us around in circles.

"We *are* surrounded by the cacophony of time's echoes; it's not coherency that's lacking, but melody. The problem is not a lack of power, however conceived, but a lack of continuity, of artistry. The echoes of the past are around us all the time, they constitute the world of the mind, just as they constitute the world of the body; we have become so used to their ever-presence that we take them for granted. It is not ghosts that are rare, whether human or unhuman, or even the circumstances that permit them, on occasion, to resonate, as it were, *plangently.* What is missing is any measured, choreographed *dance.*"

"But you think some kind of dance will be possible tonight—between three and four in the morning...the dangerous hours?"

"I hope so."

"And you really aren't afraid of harmful repercussions?"

The coachman had just suspended the replenished lantern outside the coach, and climbed into the compartment to replace the internal lamp, so there was light enough for me to see Dupin's expression of ironic astonishment.

"You and I, my friend," he reminded me, "have gone into the bowels of the Earth in the hope of catching a glimpse of something strange, and have stepped beyond its limits more than once. This is not some invasion of the Crawling Chaos that is threatened, but something in and very much of this world—but things of this world are never free of danger any more than invasions from without. If there are dangerous repercussions as well as, or instead of, pleasant ones, we shall do our best to counter or withstand them, shall we not?"

I lowered my voice again. "But what about Lucien?" I asked. "He's the one being tormented by a prophecy of death."

"He is anything but a coward," Dupin pointed out, "else he certainly would not be still in Paris, clinging to his functions as Prefect of Police. His infection is not controlling him, you know, any more than Saint-Germain's is driving him. We are all free agents, my friend, else we would not need such subtly trickery to steer us."

"But you and I....," I began, in protest.

Dupin raised a single finger; it was enough to silence me. "Mademoiselle Taglioni is right: we *are* legion, by virtue of all the echoes of the past that radiate through us...and the opportunity to find, not merely a brief note of distinct harmony in all that inchoate multiplicity, but a sustained composition, is certainly not to be missed. Now that the lanterns have all been renewed, let's climb aboard again and be on our way."

I thought that I had drawn Dupin far enough away from the Prefect not to be overheard, but I had underestimate Groix's hearing, and his curiosity. As we climbed back up into the compartment, he leaned over to whisper in my ear: "Have no fear, Monsieur Reynolds. I have no intention of leaping into the Seine—but if it so happens that I cannot help but fall in, rest assured: I can swim."

The seven of us took our seats again, in exactly the same arrangement as before, and the coachman cracked his whip. Chapelain still seemed subdued and preoccupied, and I judged from the frown on his face that he had exchanged words with someone during the halt, although I had not seen him in conversation. Jana Valdemar seemed quite serene, and Marie Taglioni merely impatient. Saint-Germain was a little less ebullient, as tiredness finally began to break through his flamboyant resistance, but when Dupin suggested that it was time for him to keep his promise and tell us what he had found in the Harmonic Society's Archives, he formed a childishly eager smile.

"As Monsieur Dupin knows," he said, as we drew away from the night-lights of the distant hamlet into the pitch-darkness, "I had never heard of Blaise Thibodeaux before last night, and would probably have remained in ignorance forever if I had not chanced to go to the Opéra-Comique last night...with no intention, initially, of watching the performance, having heard unenthusiastic reports of the preceding revival of *Robert le Diable*. When I changed my mind, though, I contrived to find a place in a distant corner in the crowded house—and afterwards, when I returned to the Rue Vivienne, I made haste to consult one of the members I had overheard talking about the performance thirteen years before. He was the one who mentioned that Blaise Thibodeaux had left an account of the incident among his papers, which were still where they had been deposited after his death, awaiting cataloguing before being properly deposited in the library—these things can take time. I found the papers in a cupboard, along with Thibodeaux's walking-stick and his old... well, I suppose I can call it a violin, although when I showed it to Anton, he merely sniffed and said that it was a gypsy fiddle of recent manufacture and no intrinsic value.

"Anyhow, to cut a long story short, I started going through the papers, searching for a document relating to the 1834 performance of *Robert*. I found it—and I also found the papers that Thibodeaux had gathered together with it, in the same envelope. In particular, I found the one of which Eugène Scribe must have heard mention when he improvised the libretto for the five-act version of *Robert* in 1831. Ours is a Secret Society and Scribe has never been a member, but people do talk, especially about trivia...folktales and the like. Thibodeaux had found the document in the library, and had never taken it back—and no one, alas, had noticed during the last thirteen years that it was missing. That's irrelevant, though...the document itself is no more than a legendary romance, the core of which must have been handed down over a long period of time, and doubtless perverted in the process, as legends always are. In all probability, no one would have bothered to preserve it had it not been for the Carolingian connection, slight as it is, and the fact that it's quintessentially Norman, and intimately concerned with the foundation of the Norman kingdom in France.

"As you doubtless all know, the Normans were originally Norsemen, who settled in France after many years of piratical raiding, under the leadership of one Hrolf, who had been forced to leave his homeland under a cloud. Hrolf's original ambitions were a great deal more ambitious than the modern territory of Normandy; having accompanied other Vikings on earlier raids on Paris, he thought that the Kingdom of the Franks was ripe for destruction, and attempted to take over the entirety of northern France. Because of those earlier raids, however, Paris as it then was—essentially, what is now the Île de la Cité—had been strongly fortified, and he could not capture it. Eventually he had to settle for Normandy—and only got that on condition that he converted to Christianity, which he pretended to do.

"It took two centuries for the Normans to be fully integrated into the Kingdom of the Franks—or France, as it was in the process of becoming—and the process was only completed when Robert the Great, generally credited with being the first Duke of Normandy, having stabilized the province, launched a further series of conquests. The Normans, more sophisticated than their Viking ancestors but with the same fire in their blood, took over England, conquered Sicily, and established other bases in Italy, as well as extending their influence more widely within France, even reaching as far as Provence.

"As well as being experts with the sword, however, the Normans also inherited their ancestors' fascination with story-telling; in a literate society, they became great masters of the pen—relentless chroniclers and legend-mongers. It was the Normans who invented the entire pseudohistory of Britain contained in Arthurian legend, and it was them, rather than Charlemagne's actual descendants, who did the same for France in creating the legendry of Carolingian knights and the entire genre of Christianized chivalric romance to which those tapes-tries of nonsense belong. Unusually, in an era in which the vast majority of literate people in Europe were monks, the Norman legend-mongers included literate women, the best-remembered of whom signed her work Marie de France.

"Almost all writers of the era wrote anonymously, pseudony-mously, or apocryphally, because signing one's own name to anything was considered to be an instance of the sin of pride, although signing a more famous name somehow escaped that stigmatization, appearing as a kind of modesty. By and large, it wasn't until the Renaissance that writers began to use their own names. The one thing of which we can be reasonably certain, therefore, is that the typically Norman legend that Thibodeaux discovered, credited to 'Rosalie de Palermo,' is not, in fact, the work of the legendary hermit, if any such real individual ever existed. Why would Rosalia of Palermo have written a legend about the Forest of Fontainebleau—indeed, about an episode that supposedly occurred during one of Hrolf the Viking's sieges? Scribe had difficulty with that one—which is why he chose to associate the legend of Robert the Devil with Robert the Great rather than Hrolf, and packed him off to Palermo to woo an entirely fictitious Italian princess.

"But enough preamble: what you want to hear is the original version of the tale he borrowed: the tale of the magic branch...or, rather, not *quite* enough preamble, because there's still one more item of context that requires specification. You're all sufficiently familiar with chivalric romances to know that, seen collectively, they describe phases of a long battle between Christianity and paganism, the latter often being represented by the fairy folk, sometimes humanized as enchantresses and wizards but sometimes defiantly themselves, like Oberon le Fay in the tale of Huon de Bordeaux. Like Robert the Devil in the Christian version of his legend, Oberon is eventually redeemed from the legacy of his dubious ancestry and an occasional tendency to play tricks, becoming a stout supporter of Huon, leaving him the legacy of his kingdom when he is carried off to Heaven by the angels. One can see why Thibodeaux wanted to conflate the two legends, in spite of the etymological falsity of the slight similarity of names.

"You probably know, too, that the fairy folk in chivalric romance are strongly identified with the forest—not with any particular forest, in geographical terms, but with a single vast hypothetical forest, usually called Brocéliande, which is imagined in *Huon de Bordeaux* to extend across the whole of Europe, from Brittany to the Near East, in spite of being hollowed out by the multiple enclaves of civilization. In Norman legend, any patch of forest can stand in for Brocéliande, and feature as a haunt of fairy folk, Fontainebleau being no exception....far from it, in fact. And if the whole of romance can be said to have a story a well as a theme, it's the story of the gradual defeat and annihilation of the pagan fairy folk by the virtuous knightly ideals of supposedly-civilized Christendom, achieved in spite of the fact that the fairy folk seem to have had magic on their side.

"The legendary romance credited to Rosalia of Palermo fits that pattern superficially—and I stress superficially. Anachronistically, because Charlemagne was dead long before Hrolf was born, and Hrolf only had dealings with Charles the Fat and Charles the Simple, the romance tells the story of a group of Charlemagne's knights, exhausted after fighting a hard battle with Hrolf's invaders, who go astray in the forest of Fontainebleau, and seek shelter in what the story describes as a 'house of women,' inhabited by seven females of various ages.

"Scribe made the 'house of women' into a convent, but in the romance it is obvious, at least to a modern reader, that it is a fugitive community of fays—which is to say, fairy folk, although many romances would categorize them as enchant-resses, or even witches. In later parlance it would be a coven, and the number would have been made up to thirteen. The magical women allow the weary knights to stay in their house overnight, but drug their wine in order to make sure that they go to sleep. One of the knights, however, contrives to stay awake with the aid of prayer, and is thus enabled to see the seven women leave the house and go to a clearing in the wood on the bank of the Seine. Naturally, he follows them, and sees them dancing by moonlight in the early hours of the morning, around what the story calls—no surprises here—a 'magic branch.'

"The knight watches the dance for a while, suitably appalled by its pagan abandon, and notices that when any of the women touch the branch, they briefly vanish from sight. They never become aware that the knight is watching, but are eventually disturbed by the stealthy approach of some Hrolf's soldiers, whereupon they all panic. They hasten to touch the branch and become invisible, but one of the seven stumbles, and falls into the river. One of Hrolf's men dives in after her, but fails to capture her, and drowns.

"The knight sneaks back to the house and succeeds in waking his comrades, who stagger out to fight the enemy yet again—but this time, they have an advantage, because the knight who has seen the dance uproots the branch, and begins tossing it back and forth to his fellows, who are thus enabled to become temporarily invisible—just long enough to defeat the invaders... and perhaps in the process, to lay the foundations for the eventual salvation of Paris from the Vikings. At any rate, the knights take the magic branch back to Paris with then, where more use is made of it against the invaders—although the epilogue of the romance relates that, once removed from the forest, it began to wither, and eventually lost its power. The epilogue also relates that the enchantresses in the forest, permanently visible now, withered and grew old for lack of it, and eventually died, leaving their house to fall into ruins.

"Superficially, as I said, the story is a conventional one of Christian triumph over residues of pagan belief and magic, but there's a subtext of sorts, in that the author often seems more sympathetic to the women than the knights—who are, after all, thieves and destroyers, no different in essence from the men they're fighting. It's the latter, of course, who will eventually become the Normans, and hence the ancestors, not merely of the pseudonymous Rosalia, but of the whole tradition of romantic legendry."

"You'll forgive me for saying so," said Marie Taglioni, with a certain edge to her voice, "But the story you've just described at such tedious length might well explain how Scribe and Delavigne formulated the libretto for *Robert*, but it hardly serves to explain anything else—including the question of where we're going, and why."

"That's because I haven't told you yet about the appendices that Thibodeaux added to the story. He was always an assiduous hunter for the supposed truths behind legends of all sorts, and having found this one, he immediately set out to search for the site described in the story. He found it—or, at least, what he believed, in his possibly-addled mind, to be the location. And having thus proved, to his own satisfaction, that the story did have some basis in fact, he slotted it into his own theories of resonance. He also contrived to convince himself that a particular tree growing in a clearing by the river had reproduced the magic branch—too late, alas, to save the unlucky fays, whose bodies were buried there, interpenetrated by the roots.

"Thibodeaux cut the branch in question, and fashioned it into a walking-stick: *this* walking-stick." He displayed the wooden stick that Dupin and I had already identified. "He became convinced that he would be able to work magic with it, at least for a while—and believed, too, that if and when the magic ran out, he could renew it by returning the branch to the tree in order, as it were, to draw new power from the roots. The fays were long dead, of course, but in Thibodeaux's worldview, everything sends forth pseudo-sound waves through time, which can bring forth resonance when they find an appropriate instrument. Thibodeaux considered that his own mind was the primary instrument, but he thought that it also needed the right stimulation, which he tried to provide using his old violin.

"Whether he had ever been a competent player, I don't know, but by the time he acquired the stick, his fingers had been crippled by arthritis; he could hardly produce a note, let alone a tune. His ankles were also afflicted, so dancing was similarly out of he question. His theories still gave him hope, however. What he couldn't do personally, he believed, the echoes that he left behind him after his death might—and those echoes themselves might be amplified, extended, and transformed if only the circumstances were exactly right. With that purpose in mind, he designed what might be called a spell: a spell that he put into operation on Toussaint Eve 1834, although it was intended to gestate and gather strength over the next thirteen years. Thirteen years later, between Toussaint Eve and All Souls' Day, that embryonic magic was to give birth. Someone working in Thibodeaux's stead was to return the branch to the tree, renew its power, and harmonize the echoes of the ancient fays, so that they might dance again.

"The purpose of the new dance was not merely nostalgic, although Thibodeaux certainly imagined it as a celebration of liberation; it was also purposive. As the present fades into the past, of course, it sends forth its own echoes into the future. The All Souls' dance could only be a temporary affair, and its dancers would soon retreat into invisibility...but it would also, in Thibodeaux's plan, serve to reinforce the pseudo-sound waves that ramified from that moment in time, and renew them in times to come as well. In brief, what Thibodeaux was trying to achieve—or what the fays were trying to achieve, using *him* as *their* instrument—was, and is, nothing less than a rebirth of Faerie, a resurrection of ancient magic.

"That is, of course, why Thibodeaux entrusted his legacy to the Harmonic Society, which is at very heart of the modern endeavor to resurrect the power and authority of ancient magic—because he was convinced, and perhaps knew, that by the time his spell reached its final phase, there would be someone in charge of the Society willing and able to do what he wanted of them: a man who would be a powerful echo himself, a reincarnation of a mage. That is what I am going to do with the magic branch: I shall return it to the tree—and it goes without saying that I hope, with all my heart, that the spell works, and that magic does indeed renew its echoes, more powerfully than ever before, in our skeptical nineteenth century and the twentieth, and the twenty-first, its sporadic ripples becoming even more powerful, and spreading ever more widely. I would do it alone, if I could, but that was not what Thibodeaux, or the fays employing him, wanted. There is magic in number as well as strength. We are seven, because the original inhabitants of the house were seven."

"But we are eight," Dupin murmured.

"Nine," Marie Taglioni added.

Legion, I thought.

CHAPTER TWELVE: THE
SKEPTICAL VIEWPOINT

Saint-Germain ignored the half-hearted interruptions. He raised the walking-stick again, holding it vertically by the shaft, with the handle that made it look like an elongated lower case "r" above his head. "Thibodeaux was right," he declared. "This *is* the magic branch—I can feel it. The clearing and the tree are there; I know it, and can find them. When the branch is returned, Thibodeaux's spell will bear its fruit. The resonance will be established. The fays will be reborn, and will dance for joy—and they will send ripples forth into the future, that will bear further fruit in times to come: not constantly, and not immediately, but in time. Faerie will reclaim its heritage. Oberon will recover his crown—and all of you will bless the day that you were privileged to see me do my work, and will know me henceforth for who and what I truly am."

Everyone's eyes focused on the stick, which had been hiding in plain view throughout our journey, virtually invisible because it had blended in so well with expectations, seemingly no different—except in matters of minor detail—from the sticks that Dupin, Chapelain, and I were carrying...those faint and mostly futile echoes of a time when no gentleman ever went abroad, especially to a wild forest, without carrying his sword.

For just a moment, I think, carried away by the flood of Saint-Germain's florid rhetoric, we all saw it as something strange and magical—but then, in a sudden deflation, as the silence that followed his final flourish extended, I for one, saw it once again for what it was: a walking-stick, no more and no less. For a moment, I became ninety-nine percent convinced that poor Thibodeaux had simply been mad—but then, as reaction followed reaction, I remembered that I had seen his ghost. Whatever he had done, he had done *something*.

"It's just an ordinary stick," I murmured, not knowing whether I was trying to convince myself of the fact, or the converse.

Saint-Germain did not let that comment pass unchallenged. "But that's exactly the point," he said. "Isn't that what legend tells us, all the way from Aaron's rod in the Bible to the modern trickery of Hindu conjuring? Legend abounds with seemingly ordinary staffs, or wands, which, when cast upon the ground horizontally, turn into serpents, or which, when stuck into the ground vertically, are capable of putting forth branches, taking root, and producing foliage and blossom."

"Always provided," Lucien Groix put in, dryly, "that the moment is right. If you try it and fail, it's not because the staff is just a staff—it's because the time has not yet come...."

"Exactly," Saint-Germain confirmed.

"And you seriously expect us to believe," the Prefect continued, as if he were an examining magistrate interrogating a suspect, "that when this wild goose chase finally gets to wherever it's going, and you jam that thing into the tree from which it was cut, that something magical is going to happen?"

"I certainly hope so," the President of the Harmonic Society replied, waspishly. "If it doesn't, we'll all have been wasting our time, won't we?"

"You're mad," the Prefect said. "I've always thought so, and every report I've had from inside our organization confirms it."

"I know," Saint-Germain retorted, brutally. "I dictated some of them, although I have people to take care of the routine material for me. You don't honestly think, do you, that *any* of your agents is reliable, let alone those who have a higher loyalty?"

Groix was furious—but Dupin put a hand on his arm, and he repressed whatever he had been about to say.

"Do *you* think that we're on a wild goose chase, Dupin?"

Saint-German demanded. "Time for your *quid pro quo*, remember?"

"I agree with you, Monsieur le Comte," Dupin said, mildly. "I certainly hope that we have not come all this way for nothing. But might I ask you a few questions, before I take my turn to tell a tale?"

"Of course," said Saint-Germain. "We are friends and colleagues now, are we not?"

"Only if you can make good on your promise," Jana Valdemar reminded him. "If the magic branch fails to perform...." She abandoned the remark there, in order to let Dupin ask his questions.

"To begin with," said Dupin, "may I clarify two points that you made in telling your story? Firstly, you said that it was obvious to you that the inhabitants of the romance's 'house of women' were fays—but does it actually say so in the text?"

"No," Saint-Germain admitted. "But what they do...."

"...Is open to more than one interpretation," Dupin said. "The manuscript you found in the cupboard where Thibodeaux's legacy as stored is, I presume, of much later origin than the twelfth century?"

"Of course. Manuscripts of that era only survived if they were repeatedly copied."

"By whom?"

"Usually by monks—but the Normans seem to have made provision for copying their romances, and this one might well have been preserved by the author's family—perhaps by other female members."

"Indeed," said Dupin. "So there is a possibility, is there not, that it really was written by Rosalia of Palermo, perhaps in her cave, and dispatched from there to her relatives in Normandy?"

"It's conceivable," Saint-Germain admitted, "but...."

Dupin did not wait for the objection. "And it's conceivable, is it not, that Scribe was partly right and that you are partly wrong, and that the 'house of women' in the story really is a nunnery, or a prospectus for one, and that the magic branch is actually symbolic of the Christian cross?"

"No!" said Saint-Germain. "That's entirely the wrong way to read it."

"Well, perhaps," said Dupin. "Secondly, you said that the scheme that Thibodeaux designed for the production of his resonance *might be called* a spell—which implies that Thibodeaux did not use that term. Is that the case?"

"Well, yes, but...."

"And what term did he use?"

"His own notes speak of 'spreading an infection'—but he didn't mean it literally. It was just a metaphor he borrowed from Raspail. Witches, who are themselves echoes of fays, were routinely accused of spreading diseases, cursing people and livestock with all manner of afflictions. The terminology of magic and disease were long interchangeable, and still overlap."

"Indeed they do," Dupin agreed, "and you're right: the notion clearly is one that Thibodeaux borrowed from Raspail, to which he probably did attach a double meaning—but even if it was only a metaphor, it was the one he chose, and I believe that there might be considerable merit in retaining it. Again, more than one interpretation is possible, and it might be as well not to take yours for granted."

"Oh, very well," said Saint-Germain, with a sigh, "the proof will come, in due course. Do you have any more quibbles?"

"Yes," Dupin said. "You said that you showed Thibodeaux's violin to Anton. Why Anton?"

"Why not?" Saint-Germain countered. "I told you that the Society is a broad Church, and that Anton is a member."

"Is he an expert judge of musical instruments?"

"No, but he knew Thibodeaux. He was he one who told me where to find the cupboard."

"And was he also among the members you chanced to overhear discussing the 1834 production of *Robert le Diable*?"

"One of them—but there's nothing surprising about that; as I said, he knew Thibodeaux, and was familiar with his work. He drove Thibodeaux to the location we're visiting tonight, way back in 1835 or thereabouts; he assures me that he remembers the way, and that he can find it even in the dark."

"So we are *not* seven after all," Dupin murmured, "and the eighth, whom we have all been taking for granted, might be the most important of us all, the prime mover in this entire affair."

"Anton?" said Saint-Germain. "But he's...." He stopped himself from saying that Anton was only a coachman just in time, remembering his own observations about the broadness of the Harmonic Society's Church, and the fact that Anton had been a member of the Society far longer than he had. Instead, he said: "One of us is obviously only here to observe: a super-numerary."

"One of us is," said the faintest of whispers—which I took to first to have been spoken by someone invisible, until I decided that it must have been Jana Valdemar.

"It's me," I said, quickly. "I'm not really part of this; I'm merely—as Saint-Germain said himself—a recorder, who will one day write the story.

"Alas, my friend," said Dupin, "you are closer to the heart of the matter than that."

"Do you really think that Saint-Germain *infected* me by putting a curse on my opera-glasses?"

"It is a possible interpretation," Dupin said. "Just as you then infected Chapelain, who infected Mademoiselle Valdemar in his turn."

"Me!" I protested. "If any infection were needed in that direction...." I stopped, thinking that it would be impolite to level such an absurd accusation against Marie Taglioni.

"Well, perhaps," said Dupin, "but of our own infection there can be no doubt. If seeing Thibodeaux's ghost were not enough, your subsequent impression of seeing something in Madame Lacuzon's eyes would confirm it. What you saw then, my friend, was in the eye of the beholder."

"Well, if I'm not the supernumerary, who is?" I demanded. "You?"

"Certainly not. If Saint-Germain is correct about only seven of us being required to trigger Thibodeaux's resonance effect, the exception is more likely to be Mademoiselle Taglioni."

"Do you think so?" the dancer asked, more surprised than incredulous.

"But she's been afflicted for thirteen years!" I objected, on her behalf.

"That is one anomaly in the pattern," Dupin pointed out. "An anomaly that Thibodeaux would undoubtedly have sought to explain by evoking some additional factor...a Titania to complement his Oberon, so to speak."

"A Titania!" exclaimed Mademoiselle Taglioni, clearly not displeased by the label—as, indeed, Chapelain had anticipated.

"With all due respect, Dupin," Lucien Groix put in, "you're letting yourself get carried away by Thibodeaux's craziness, just as Saint-Germain has. All this is poppycock."

"Perhaps," Dupin conceded, his voice falling to a murmur. "The world certainly has no shortage of appealing nonsense, which often seems to strike a chord more readily than the humble truth, in the most brilliant minds as well as the most cretinous. I certainly cannot deny the temptation of the exotic." In a louder voice, addressed primarily to Saint-Germain, he said: "Anton has doubtless packed Thibodeaux's 'gypsy fiddle' in the luggage compartment, along with candles and oil, fresh water, blankets, and the like?"

"Everything that we might need," Saint-Germain confirmed. "And now that you know everything I know, even though you seem determined to cast aspersions on it with your ridiculous quibbles, perhaps you will deign to tell us what *you* think. What is your interpretation of our circumstances? *Will* something happen tonight, in the forest of Fontainebleau? And if so, what, how and why?"

Saint-Germain's own voice was as abrasive as it was demanding. The gauntlet had been thrown down in no uncertain terms. All eyes were now on Dupin.

"That rather depends on whether there is any truth in Thibodeaux's theories," Dupin answered, equivocally. "But the appearance of his ghost, as promised, and Mademoiselle Taglioni's experiences, surely offer powerful evidence that there is *something* in them. Given that, yes...I think there is a strong possibility that at least seven of us will be party to a manifestation to some kind when you plant your stick in the tree. It will, I suspect, be more subjective than objective...but if, even in only in our minds, we have crossed the invisible border between Fontainebleau and Brocéliande, then we shall very probably see *something*, although we might interpret it in different ways.

"Mademoiselle Valdemar is, I think, correct to say that there are many more possibilities contained in Thibodeaux's theory than vulgar accounts of reincarnation and ghostly apparitions have grasped. We really do not know what kind of entities might be echoing in time, awaiting resonance. Whether or not we are literally haunted or literally infected, or both, or neither, something has affected us, which might indeed be very ancient. The suspicions filtered through folklore, while by no means irrelevant, are far too vague to give us an accurate picture of what it might be, and Thibodeaux was never able to frame a convincing account himself, in spite of all his long discussions with me, with Lucien, with François Raspail, and, it now appears, with his good friend in the Harmonic Society, Anton the coachman."

"With a set of friends like that," Lucien Groix put in, "it's hardly surprising that he remained deeply confused."

"It's true that he was unlikely to find much common ground," Dupin conceded, "but he did not come to us in search of common ground. He came to you for statistics relating to crime and suicide rates, and he went to Raspail for statistics relating to epidemics of plague and cholera, just as he went to Arago and the Observatoire's Bureau of Statistics for astronomical data, and to the Harmonic Society for occult lore. He looked for patterns everywhere, as you know...including political upheavals, and the rise and fall of entire civilizations. Your vision has necessarily become narrow since you were appointed Prefect, but his was anything but, and he remained a highly original, if overambitious, thinker until the very end."

"You're procrastinating, Dupin," Saint-Germain suggested.

"Am I?" Dupin countered. "Perhaps because I'm tired, or because I'm still not entirely sure what story to tell, where to start it—or even whether to bother at all, given, as you say, that the proof will arrive soon enough. I did promise, though, so I will offer you an alternative interpretation of what is happening to us. I cannot promise that it will be any more or less accurate than yours, but at least it will keep us away from *common* ground. It might, I suppose, be as convenient to start with Raspail as anywhere...or, I suppose, with Athanasius Kircher."

"The alchemist?" Groix asked.

"He is often stigmatized as such, but he was a man of exceedingly wide interests and learning. He was an early microscopist, and one of the first to make a leap of the imagination that others have made since, including Raspail, in suggesting that the agents of infectious disease might be tiny organisms, at or beyond the limit of microscopic vision, which are passed from one human to another by physical contact, or contact with objects that others have touched.

"On the basis of that supposition, Kircher made several suggestions about the manner in which the spread of infectious diseases might be checked—which, if adopted widely, could have saved countless lives. Raspail has been attempting to institute similar hygienic measures in Paris for more than twenty years, where they would undoubtedly save even more lives, but he has run into solid opposition from the administration—which is one reason why he is so enthusiastic to see it overthrown. Whether a new government would be any more interested than Louis-Philippe's in addressing the problem of the city's cesspits and investing in proper sewerage, or in actively promoting the use of antisepsis, it is difficult to tell—poor Ignaz Semmelweis is having no success at all with his similar campaign in Vienna, if rumor can be trusted—but it is certain that very little can be done until the barriers of intolerance are smashed.

"Perhaps it is merely my recent experience that has inclined me in this direction, but while listening to Mademoiselle

Taglioni's story, and Mademoiselle Valdemar's conjectures, earlier tonight, I was forcibly struck by the resemblance between what is happening to us now and Raspail's theory of disease. If there are actual entities involved in this, apart from the force of Thibodeaux's desires, it might be more helpful to think of them by analogy with imperceptible organisms than relying on traditional notions of devils or fays. As Mademoiselle Valdemar has suggested, their action might not be intelligent at all, but merely instinctive, and might be following some agenda that is entirely separate from our own.

"Kircher and Raspail, having hypothesized the existence of submicroscopic entities, immediately focused on the possible agents of the plague, cholera, and other so-called scourges of humankind. By so doing, they have, in effect, demonized the concept of such submicroscopic creatures. We must remember however, that it is an inefficient parasite that kills its prey. In the same way that what is good for sheep is good for the wolves that rely on them for nourishment, and whatever harms the sheep indirectly harms wolves, what is good for a host is good for its parasites—and perhaps even more so given that, from the viewpoint of a very tiny parasite, its host is, in effect, its whole world, even its universe—and whatever harms a host also harms its parasites.

"I once suggested to François that his antiseptic methods might have unintended side-effects—that in trying to wipe out the entities causing serious diseases, he might also be wiping out legions of other parasites that do no harm, and perhaps some whose effects are actually beneficial. The ultimate wolf, after all, is the human farmer who labors long and hard for the welfare of his sheep, until the time comes to slaughter them...or perhaps the dairy farmer, who contents himself with drawing milk from his livestock until they can give no more. Perhaps, I suggested to him, every one of us is a host, not merely to occasional infectious agents, but to perpetual infestation, so that each of us really is a world and a universe to a multitude of unobtrusive passengers. That, I told him, is what the logic of his thesis would actually predict. His interest being strictly confined to human health, he probably did not think my argument relevant to his concerns—but Blaise Thibodeaux was interested in *everything*.

"Raspail imagined his disease-causing organisms as tiny worms, potentially visible to sight be more powerful microscopes, but that might be too narrow a view. If there is such a microcosm-within-the microcosm, who can tell how complex it might be? He also considered that the delirium that accompanies many infectious diseases, when their fevers reach crisis, could be seen simply as a disruption of rationality, a mental upheaval sowing chaos. But if inefficient parasites can do that, I could not help wondering, what might my hypothetical efficient ones do? What kind of input might they have into our dreams, or even our conscious intellect?

"My memory is slightly hazy, and in any case, I would only have been playing with ideas, but I believe that I suggested once, when I happened to be in the company of both Raspail and Thibodeaux, that submicroscopic entities might conceivably be an important factor in processes of temporal resonance: that they might, in the right circumstances, be active agents of the transmission and reproduction of both the typical substance of dreams and the recurrent substance of philosophy. Perhaps, I suggested, superstitious, religious, and political ideas might be associated with action and activity within the submicrocosm. Raspail, I do remember, called such notions poppycock—but Thibodeaux was never a man to let any idea slip away that might be recruited and adapted to serve his own hypotheses. Indeed, had I given him the seed of such an idea, he would surely have let it germinate and grow in his own mind, cultivating it according to his own skills and tastes.

"It is impossible, of course, that Thibodeaux could have discovered anything at all in the submicrocosm, for he was certainly no microscopist, but he was also a friend of Puységur's, and a member of a society that had practically every mesmerist in Paris in its ranks. He must have been very familiar with the ideas that lie behind Dr. Chapelan's theory of suggestion: the idea that suggestion can sometimes induce the symptoms of disease and often cure them. He cannot have found anything particularly strange about the notion that, by means of self-hypnotism, he might be able to develop symptoms of disease in himself—and I am perfectly certain that he strove for many years to cure his own arthritis by means of self-magnetism. He never managed that, but he was not a man to abandon a conviction on the basis of failure; he was always able to invoke some supplementary explanation. Given his general theories, I suspect that he would have told himself that the moment was not propitious, or that he simply had not found the right combination of circumstances. Perhaps he believed that he might have greater success if he employed a more elaborate caution, with respect to something less intimately personal and more important.

"Unlike the Comte, I have not read Thibodeaux's papers, but the mere fact that he described his plan, not as 'casting a spell,' but as 'spreading an infection,' suggests to me that I am thinking along the right lines. And no matter how implausible it might seem, in 1847, to suggest that the power of human thought and desire might be capable of creating, or modifying, inhabitants of the submicrocosm in such a way as to design an infection capable of acting over a period of thirteen years, in ways that can only be described as utterly bizarre, I submit that it is no more inherently implausible that Saint-Germain's story of the magic branch that will pave the way for the future renaissance of the fays. And however we elect to envisage the situation, we are in it, are we not? We are on our way, at least to Fontainebleau, and perhaps to Brocéliande, following Thibodeaux's plan, not merely intending to replant his branch, but actively hoping that when we do, we shall see something miraculous...even if it is only a benign delirium, caused by an efficient parasite."

Saint-Germain, I think, might have cried "Poppycock!" had he not thought that he would merely seem to be echoing Lucien Groix.

Jana Valdemar, with no such inhibitions, actually did

murmur: "Bravo!" in an abstracted manner.

Chapelain and the Prefect shook their heads, in a chorus of bewilderment.

"And where do I fit in, Monsieur Dupin?" demanded Marie Taglioni.

"Perhaps you don't," said Dupin. "That's the point I was making earlier. You're the anomalous case. Unlike Lucien and myself, who blithely accommodated the parasites with which Thibodeaux infected us thirteen years ago, your body and mind reacted. For thirteen years, you have been fighting your infection. You are here, of course, with the rest of us, but your role and fate might well be distinct...if seven really is the magic number."

"Do you really believe that, Dupin?" asked Chapelain.

"It's not a matter of belief," Dupin replied, predictably. "Because we cannot see into the hypothetical submicrocosm, we have no information, and can only speculate. The point I am trying to make, and have tried on make repeatedly, is that events might be subject to more than one interpretation. Even if we could guess Thibodeaux's own explanation correctly—and he was such a muddled thinker that I doubt that even he could have explained himself coherently—that certainly would not mean that it is the correct one."

"But something *is* happening," I reminded him.

"It is. We might never know what it is—or, afterwards what it was—but that should not prevent us from trying to understand it, because we might be able to glean some insight therefrom into much wider questions. In exactly the same way that, when we fall ill, we usually have no idea what the ultimate cause of our illness might be, and routinely live with all kinds of symptoms that we simply have to suffer, but that we have nevertheless discovered palliative treatments that we have successfully applied, perhaps we can learn something from his experience that will arm us against future infections of a similar sort. It is possible that we routinely entertain many phenomena that Blaise Thibodeaux would have characterized as temporal echoes or resonances—some few of which at least resemble living beings. We are only marginally aware of such phenomena—the images that echo unbidden in our dreams or in our reveries, for instance—because they are so commonplace that we simply take them for granted, and ignore them. Sometimes, however, the infection becomes acute, and we can no longer ignore the temporal echoes that have somehow attached themselves to us, although we still have no awareness of precisely what they are. They might, in such circumstances, drive us mad, cause us to become obsessive, or furious, or to mimic the symptoms of intoxication, demonic possession, or what is sometimes called pixilation.

"I am correct, am I not, in assuming that everyone here, with the possible exception of Monsieur Reynolds, does not seem *quite themselves* tonight—that everyone is to some extent *in distress*?"

"I would have thought that was obvious by now," Groix growled.

The others allowed him to speak for them, but I did not look around in an attempt to judge their reactions more accurately, I was busy wondering whether I too was 'pixilated'—and whether, if so, I might free myself of that pixilation by the power of self-suggestion. I rapidly came to the conclusion that it was unlikely to work, even with the aid of an expert magnetizer.

For all Dupin's reluctance to join in the storytelling game, now that he was in full flow he could not resist adding further thoughts as they occurred to him. "Thibodeaux's consultations with Raspail must have led him to realize that the sporadic nature of disease, both spatially and temporally," he mused, "arises from two factors: firstly, that not everyone who comes into contact with the germ of a disease develops symptoms, or develops them to the same extent; and secondly, that the germs of disease sometimes lie dormant for long periods of time, and that even when they begin to develop, there is an incubation period before symptoms appear and progress to their climax. Thibodeaux probably adapted both those notions to his own thesis regarding temporal resonance in general, and came to believe that the imperfect reproduction of apparent patterns was partly due to recurrences not becoming fully manifest, and partly to the complexity with which resonances not only had to find appropriate receivers, but had then to operate within those receivers over a period of time, calculable in terms of his various significant numbers, usually in days, but sometimes, with respect to far-reaching manifestations, in years.

"Thibodeaux always hoped, of course, that if he could fully account for the variability in the manifestation of patterns of resonance, he might be able to affect that variability. He certainly began to carry out experiments of various kinds in his later years, although you will have to look at the papers he left to the Harmonic Society for details, because he confided very few to me. Indeed, he became increasingly secretive toward the end, and his behavior became gradually more erratic. I think it highly likely, now, that he tried to infect himself, deliberately, with an entity akin to the ones that have infected us, perhaps knowingly—and came to believe that he had succeeded. It would have been entirely typical of him not only to seek out echoes that might reverberate in his own person, but to reach out to them and embrace others...and he would have made a particular effort to cultivate any such echo that he thought capable of intellectual effort, whether it was the echo of a human or something else.

"It would have been entirely typical of him, too, to assist in the spread of such infection, all the more so if the spread in question required intricate and ingenious planning. To what he extent he was personally responsible for the effects that he anticipated in 1834, and which are now coming to fruition, and to what extent they might have been the work of some other entity—the one that we think of, and might even think of itself, as Robert the Devil or Oberon the Fay—I don't know. It probably doesn't matter, since it was undoubtedly a willing collaboration on both sides...and since the entity still seems to be active, in spite of Thibodeaux's death, having indeed been spread.

"I suspect that Mademoiselle Valdemar and Mademoiselle

Taglioni were correct, last evening, to emphasize the point that the entities that have infected us are not evil, and have no more malevolent intention toward us than the germs of an ordinary disease—but just as diseases sometimes kill, and often cause collateral distress, while they are going about the business of their own reproduction, something of the kind might conceivable happen to us. We may take some optimism, however, from the fact that at least one of the entities involved, including the one that seems to be, as it were, leading the orchestra, seems to be conscious, and to have a degree of intelligence, and is hence capable of moral discrimination. Given that, it is conceivable that it might have deliberately organized its own plan so as to minimize potential harm to us."

"Unless it is, in fact, malevolent," I put in, remembering the ghost's eyes yet again, "in which case the converse might be true."

"Granted," said Dupin. "Which brings me to my next, and perhaps final point: what should we do about our situation, if it really is as I have described it? We are still free agents, after all, hag-ridden as we might be. We are under no real compulsion even to plant Monsieur de Saint-Germain's walking-stick, but we have already agreed to do that much. The question is—and it is a question that we must each ask ourselves, in order that we might be ready to act when the time comes—what shall we do if and when the miracle begins to unfold, and the magic branch is reactivated?"

"Rejoice, and glory in our achievement," Saint-Germain was quick to say, but then added, a trifle mischievously: "But Dupin is correct to say that no one here is under any compulsion. If all his prattling about disease has frightened anyone, I am perfectly willing to leave those who do not want to take part in the adventure behind, and pick them up on the way back...unless, of course, I have been struck dead by plague, dragged down to hell, or suffered some other fate worthy of a devil opera...."

He giggled. Now, the giggle seemed sinister—but he knew that no one would accept his offer. We were all committed—

and no one wanted to be left behind in the Stygian gloom, for hours on end.

"Of course no one wants to opt out now," Dupin said, without the hint of a sigh. "Personally, I wouldn't miss it for the world, even if my fertile imagination turns out to have magnified the prospect out of all proportion. I assume that there's no need to collect Anton's vote...which would surely be Robert the Devil's, at present."

The opera, I remembered, had a happy ending—for everyone that is, except Bertram, who had sold his son's soul and then failed to deliver it. But the opera was an opera, and operas are supposed to have happy endings, at least for those who do not play fast and loose with souls, and those in love. The opera was based on a series of misunderstandings, since Robert the Great really had nothing to do with Robert the Devil, the magic branch probably had nothing to do with Saint Rosalia, and the convent could not be a real convent. And none of us was in love, with the possible exception of Jana Valdemar—and although some of us, at least, had a slightly casual attitude to our souls, I did not think, then, that any of us would have sold our sons to the Devil.

The carriage had made a left turn off the highway, and the track we were now following was far less even; it jolted considerably in spite of Anton's uncanny skills. I knew that we were following the course of the river instead of heading for the town of Fontainebleau—and I knew, too that we could not be far from our destination. At least, I hoped so, for the jolting threatened to become quite nauseating if it went on for very much longer.

CHAPTER THIRTEEN:
THE MAGIC BRANCH

When the carriage finally came to a halt, I took out my own watch and consulted the hands. They marked half past three—the supposed time of maximum fatigue, when the body reached it lowest ebb. I cannot say that I did not feel drowsy at all, but I didn't yet feel that I was incapable of staying awake. The jolting of the vehicle over what was little more than a hunting track had given me a thorough shaking, but hadn't quite brought me to the point of nausea. Nor did my companions seem unduly nauseous—with the possible exception of Jana Valdemar, who was the first to take Anton's hand when he opened the door—although they certainly seemed terribly weary.

As before, I got down on the other side, but this time I let Dupin open the door and get down first, while I tried to get a good look at Anton's face by the light of the external lantern. He was younger than the ghost of Thibodeaux I had seen to the opera, but he had trimmed his black beard in the same style, and when he met my eyes—which he did frankly, and almost insolently, the creature that looked back at me through the dark pupils gave every impression of being far older than the thousand-year history that connected it to the era of Hrolf the Viking, the scourge of Charles the Fat and Charles the Simple.

By the time I had walked around the coach to join the others, Anton had made his way round to the rear luggage compartment and was rummaging around therein. Having taken out a violin and bow, he left the compartment open, with a coil of rope hanging over the rim.

Again I met his eyes. "Can you play that thing?" I asked.

"Yes sir," he assured me.

"But can you play Berlioz on it?" I asked.

"That will not be necessary, sir," he said.

"So what do you intend to play?" I persisted.

"You will recognize it readily enough, sir, once it begins," he said. "It has been echoing in your dreams for many years, perceived but unheeded by consciousness. The ancient race is no more, but yesterday never dies. Its rhythm will echo for thousands of years yet, and will echo still when the new race has reached its own terminus...and far beyond."

"Even the Harmonic Society's coachman is a seer, I see," I observed, dryly.

He smiled. "Yes, sir," he said, politely. "Those who think they see, but only sit and talk, have no need to be true seers—but a coachman must have keen eyes, in order to follow the road, and find his way."

"You have not always been a coachman, I suspect," I said.

He actually seemed to consider that question for a moment or two, before replying: "Not literally, sir—but thank you for asking. One becomes so accustomed to following the road, that one sometimes needs to be reminded that there are other things to be, and other places to go. From the perspective of the future, the past cannot help but resemble a path leading inexorably to the present, but in the present, at least unless one dies...but you must hurry, sir, and catch up with your friends."

He was right; the others were already drawing away into the darkness, led by Saint-Germain, who had taken possession of a lantern. The coach could go no further, because the trees were too tightly packed, but it seemed that we still had a little way to go to reach the tree whose roots were nourished by the dead of Brocéliande.

"Do we have far to travel?" I asked.

"Not in distance, sir," said the enigmatic coachman—but he added, as I moved away: "But be careful of the water's edge, sir. Don't worry about the carriage—I'll leave a lantern here, so that they will find it easily enough in the dark."

He was right about the distance. Had we not been moving tentatively, because of the darkness, we would have reached the clearing in thirty or forty strides, although it was more a terrace than a clearing, cut into the steepest part of the hillside.

I could not see the river, although I could hear it, away to the left, beyond the rim of the terrace; but I could tell that the slope was shallower there, because I could see the crowns of the trees extending away, their glittering leaves reflecting the yellow lamplight like a shower of sparks. I could not identify the trees—especially the one that grew in the center of the clearing, which bore red fruit. They were the size of apples, but it was not an apple tree. That was not surprising, though; we were supposedly in Brocéliande now, where exotic trees bearing strange fruit still grew, as they once had in the Garden of the Hesperides, or in Eden.

Saint-Germain was in no doubt as to where to go. He had only to trust to his intuition. While the rest of us remained on the edge of the terrace nearest the place where the carriage was waiting, its remaining lantern still visible through the foliage, he went to the tree. There was a bank of earth on the edge, on which humans could conveniently sit, and we did sit, even though we had been sitting in the coach for what seemed like a eternity. Once stretched, it seemed that our legs were reluctant to hold us up, so weary were our bones.

I took care to make sure that Lucien Groix was not sitting anywhere near the far rim of the terrace, where the slope resumed, running down to the water's edge—and, indeed, that no one was. My companions had not spread out very far; with the temporary exception of Saint-Germain, they formed a ragged line only a few meters from end to end, all watching Saint-Germain with rapt attention and expectation. Dupin was in the middle of the group, with Marie Taglioni to his right and Chapelain to his left. Jana Valdemar was sitting next to Chapelain, with the Prefect at the other end of the row. Lucien

Groix and Chapelain had both lit fresh lanterns, making three, with Saint-Germain's, so the stage on which the tree stood was adequately lit, although the trees of the forest surrounding it were nothing more than a mass of shadows sprinkled with the dust of jaundiced stars.

I hesitated as to whether to insinuate myself between Dupin and Chapelain, but decided in the end that I ought to stand beside Jana, so that she would be bracketed by the physician and myself. That put me nearest to the river by a meter or so, but with the entire terrace between myself and the far rim, I judged that I was in no conceivable danger, and obedient to Anton's injunction.

Why Anton? I wondered briefly. *Why nor Robert or Oberon?* Because, I supposed, he was in hiding, and had taken on the coloration of his hiding-place, mimicking the name of its honored founder. I no longer doubted, however, that he was the guide and driver here, and that Blaise Thibodeaux had merely been a privileged passenger, like the seven of us. Anton was the one located outside the company, who did not contribute to the magic number. He was the one who cracked the whip.

I looked for evidence of a ruin on the edges of the terrace, for some fugitive reside of a "house of women" or witches' lair—but any building that might have been standing in the vicinity in the ninth century would have been obliterated by the forest centuries ago. If the place where we were standing had really ever qualified as a literal clearing, it was a perfectly anonymous location by now; we could have been anywhere in the forest.

Saint-Germain, while holding his lantern above his head, was using his free hand—ungloved—to clear ivy from the tree's bole, above the master branch. He was obviously looking for something very specific: a slot of sorts.

When Saint-Germain looked back briefly, perhaps searching for Anton, his eyes briefly met mine. They did not have the seeming depth of thousands of years that Anton's had, but they did seem wild and bloodshot. Before resuming his search, he winked at me—and that, even in the absence of a multitude of other indicators, would have convinced me that Saint-Germain was not himself tonight.

Anton had taken up a position on the far side of the clearing, with his back to the river's edge, although he had not moved through our line, and must have made his way there through the trees. Saint-Germain eventually had to turn round in order to locate him. Perhaps he winked at Anton too—or at Oberon, that surely being the more appropriate name, now that we were in the forest and no longer in the theater—but if he did, I was not in a position see it. Either way, it seemed their gazes came to an understanding. Saint-Germain carefully set his lantern down, and then reached up, raising his walking-stick high above his head—and slotted it into the tree, where at least a third of its length was swallowed by the wood, leaving the protruding handle pointing obliquely downwards, more like the head of a tiny horse than the cap of a lower-case "r."

And nothing happened.

The stick stood where it was, seemingly firmly embedded, but it was just a stick. Saint-Germain stepped back two paces, without retrieving the lantern. He made a signal with his hand, which I interpreted to mean that Chapelain and Groix should put their lanterns down too, but they could not have understood it in the same way, because neither of them did.

Anton—Oberon—began to play.

He was right. I did recognize the tune, even though I had never heard it before. There was nothing complicated about it— it certainly was not worthy of Berlioz—but it had the kind of insistent rhythm that "gypsy fiddles" often have, to which one might dance a slow jig of sorts, if one felt the urge.

I didn't.

Nor, it seemed, had anyone else.

Scenting wild geese, I relaxed, but I was prepared to wait, at least until the tune finished.

Saint-Germain came back to join us. Gently, he took the other lanterns from the hands that held them, one by one, and placed them on the ground himself. Then he sat down on the far end of the row, next to Lucien Groix, so that he and I bracketed the party.

The tune did not finish; it went on and on—and I had the curious sensation that time outside the clearing had stopped. I looked up at the sky, as if I might have been able to tell whether the moon and stars had ceased in their apparent rotation—but the cloud cover was still solid, and the fragility of the lantern-light gave me the illusion that it was very low. It seemed so low that illusion told me that I might almost be able to touch it by raising my hand. Indeed, the whole world seemed to be shrinking, and I no longer had a sensation of distant horizons beyond the enclave of the forest where we were standing.

I looked behind me, to check that the carriage and horses were still there.

The lantern was still burning, and by its light I could still see the rear end of the massive coach, and the rim of its open luggage compartment.

That was reassuring—but a frisson went through me regardless, as if I were looking at the familiar object from the viewpoint of another existence.

I felt a second frisson when I turned back to look at the tree, lighted from below by the lantern that Saint-German had left beneath it. The leaves were rippling, as if in a slight breeze, although I could feel none on my face; as they wavered, alternately exposing their varnished upper sides and their paler underside, they were reminiscent of a host of fluttering eyelids.

The walking-stick was no longer a walking-stick. It was now a branch.

It had begun to put out subsidiary branches, which were already coming into leaf, and it was growing at a prodigious rate, easily perceptible to the naked eye.

Perhaps I should have been terrified, or at least alarmed, but in fact I was profoundly glad. This was something else that was echoing within me, emerging from an unimaginably distant past—which had always been there but had never before struck a resonant chord....

But I really was myself, and wholly myself. The echoes were within me, but the resonance they found now was unique. I was myself, undissolved and unimpaired.

The lanterns that Pierre Chapelain and Lucien Groix had been holding up, but which Saint-Germain had laid on the ground, were no longer providing as much clarity, because their light was partly masked by tall grass and fern-leaves, whose shadows they cast upon the glitter of the forest and the crown of the isolated tree. Everything around me was nine-tenths in shadow, everything seemed ghostly—but I could see it all, after a fashion.

I thought at the time that I was the only passenger who could and did, because it seemed to me, when I looked along the ragged line, that all six of my companions had fallen asleep, or unconscious. I did not imagine that they were dead, however; I was confident that they had only surrendered to the pull of sleep, which had abruptly become irresistible. I did not doubt that they would dream—that they were already dreaming—and I presumed that some of them, at least, would remember what they dreamed; but none of them, I thought, would quite be able to believe that what they had dreamed was real...for that, after all, is the nature of dreams.

Why did I think those things? Why, indeed, had I thought so many of the things that I had thought since I had seen Blaise Thibodeaux's ghost in the Opéra-Comique? If I had fallen asleep myself, I certainly had not done so suddenly; the dream had been consuming me for some time, gradually and insensibly. I believe, now, that I *was* dreaming, and that the dream had been intruding upon me for at least forty-two hours, but I also believe, in spite of the evidence to the contrary—which I have reported faithfully thus far, and will continue to report faithfully—that I was also wide awake, perhaps more fully conscious than I had been before I saw the ghost. Perhaps I, too, will never quite be able to believe that what I saw was real, but I do believe that it was *true*.

At first, there were only shadows. The dance did not begin

immediately, but that was not because the dubious aristocrats of some fairy court were waiting for Oberon and Titania to lead then in a parodic pavane. I could not see from where I stood whether the shadow playing the violin, as it ground out the inappropriately slow but oddly insistent jig, still had Anton's human form, but it was not that of a humpbacked dwarf.

Suddenly, I became aware that I was no longer on the end of the line of sleeping watchers. Someone else had slipped out of the forest, unobtrusively, and was standing beside me, as if waiting politely for him to notice me. He was standing very stiffly at first, but as soon as I turned toward him the stiffness seemed to flow out of him. He flexed his fingers, massaged his neck, and hopped up and down, testing his ankles.

His arthritis had been dispersed. He was young again— younger than before, at any rate. He was probably nearer my age than twenty-one, but he seemed to be reveling in rejuvenation nonetheless.

He bowed to me, and said: "Blaise Thibodeaux."

Had we been in a theater I would have returned the gesture and told him my name, but we were in Brocéliande, where a different etiquette applied.

"I know," I said. It was not rude; it was the correct thing to say. He needed to know that I knew, not what name I went by. He knew how unreliable names were, with the possible exception of his own.

He linked arms with me, as if we were the oldest friends in the world, and said: "Walk with me, my friend."

Was I his friend, I wondered? Was he grateful to me because I had been able to see him at the theater, thus helping to confirm his reality, his resonance?

He tried to lead me toward the river. I did not wish to miss the dance, if the fays really were going to emerge from the ground and dance, and I was reluctant to be drawn.

"It's quite safe," he assured me.

I was slightly insulted that he seemed to be under the impression that I was afraid of falling in. "The dance," I said.

"You won't miss it," he assured me. "That's not why you're here, though. You gave me quite a shock, you know, when I first saw you on All Hallows' Eve. Everything was different: the hall, the stage, the music, the dancers...and I was expecting to see Dupin. Dupin was the one man in the world I thought I could rely on. And I saw *you*. Imagine how anxious I felt!"

"He was unavoidably detained," I said, apologetically.

"I know that *now*. I knew that it was all right *then*, as soon as I had looked into your eyes and saw Oberon looking back at me, from the depths of the ages."

"But he was in *your* eyes," I objected.

"An easy mistake to make," he said, as we moved down through the trees to the river bank. There, it was exceedingly dark, hardly any lamplight filtering through, but while my arm was linked with Thibodeaux's, I felt sure of my footing. Indeed, I felt quite at home in a world where there was nothing but shadow. I could no longer see his face, but I could hear his voice.

"I had my doubts, you know," he said. "I wasn't by any means sure that, when the resonance was confirmed, I'd be fully conscious, possessed of a viable phantom of flesh, able to walk and talk and breathe and see...but here I am. It's my first time, of course, following the stream as I'm bound to do. In time, though...in time, everything will be possible. I won't just remember; I'll be able to swim against the current, and become eternal. That will be so strange and so wonderful...I thought of it, you know, when I was working out my theories, but I never quite grasped it.

"Isn't it strange that the dead can doubt? It's hardly surprising that they can dream, because dreaming is all they possibly can do, once their bodies have turned to dust, but that they can doubt...that's a boon of which Plato never dreamed. You know the *Republic*, of course—the dream at the end, where the dead choose their reincarnations, knowing everything, with no further room for doubt? An idle dream! Death is no more a Republic, in which everyone has a vote, than it is a monarchy, in which some omnipotent king deposits souls despotically, wherever the Order of the State requires that they should be. Neither is it anarchy, though, devoid of leaders, let alone laws. But the dead can doubt, my friend, believe me! The blessed uncertainty of existence survives."

"Am I dead?" I asked him, suddenly anxious.

"Not yet, my friend. Don't be in such a hurry. You'll be dead a very long time, and no matter how you long to dream...I'm one of the fortunate ones, of course. Even if I hadn't met Oberon, I wouldn't have been one of the dead whose dreams are nightmares. It *is* luck, though. One might like to think that the dead whose dreams are nightmares are the ones who treated others badly in life, and that their nightmares constitute some kind of punishment—some echo of moral order, so painfully absent from the world of the living—but that's not the way it works. The dead whose dreams are nightmares might have been pusillanimous in life, but I doubt even that. It's simply one more instance of the uncertainty of existence. Even with eternal aid, there's no possibility of utopia. Some might perhaps be glad to spend eternity in Brocéliande, while others would prefer Babylon, but doubt remains, and hesitation, and even the dead may change their minds.

"The nightmares aren't continuous, though, for those who have them, nor consistent. Nothing is continuous or consistent—not even quotidian existence, and not just because of the need for sleep. The seeming continuity of life is an illusion akin to the persistence of vision; it's an artifact of the slowness of thought, the inability of consciousness to perceive the true pace of time. Everything is discontinuous—time itself is discrete and particular, if you'll forgive the puns...although, to be honest, time is also discreet, and particular too, in the other sense of the term, so both double meanings are literally applicable. If we could only see things from Oberon's perspective... but that's a long way off, as yet, for the likes of you and me. It's a paradoxical thought, but it isn't until the *fullness* of time that one can become eternal. We can *remember* the past, with a little help in escaping from the refuge of consciousness—oh, very briefly, for we're not yet made for freedom—and we can even *reproduce* it, after a fashion, but we can't *dwell* in the past in the sense that Oberon can and does."

"*Can* we remember the past?" I queried. "Not just our own past, that is, but the world's? Can we remember our previous incarnations?"

"Our past *is* the world's past," Blaise Thibodeaux told me, as if it were obvious—as, in fact, it is. "And yes, we can remember previous incarnation, with only a little effort—but not in the sense that we can remember being other people, because that's not the way it works. Living other lives is something that can only be done in dreams. Flesh inevitably turns to dust, and the memories it retains, when it's reconstituted into further flesh, thus acquiring new individuality, are the memories of dust.

"It's possible to obtain sporadic flashes of insight—to remember the momentary sensation of being eaten, when a part of one's being was once a fruit, or of biting, if a part of one's being was once an insect...but we have such an infinitely tiny residue of the emperors, generals, goatherds, goats, and fish of the past that it's hard to recall even the briefest resonance of their consciousness. And we have to remember, given the implications of the calculus of probability, that of all the lives our flesh has lived in the past, and all of those that it will live in the future, all the way to the fullness of time, when our ultimate descendants will master time itself and remember us *fully*, the overwhelmingly vast majority must be so small that our optical instruments cannot even perceive them as yet."

"The agents of disease?"

"No, no...the agents of disease are even rarer, in the realm of the very tiny, than fruit or insects; goats and fish are in the realm of medium size—perhaps as rare as goatherds, or even generals and emperors. We notice them, of course, because of the harm they do us, just as we notice emperors and generals, but we ought never to forget how very few they are, by comparison with the vast hosts of the harmless and the benign. Yes, it's possible to catch glimpses of the components of our flesh that were once, or will be, scourges and afflictions, which spread terror and pain...but even they were and will be merely reckless, unaware of the damage they did and will do. There should be no nightmare in that.

"The nightmares of the living, who must endure the troublesome presence of emperors, generals, pain, and disease, are another matter...but they don't arise from the fragmentary memories of past incarnations. The temporal echoes we receive of the past and the future are, in the overwhelming majority, harmless and benign. You need have no fear of them."

"And yet," I said, "*this* is possible. *You* are possible. Saint-Germain might or might not be possible, but he does seem to believe in himself. Reincarnations are not always fragmentary. Coherency is possible, even if only briefly."

"Yes it is," he agreed. "With the right assistance, brief coherency is possible. I am possible. You are possible. But such dreams as you and I are made on are not contrived without effort, skill, and sacrifice. Were it not for Oberon, and the magic of the fays... you know, of course, that that is only a manner of speaking?"

"Yes," I said, "but it seems that the time has not yet come when we are capable of devising another way of speaking about it. It's marginally better than talk of the Devil, I suppose, although talk of the Devil replaced it for a while."

"So it seems, given the river's drift. That too is a manner of speaking, of course; time is not really a river, and does not even flow, in any real sense—but that is the way that we are bound to perceive it, as figments of consciousness, all the more so as figments of flesh. We have no manner of speaking about the eternals, except to call them eternal, and cannot understand how they have always been in existence, at least sporadically, and have always been active in our lives, at least sporadically, when they will not be born for billions of years, after an exceedingly long and difficult engineering of their own evolution.

"Timebound as we are, we do not have their privileges, and can only take refuge in the illusions of coherency and fate...but we do, at least, have the intellect and the courage to rail against fate, and we can, I think, take some comfort from the fact that the ultimate ancestors of matter and life will be able to swim upstream, even if they are not directly descended from our own flesh and blood. They are interested in us nevertheless. I do not say that they are medium in size, let alone giants, and they might in themselves be so tiny as to be beyond the range of our microscopes, but they are interested in us nevertheless; we have a role to play in their story...we have a resonance in their souls."

There are, as Dupin had remarked, forbidding texts as well as forbidden ones: texts that are willingly, even eagerly, imparted, but which remain unread because they are simply too difficult. As a ghost, Blaise Thibodeaux was no easier to comprehend than he had been as a man or a book...but as Dupin had also said, simply because a book is forbidding, that does not mean that there is nothing in it.

The night was very dark, but I was aware of the forest, and the gentle grip on my arm. I was aware of a direction, and I was aware of the proximity of the river, into which I had no intention of falling. I knew that I had to concentrate on what he was saying, so that I might remember it for future reference, even if I did not quite understand it. I had my duty as a recorder to observe and maintain—and Dupin would not want me to miss a single word, even if his dream turned out to be a much clearer and more abundant revelation..

"Why are you telling me all this, Monsieur Thibodeaux?" I asked him. "Is there nothing better you might do with your brief reincarnation than try to explain yourself to a blockhead like me?"

"I've already tried to explain myself to Dupin," he said. "I might have tried again—but he sent you to the theater in his stead. And no, there is nothing better that a man like me can do with even the briefest of reincarnations but try to explain himself. Others, I suppose, might have different priorities—but you and I are alike, are we not?"

Are we? I thought—but said nothing.

"What else is a mind like yours or mine for *but* to try to

explain itself?" he continued. "It is not everyone's chosen purpose, I grant you, but it is surely the primary purpose of every *thinking* mind. What else is Oberon himself doing, in remembering all of time, and molding it to his own purpose, but trying to explain himself...and in so doing, to create himself, so to speak, in his own image? Since we *are*, what else can we do but investigate *what it is* that we are, and try to make it better?"

"You're right," I said, with a slight sigh, "in saying that not everyone sees life that way."

"I'm very well aware of that," he said. "I have lived—and although I no longer live, I still dream. I pass no judgment on others, but I do pass judgment on myself, and my own sanity and purpose. You and I, my friend, are kindred spirits, and you are in sympathy with me. If you wish, you too might eat of the fruit of the tree. The fruit is as red as blood, but this is a golden opportunity. It will not last long, and its continuity is pure illusion, but still...I am here, and you are here, and the future lies ahead of you in the drift of time. You can follow my example, if you wish."

"A saintly man might think that you were playing the role of tempter now," I pointed out.

He laughed. "Am I a serpent, then?" he asked. "Am I a man who would sell another's soul to the Devil? You know better than that, my friend. You know that the fruit of the tree of good and evil, bitter as it might be, is the only nourishment that the brave human soul needs. We're not in Eden now, much less in Babylon, but in Brocéliande; and the gifts of the fays, precarious as they might be, are not to be scorned. The kingdom of Mommur is yours for the taking, and that it not a gift that comes within the reach of very many men, most of whom must make do with the rations of Tantalus. Can you see the light now?"

I could, in fact, see a light, although I wasn't sure that he had meant to be taken literally. It was, in any case, paradoxical that we should be able to see what was obviously lamplight, for we had been walking along the riverbank—downstream, I think, in the direction of Paris—and I had certainly not been aware of circling back. Nevertheless, the lamplight was there distantly. Nor was it the only light I could see, for there were myriads of tiny sparks moving among the trees now, and descending from above like rain. They did not give off a great deal of light, but they were visible.

So much, I thought, for the nightlights of some obscure hamlet. We have not been alone for some time, and they are gathering now.

Thibodeaux was urging me on now, toward the yellow lamplight. Paradox or not, we were returning to the terrace, and the tree.

In spite of what Blaise Thibodeaux's ghost had promised me, the dance had already begun; not only that, but it had already become furious.

The shadows within the dance seemed vaguely humanoid but not exactly human. They were short of stature, for one thing. Perhaps there were other differences, but the movement was too fast. I could not tell for sure. I could not even see their eyes...if they had eyes.

They were not always visible from the edge of the terrace; when one of them happened to touch the branches of the marvelous tree, it would disappear, at least for a moment or two...or, perhaps slip sideways into some other space, some dream dimension within crowded space, where it presumably executed a quick pirouette in order to slip back again.

It was all familiar to me; it all awoke resonance in my own being. It was amazing, bizarre, and absurd, but it was not alien. I had been bathing in its temporal radiation all my life. It was part of me...or I was part of it. It was part of the fabric of the world that had given me birth, and I knew that I would never be separate from it, even if I never heard the music again, and even if I could not bring its fantastic rhythm to memory.

For a brief interval, I felt comfortable there, as if I had returned to a country fondly known in my childhood, after a long absence. It lulled me....

And then it began to change.

CHAPTER FOURTEEN:
THE DANCE OF THE FAYS

As the dance of the fays was transformed, I had another, perhaps belated, flash of insight into the secret that Blaise Thibodeaux had been trying to impart to me. I caught another momentary glimpse of what the entire insanely complicated scheme had all been *about*, and what it had all been intended to *achieve*.

Echoes are only echoes; that is supposedly their tragedy. They are not supposed to be able to innovate, but only reflect, perhaps in distorted form, but nevertheless following strict rules of conservation. Such, at any rate, is the theory. But Oberon was cleverer than that. Perhaps it had taken him an exceedingly long time to learn that cleverness, but whatever he had been a thousand years ago, and whatever he was now, while still in the margins of the world, he would not always be, and would not always have been. And like me, he was not alone.

I had referred to his potential counterpart, on a passing whim, as his queen, Titania, and to the remainder of his company as his court, but as soon as the dance began to change, I realized that it was an absurdly limited analogy. I do not mean that I reconceived him as a Republican, let alone a Revolutionary, but I did catch a brief intuition of the fashion in which he was more than a prisoner of ancient convention, more than a blind follower in the leaden footsteps of tradition. He became, at the very least, a Reformer.

Marie Taglioni's *other* had been released now; the thirteen years of turmoil that she had inflicted upon her carrier had come to an end; the *prima ballerina* had served her purpose, and taught her recalcitrant pupil a little—just a little, but enough—of the art of ballet.

I would like to be able to comment on Titania's *en pointe* work, and describe her *entrechats*, but I could not even tell whether she was wearing some form of skirt, and it is possible—far too easy, in fact—to take any manner of speaking too far. The dance was too fast, the light to poor, for me to see anything but shadows—but what I can say, for certain, is that the company of fays, following the lead of their reeducated sister, began to dance in manner that was not merely an echo, or a mere distortion of a echo, of the dances they had performed before, in brief and sporadic moments of opportunity. Unlike the nuns in the opera's ballet, they were no longer content to remember, to echo, to replicate, nor were they content to remember, echo, and replicate mere debauchery. They were determined to do something new, to create, to be artists.

And they could.

That was the most amazing, bizarre, and absurd thing of all.

They were, in essence, echoes; they were phenomena created and defined by the resonance of time—but they had fragmentary minds of their own, even if those minds would not be born for billions of years, and they were no longer content to follow their instincts blindly, to do nothing but repeat.

The ancient folk might have been long gone, in terms of their capacity to interact with human beings on a physical level, but they would never be absent while the waves of time carried the potential resonance forward...and they would never be entirely passive; they were still alive, still evolving, still capable of making something of themselves.

Their dance was, in one sense, the very opposite of the kind of ballet of which Marie Taglioni had been the world's greatest exponent. The latter was highly-ordered and wholly artificial, making great demands on the athleticism of the body. The dance of the fays was wild and free, entirely natural and unbound by the restrictions of organic muscles and sinews. That contrast did not mean, however, that there was nothing that either art could learn from the other; even within the most orderly artifice, there had to be something of the free expression of the fays' dance, to provide the raw material for the patterning of choreography; and even within the hectic exuberance of the fays' dance, there had to be an underlying structure, an organizational framework. In either case, there was room for improvement, augmentation, and enhancement; in either case, there was progress in the art, and there was fuel for that progress in the possibility of exchange.

To describe the fays' dance would be impossible even if I had been able to see it far more clearly, in better light; even if that flock of fluttering shadows had been laid bare by daylight, possessed of color and distinguishable form, their movement would have been too rapid, and too mercurial. It was, however, unmistakable that what they were doing was dancing. Indeed, as Marie Taglioni had said of her seemingly troubled passenger, dance was the very essence of their being. They were creatures of vibration and resonance, rhythm and reflection.

In a sense, I thought, *we all are, not simply because the echoes of time course through us incessantly, but because we are products of all the other rhythms that shape and organize life: the rhythms of the day, the month, the year—and, more intimately, the rhythm of the beating heart and the blood it drives to nourish our being, the rhythm of love and sleep, music and affectionate touch. We dance through life, in our own awkward and bewildered fashion, always aware of its reverberation and its patterns; even in the midst of seeming chaos, even though we do not know the steps of our lives, the choreography of its scheme, at least we know that we do not know them, and are prepared to make our tentative attempts to learn. And while the echoes of our actions and our ideas are sustained, in one way or another, by the fabric of time, we never truly die—and, more remarkably still, never entirely lose our capacity for change, for the alteration of our effect.*

While I watched the dance from the edge of the terrace, my

attention was inevitably absorbed by it, but not completely. From the corner of my eye I perceived that I was not alone, and not merely in the sense that my arm was still linked with Blaise Thibodeaux's. I was, in fact, part of a larger audience than I had been some thirty hours before, when I had watched *Robert le Diable* at the Opéra-Comique. My immediate neighbor, now as then, was the ghost of Blaise Thibodeaux, but the house was full. The tiny lights that had gathered so rapidly, in such profusion, had aggregated now, not to replicate the forms of human or animals, but something stranger and freer. They too were dancing, even though they too were spectators, not fays. I wondered if the individual lights would even be visible, without a microscope, and whether human eyes could resolve their collectives.

I could not. I knew they were there; I could see that they were there, after a fashion, but what they were was beyond the scope of my thoughts, let alone my technical terminology.

I spared a moment to look at Thibodeaux again, now that there was light enough to let me see him, and he responded, reflectively, by meeting my gaze momentarily—but it was merely an automatic reaction. There was no longer any active seer looking through his eyes from the utmost depths of time; he was no longer accompanied by anyone but me, and the crowd around us. He was an echo now, but because the moment was propitious, the echo had put on substance of a sort; it could see and hear and think; it could watch and listen, and appreciate artistry. The words it had spoken in the box at the theater echoed once again in my memory, as if evoked by setting, the stage and the dance.

"Yesterday never dies," Blaise Thibodeaux had said then, expressing the dominant idea of his obsessive life, his stubborn search, "but such is the rhythm of time that one has to grasp its echoes on the wing."

He had explained himself more fully now, because he had had the time to do so. Although it seemed a slight sacrilege to murmur now, in the course of what was, after all, a public performance, I spoke to him again, in a whisper, convinced that he might want to listen to me, even while he watched the dance.

"One can see why people, catching fleeting glimpses of such dances on the Breton Heath, or forest clearings, or in the sky beneath the stars, might mistake them for nostalgic memories of past debauchery," I observed, "even though they are nothing of the sort. It is only in erotic experience, I suspect, that many humans ever come close to that kind of abandon—and even call it abandon, on occasion, although it is a feeble echo of this. If these spirits were ever flesh—and I beg leave to doubt it—I doubt that they are nostalgic for that limitation. I might be wrong, though, for I have long labored under a curse of sorts in that regard; and although I cannot imagine ever being nostalgic for debauchery, it appears that others can. But there are other forms of human abandonment, are there not?"

"There are," he said. And he drew me forward again, insistently. This time, I resisted him because he was pulling me toward the dance, and I thought for a moment that he wanted me to join it—but in fact, he wanted to draw me into the shade of the tree.

"Don't be afraid," he said. "We can pass through safely, and will not disturb them.

He was right. We could and we did. And when we looked back, with the lantern now at our feet, the dance seemed brighter and clearer, but wrongly orientated, as if we were watching from the wings of a theater a performance designed to be witnessed from the auditorium.

I could no longer see the shadows of the crowd, but I knew that they were there: soldiers of Charlemagne and Hrolf the Viking, as well as countless other strays from the forest of Fontainebleau, and Anton's other passengers, brought to complete a set of seven, and thus to facilitate, by some mysterious magic of mathematics, the advent of strange legions.

Blaise Thibodeaux reached up with his supple hand, and plucked one of the fruits from the tree. Although it was red, like an apple, it was round, with an outer tegument more reminiscent of some kind of citrus fruit.

He offered it to me, and I took it.

"Try it," he invited. "It's an acquired taste, I admit, but worth persistence."

I bit into it—and had yet another flash of memory, this time of having read about the fruit that grows by the Dead Sea in the Holy Land, which is bright on the outside, but desiccated within, filled with the ashes of Sodom and Gomorrah.

The fruit from the Tree of Knowledge of Good and Evil contained no such ash, but it was, as I had been warned, more than a trifle bitter. Nor was its texture inviting, for it felt like dust: the dust of the past; the dust of millions upon millions of bodies that had once lived, but had long decayed. It was like biting into the past...because it *was* biting into the past, but it was a past unsweetened by the sap of spring and the unalloyed desire of reproduction. It was the truth of the past, and the true taste of the past, bitter and sour and full of tragedy.

And I spat it out.

Perhaps that was a moment of destiny, when I might have changed the entire direction of my life. Perhaps it was a moment of potential metamorphosis, of transcendence, of apotheosis... and perhaps it was a mere threat of pixilation. Perhaps I was the worst fool in the world, or perhaps I was merely obeying a reflex.

Perhaps....

But there is no end to perhapses. What I did, I did. What I was, I was. If I disappointed eternity, so be it. I'm only human, after all.

The moment into which I had briefly strayed could not last for very long, and the human mind's ability to stretch time subjectively is limited; we are imprisoned by time as we are by matter, and do indeed have to catch yesterday, today, and tomorrow on the wing, momentarily, if we are to catch them at all.

The dance did not stop abruptly, but it faded away with what seemed like undue rapidity. The fluttering shadows melted into darkness, and the galaxies of tiny lights faded too, still whirling;

the music of the violin faded to a whisper, and then to inaudibility.

The magic branch contracted, before I had had a proper opportunity to study it. By the time I focused my attention on it fully, it was nothing but a walking-stick again, jammed into hole that might have been made by a woodpecker, in the bole of the tree above the master branch.

I had an overwhelming sensation of the return of substance, although I had never been aware of losing substance. It was also an overwhelming sensation of returning reality, although I had only been marginally aware of losing that. Until reality returned, in fact, I had no consciousness of how far from it I had strayed.

But I *had* strayed, and the returning reality fell upon me like a hammer, surged through me like a blade, gripped me like a vice. It almost knocked me down, but I contrived to remain on my feet, awake...and more alert than I had been for days, although I was not aware, at first, of exactly what it was for which I was striving to be alert.

My companions were still on the bank on the edge of the terrace, seemingly still asleep—but one of them missing. I looked around, wildly, and just managed to catch a glimpse of her as she moved between the trees, walking unhurriedly but purposefully. She was twenty meters away before I realized it, barely visible any longer between the trees as a distant glint of reflected lamplight, more ghostly and fey than any actual ghost or fay—but I knew that she must be at the water's edge, and that she would not hesitate for long.

I began to run, having already thrown away my stick and hat, tearing off my jacket and kicking off my shoes as I ran.

I did not doubt for a moment that she really was still asleep, that she was a true somnambulist. I did not doubt for a second that she did not really want to drown, that what she wanted—or would have wanted, if she had been capable of wanting anything in her present state of mind—was to be saved. I remain utterly convinced that that was what she would have wanted, had she not been entranced, so very far from her true self....

Abandoned....

I did not see her fall; the darkness had swallowed everything up. I heard the splash, while I was still seven or eight meters short, still running but stumbling and making too little progress, impeded as I was by the undergrowth, which grew far more thickly beside the bank, although I had not noticed it at all while strolling there with my ghostly guide.

By the time I reached the water's edge, three or four precious seconds must have gone by.

I dived in, and aimed for the point where instinct told me she had to be, only a little way downstream, not yet caught by the full surge of the midstream current. About that, at least, I was right; I managed to reach her. Three or four seconds more had passed, but I did reach her. I was able to take hold of her, to grip her solidly with my arms.

She struggled, but she wasn't fighting me. It could only have been the stupid reflexes of her body, reacting to desperation. She wasn't struggling with her mind, but only with her muscles. She wasn't fighting me; she wasn't fighting to drown.

And yet, she struggled. Her reflexes made things difficult for me, even though I was trying to save her, and needed her to cling to me, or at least to lie still.

She struggled.

I struggled.

And then....

The same newspapers that have made a cliché of the Unknown Woman of the Seine regularly carry reports of people saved from drowning. It is the most common form of heroism, now that we carry walking-sticks instead of swords, to save someone from drowning—usually a woman or a child. It is the everyday fuel of reportage and rumor.

But the newspapers only report the successes; they do not provide the true statistics. They give an entirely false impression of the ease and simplicity of the task, of its seemingly routine nature.

Can you swim? Dupin had asked me. *Yes*, I had replied. It had not occurred to me to think that twenty years had passed since I had actually swum, and to be anxious about it, because the ability to swim is one of those things that, once mastered, one is supposed never to forget.

What Dupin should have asked was: *Can you swim in icy water, in sodden clothes, with both hands wrapped around a reflexively struggling body, fighting the clutches of eddies, undertows, and tangled weed?* To that, I would have had to answer, *I don't know.*

I know now.

In truth, the eddies, undertows, and weeds were trivial. Once the shock of diving into the cold water had passed, the effect was not so very bad. As for swimming while holding a reflexively struggling body, it can obviously be done—and in any case, the body had stopped struggling, and become inert, before I lost my grip. Heroes hang on to struggling bodies all the time, and when they become inert, they continue to hold on; for them, it *is* routine. Presumably, there is a knack to it, which I had never had the opportunity to forget. Perhaps the true odds were against me, and perhaps I was simply woefully incompetent. Perhaps the moment was against me, or perhaps I simply failed, through culpable neglect, to catch it on the wing.

At any rate, I not only failed to save Jana Valdemar from drowning, but very nearly drowned myself. By the time I lost my grip on her unconscious body, I could not keep my own head above water, let alone hers. I swallowed water, and sucked at least a little into my lungs.

Even though I was some way upriver of Paris, the water was horribly polluted. Human life has polluted all rivers by now, save for the remotest mountain streams. We are agriculturalists and livestock-keepers; we build mills and wineries; we export our own excreta recklessly, for want of efficient sewerage. River water is filthy, foul, and sometimes fatal—but it is not evil; it means no one any harm. Its pollutants are, after all, merely the dust of the past, and even their dangerous component is merely the molecules of entities that have lived before and will live again.

I tried to spit it out. I tried with all my might—but I could not.

It nearly killed me, and probably would have done, had my friends not woken up in time.

Lucien Groix was the hero. He was the one who dived in after me and pulled me out—but he might have drowned too, extending the chain of failure, had Auguste Dupin, the great logician, not done the rational thing. He it was who ran back to the carriage and got the rope, and threw one end of it to the Prefect, so that he, Chapelain, and Anton could haul both of us out.

It was, of course, Anton who had brought the rope—but it was Oberon, who would not even be born for billions of years, but was nevertheless eternal, who had carefully left it overlapping the rim of the open luggage-compartment of the coach. He, she, or it, not Anton or Thibodeaux, was the true expert on the echoes of time, and their ramifications.

It was Dupin that I saw first, as he applied some method of his own to get me to cough up and vomit up at least some of the river water I had taken in, and who brought me back to consciousness. Then I saw and heard Groix, who was sitting up beside me, complaining volubly, bitterly, and very loudly about my foolishness, and the fact that I had forced him to get wet, and ruin his clothes, and risk his life—a life, although he was too polite to say so in so may words—that was infinitely more precious, to Paris, to France, and to existence in general, than mine.

It wasn't until I was able to look him in the eyes and say: "Jana?" that he sobered up, and shut up, merely shaking his head. Jana Valdemar was lost. I had failed to save her. She would float downriver, perhaps all the way to Paris—but whether her corpse washed up on the bend between Fontainebleau and Melun or beneath one of the bridges of the city, she would still be the Unknown Woman of the Seine to the newspapers. Even though she would be swiftly recognized in the Morgue, and immediately named for entry into the record, she would still, and always, be the Unknown Woman of the Seine.

"It wasn't suicide," I said to Lucien Groix, the Prefect of the Parisian Police. "She was sleepwalking. She was a somnambulist. She was entranced. She didn't know what she was doing. Make sure that goes into your records, into your statistics. It wasn't suicide."

He nodded, silently.

It wasn't until I was able to stand up again, and to start searching for my hat and stick, jacket and shoes, that I saw Chapelain. He was standing on his own in the trees, in the shadows, avoiding everyone. He didn't want to meet my eye, but he had to. I gave him no alternative, and I hope that he found my gaze terrible, all the more so because he was my friend.

"I don't blame you," he said.

He didn't blame me!

I stared at him, and said nothing. I didn't bother to ask him whether she had been pregnant, because I knew, now, that she had been, and he knew that I knew. I didn't bother to ask him whether he had intended to marry her, because I knew that he hadn't, and he knew that I knew. I just stared at him, and hoped that he found my gaze terrible.

In the end, he whispered: "How could I?"

I couldn't even say: "How could you not?" He was my friend, and friends do not say that kind of thing to one another, even in a forest, where etiquette does not apply.

I was able to speak a little more freely to Saint-Germain when I found him standing by the water's edge at the spot where Jana Valdemar had fallen in, in her somnambulistic trance, and I had dived in, fully awake.

"She was the finest medium in Paris," he said. "Perhaps the world. She had so much potential. There was no limit to what we might have accomplished together."

"Yes," I said, as I finally contrived to locate my second shoe, "but would you have married her?" Saint-Germain was not my friend, but even so, I refrained from making the question more difficult by adding: *while she was carrying Pierre Chapelain's child?*

That was probably not what enabled him to lie, because he was a habitual and accomplished liar, but it helped.

"Yes," he lied. "I would have married her."

One day, I knew—and he knew, too—he would marry money. The opportunity would eventually come along to secure his own ill-made and somewhat precarious fortune with more solid wealth, and he would take it. He was a practical man. He was, in his own eccentric fashion, a conventional man. He would not have married Jana Valdemar, even if she had been carrying his own child.

That, I think, entitled me to be brutal. "But she didn't want you, did she?" I said, malevolently. "She wanted Chapelain."

He didn't find my stare terrible. "I could have brought her round," he insisted, "if only I could have got to her in time. I tried—you know that I tried. You were there."

"You took the words right out of my mouth," I said, bitterly.

And he looked at me, almost with pity, and said: "I don't blame you."

He didn't blame me either, any more than Chapelain did. They were prepared to forgive me my failure; it would have been ungracious to do otherwise. Dupin would not dream of blaming me either, and would not have seen anything in my failure to require forgiveness.

I blamed myself, though. Of all the people I could have blamed, I blamed myself.

CHAPTER FIFTEEN:
THE UNCERTAINTY
OF EXISTENCE

When I had been possessed by an egregore a little over a year earlier, the aftermath of the experience had put me in bed for a week—perhaps not at death's door, but in a parlous condition nevertheless—even though it had never meant to harm me. On this occasion, if I had been possessed at all, I had only been possessed with exceeding discretion, and sporadically, by an entity that actually wished me well, and had offered me a golden opportunity that I probably should not have refused—but still I ended up in bed for a week, at first experiencing symptoms that are too disgusting to be reportable.

This time, Dupin was not available to care for me, because he suffered the same fate—not because he had swallowed polluted river water, but probably because, in spite of all his antiseptic precautions, he had caught whatever infection it was that had felled Madame Lacuzon, and had been felled in his turn once it had had time to incubate. Lucien Groix was ill too, but that probably was the river water. So were Chapelain and Saint-Germain, although it wasn't obvious how they had picked up any infection. I had no news of Anton the coachman, but I had my suspicions. I could at least imagine, once I was capable of imagining things again, that he was lying in some meager bed in the Marais or Montmartre, spewing the contents of his guts in all directions, having no immunity at all from the shocks that flesh is heir to. I hoped, if so, that he had someone to care for him, and trusted that he had.

I, of course, had Madame Bihan. Dupin had Madame Lacuzon. Chapelain had his own servants, Saint-Germain had every physician in the crowded ranks of the Harmonic Society, and Lucien Groix had the authority to call not only upon the resources of the state but all the Sisters of Mercy a man could desire. Groix needed that extra assistance; he came off worse than any of us, with regard to the illness, although we all made a full recovery in the end. Groix never returned to the Prefecture; no one ever found out for sure—perhaps not even him—whether he had resigned of his own accord, or whether he had been discreetly dismissed.

Madame Lacuzon was by no means entirely well herself, but there could be no question of convalescence in her mind while Dupin was ill. She had to look after him, and to do it alone, barring access to his room to anyone and everyone else. That exclusiveness at least had the side-effect of freeing Madame Bihan to care for me—"exactly," I was assured, "as Amélie would have done." Her policy was not quite exact, though, for she did allow me visitors once the worst of my symptoms were over and the room had been thoroughly cleansed. She even apologized for not being able to let Chapelain come to examine me, even though she was a confirmed non-believer in "magnetic mumbo-jumbo," because he was too ill—although she made no apology for not calling in any substitute physician.

Madame Bihan was, however, able to allow Marie Taglioni to call in to see me before she went back to Venice. I was still feeling ill at the time, but was no longer feverish, and felt capable of conversation. Indeed, I was hungry for conversation, Madame Bihan being only garrulous without being capable of listening to anything except household instructions.

The dancer had not escaped the dread symptoms entirely, but in her case they had been mercifully slight, and had cleared up after twenty-four hours or so. She, it seemed, had more resistance than any of the mere males who had accompanied her on the lunatic excursion. Nor had she forgotten the extraordinary circumstances of the journey, and its even more extraordinary conclusion, although she did not remember it as I remembered it, and I did not feel that I had the authority to suggest to her than she might have been mistaken, even if etiquette had permitted it.

"I've tried to see Monsieur Dupin," she told me, "But his concierge would not let me in, even though she seemed to know perfectly well who I am. She really is the most fearsome woman I've ever met—and as you can probably imagine, I've met more than a few. I wasn't allowed to see Monsieur de Saint-Germain either, although in his case, it was a veritable wall of mesmerist physicians who forbade me access, on the grounds that he was far too ill. At Monsieur Groix's home, I got the same story from a nun, who reminded me very forcibly of the abbess in the opera, and must surely be one of those who really did have a colorful past before finding her vocation. Dr. Chapelain I did get in to see, since his servants have become as accustomed to taking orders from me as they were from him, but I found him rather uncommunicative. Doctors are by far the worst patients, aren't they? Perhaps he is grief-stricken over the loss of Mademoiselle Valdemar...or conscience-stricken."

She paused at that point, as if expecting a reaction.

When she got none, she added: "I heard what you said to Monsieur de Saint-Germain by the river bank, and what he said in reply. He was lying, of course."

"Of course," I said. "Not a reliable man, as I told you."

"It was an unfair question, though, was it not? You might, perhaps, have asked it of Chapelain, but...after all, would *you* have married her?"

I was not so unwell, by then, as to have lost my ability to parry. "Would you believe me if I said that I would?"

"No," she said.

"There's no need for me to answer, then, is there?"

She might have taken offense at that, because my tone was less than polite, and she was, after all, a person entitled to the utmost politeness. She did not, however, perhaps feeling that we were friends now that we had both been press-ganged into the Harmonic Society.

"She did have other options," the dancer said, a trifle defensively.

"Options didn't come into it," I told her. "She was walking in her sleep. She didn't know what she was doing."

She didn't press the point by suggesting that I might have been wrong about Jana. Instead, she accepted the cue to move in a different direction. "Were you still asleep too?" she asked me. "Did you know what you were doing?"

"I was awake," I told her, and left the second question unanswered.

"While you were asleep," she said, "did you dream?"

It was, I imagined, a question that she had already asked Chapelain, and would have asked the others had she been allowed to see them. She didn't really want to know. What she wanted was to tell me what she had dreamed...except that she would not represent it as a dream, but as a waking experience. That was what I wanted too, so I told her that I didn't remember. I excused the lie as a matter of etiquette, although that was a dissimulation to.

"I thought not," she said. "I don't think any of you remembered anything—including Mademoiselle Valdemar. Monsieur Dupin was right about my superior resistance, though, as evidenced by the inability of the infection to master my constitution. I contrived to stay awake, in spite of the fact that I hadn't slept for forty hours. Something did happen, you know. It wasn't the complete failure that you might assume. Rational or not, something did happen—and I saw it."

"I believe you," I said. "Lucien Groix did throw himself into the Seine, as Blaise Thibodeaux had prophesied, so I imagine that you did see the dance of the debauched abbess performed as your father had intended. The theory of resonance demands it...not to mention the rules of esthetic propriety that I shall have to observe when I eventually write the story."

She seemed slightly disappointed that I had guessed, having wanted to spring it on me, but she was also pleased by the endorsement, because she had been afraid that I would not believe her. Doubtless she would have preferred Dupin's endorsement, but probably felt that mine would do, given that Chapelain had been "uncommunicative."

"It wasn't quite that," she said. "In fact, it wasn't what I would have expected at all—but yes, there was a dance. It wasn't Monsieur Berlioz' music, and it certainly wasn't Meyerbeer's, and it wasn't my father's choreography...but I felt, somehow, as if it really was the dance as it was supposed to be performed. It was like no ballet I'd ever seen or imagined, but it was balletic, and not merely balletic in some abstract or formal sense, but in a very personal sense. I felt that the sylphide really was dancing *my* dance, that she really was dancing for me."

"You saw a sylphide dancing?" I queried.

"Not in a literal sense. That's only a manner of speaking—but yes, I saw an entire corps de ballet of sylphides, led by a *prima ballerina*. She was my other. I'm no medium, and wouldn't want ever to be, but for the duration of that particular moment, I was glad that I could still identify with her, while she enjoyed her transient moment of full existence...although she wasn't really a *she*, was she...it...." She trailed off.

"People imagine them differently," I said, "on the basis of the glimpses they catch. Some see ugly, dwarfish korrigans; others see beautiful women. That ugliness or beauty really is in the eye of the beholder, though. It's just an attempt to make sense of something beyond our grasp. No, they don't have any sex, really, and perhaps never did...or ever will."

"How fortunate," she murmured, very faintly—but she didn't really mean it. Perhaps she was thinking about poor Jana—or perhaps she was thinking that she, too, by force of necessity, had been compelled to make her affections subservient to her art and her career, and had thus lost, or warped, something that some other women found fulfilling. She was no nun, but she was no ex-debauchee either. Her murmured "how fortunate" was not a lament, but an ironic observation.

"Was the dance the whole of it?" I asked her, curiously.

She hesitated before answering.

"No," she said, finally, "I couldn't resist the temptation to try one of the fruits on the tree, even though the red coloration suggested that they might be poisonous. There's still a little of Eve in all of us, I suppose. It was extremely bitter, though, and I spat it out immediately. The dance ended immediately thereafter, and I wondered whether I'd done the wrong thing. People do routinely do the wrong thing in romances and fairy tales, don't they? Was I silly, do you think?"

"No," I said, readily offering the endorsement that she still craved. "Resonance has its imperatives, even though we sometimes need to work hard to produce it. After all, it couldn't go on forever, could it?"

Again, that was partial dissimulation. It could, it had, and it would, albeit discontinuously—but everything is discontinuous, so as well as everything going on forever, nothing does. The propagation of the world is more like a sound wave than a river—although even a river consists of discrete molecules. At any rate, I was able to imagine the world, then, as a musical note extending into eternity, perhaps audible to an external viewpoint. In fact, all the parallel universes that share the frame and fabric of space with ours must propagate in the same way, sounding their own notes, making up a near-infinite orchestra, or chorus. It is, I suppose, a cacophony now...but might not always be, if Oberon and his kin can complete their eternal work.

"I wanted to thank Monsieur Dupin in person," Marie Taglioni added, "but as I was unable to do so, would you be so good as to do it on my behalf?"

"I'll be sure to tell Dupin that you tried to see him before you left, but you really don't have anything to thank him for. In the end, he didn't actually *do* anything. The problem sorted itself out."

"On the contrary," she said. "Monsieur Dupin—and you, and Dr. Chapelain, and poor Jana—did *everything*. Between you, you persuaded me that I was not mad, and you gave me a glimpse into the true strangeness of the world, for which I shall always be grateful. I shall not return to the stage, I think, but nor will I retreat to Venice and live as a recluse, as I might well have done had the memory and fear of my affliction lingered as something inexplicable and incurable. If I had not seen you at the *Comique* and sent poor Jana to summon you the following morning, I might have had to bear my affliction permanently— and so might she. I don't know yet exactly what I shall do in future, but I shall certainly do *something*. The art has not heard the last of me, and it has a deal of progress yet to make."

She was right about that, of course—and her decision to continue working for the progress of the art was one for which Paris, in particular, had cause to be grateful, once it had recovered from its own dire fever.

Eventually, the others recovered, but I did not hasten to see them even when I could. For a while, I was content with my own company.

I expected Dupin to be the first to come, but in fact it was Saint-Germain, a trifle pale and queasy but irrepressible. I was able to receive him in the reception-room, and even offered him a cup of tea—which he accepted.

"The dragon still won't let me see Dupin," he complained, "even though I know full well that he's up and about. She really is the most infuriating hagwife in the world. You've seen him, I suppose?"

"Actually, no," I admitted, "but I doubt that you need to worry. I suspect that Dupin knows—as I do—that you kept your end of the bargain. The magic branch delivered on your promise, even if most of us slept through it and saw what we saw in a dream. Dupin is now a member of the Harmonic Society. I see that you're carrying your old bamboo cane, though. I had assumed that you would retain the other, ugly as it is, now that you know what it can do, when the time is ripe."

"I've set people to do study that," he said. "I've put three of the more ambitious members onto the book and the papers. If I can calculate the next time that, as you put it, the time will be ripe...but would you believe that that rogue Anton has disappeared? Vanished from the face of the earth, it seems, without so much as an *au revoir*. After all I've done for him! As for the stick, I replaced it in its cupboard, to await developments. I did think of giving it a place of honor in one of the display-cases, but just between the two of us, most of that material is mere trumpery. True magic shuns excessive display. Thibodeaux deserves to have his heritage remain intact. I put the violin back too, although that oaf Anton must have dropped it at some point, for the body of the instrument is cracked. I doubt that it will ever be able to resonate properly again."

"No matter," I said. "It's not as if it were a Stradivarius or a Guarneri. Any old fiddle would probably have sufficed, with the right player."

"You don't remember the tune, by any chance?"

"Alas, no," I said. "If only we'd had Monsieur Berlioz with us...."

"Mademoiselle Taglioni's gone back to Venice, alas—although I've heard a whisper that she doesn't intend to stay there forever—but Dupin plays the fiddle, doesn't he? There's a rumor floating around that he and Groix smashed up a Stradivarius in the old Rue Auseuil for some unaccountable reason."

"He can play," I admitted, "but I'm not sure that he'll be able to remember Anton's tune, all things considered. Can't you remember it?"

"No, alas. I didn't even retain a clear image of what I saw—it was too dark and too fast—all shadows. But there was a dance, wasn't there?"

"Yes there was," I confirmed.

"And the renaissance of Faerie is underway."

"I can hardly be expected to offer a judgment on that," I said. "We'll have to wait and see, won't we—if we can survive the Revolution."

"We'll survive," he said, confidently—and then changed tack: "You're a member now, of course, and you'll be able to write an account of it for the Archives, won't you? I always knew that scribbling of yours would have its reward someday."

"My notes of past adventures are still too chaotic," I told him, "and they'll be even more chaotic once I've had a chance to record my memories of this one. One day, though, I'll doubtless find time go through them more carefully, and write the stories as they ought to be written, more carefully if not more elegantly...."

"Don't wait too long," the Comte advised. "Remember what happened to Thibodeaux."

"I do," I assured him. "In any case, I'm not sure that I want to deposit my accounts in your Archives. There are issues of confidentiality involved—not that it will matter much, if they're simply stashed in a cupboard or a trunk, to wait for ten or twenty years before anyone even can get around to cataloguing them."

"Don't worry," he said, cheerfully. "I'll make sure they take priority. After all, they're a precious record of one of the greatest minds of the century, and I can't imagine that Dupin will ever get around to writing his own memoirs, or even condensing his theoretical thoughts into an impenetrable book, like Thibodeaux's. He really is an infuriating man, in his way—but now that we're colleagues, I'll be able to make more strenuous efforts to reform him."

"He would probably disagree as to which of you needs reform," I said, dryly.

"No doubt," he said. After a long pause, he added: "I really would have been able to save Jana, if only I had got to her in time. If only she'd been at the theater that night...."

"She was indisposed," I told him. I didn't tell him that she *had* been at the theater, but that he had missed her, or that she had been in my house the next morning when he called round, sitting on the stairs and listening to him ramble. There were issues of confidentiality involved.

"She should have come to me," he insisted. "If she had only put herself in my hands...."

There was no point in telling him that she considered him

to be a traitor, a rapist, and a pimp, and that she had preferred delivering herself to the unkind river to the prospect of putting herself in his hands again, once Chapelain had proved to be a weak reed. It would have been a futile cruelty, because it wouldn't have hurt him. In the absence of an adequate receiver, the resonance of guilt is impossible.

"I can help you too," he told me. "The Society can help you."

"No thank you," I said. "Madame Bihan is looking after me very well, and I have no need for a magnetizer now. If I do have need of one, in future, I'll probably call Chapelain."

"Everyone prefers Chapelain," he muttered, to himself. He really had no idea why. I was no longer entirely sure myself.

Dupin, I thought, probably had the best of it, where care and convalescence were concerned. If ever there was a person entirely to be trusted, and entirely to be admired, it was surely Amélie Lacuzon.

"You will stay in Paris, won't you?" Saint-Germain said. "There are dark days ahead, as we both know, but you're not thinking of returning to America, I hope?"

"I had no idea that you cared," I said, ironically. "Indeed, I've often suspected that you'd far rather I were out of the way—even at the cost of having to subsidize Dupin's cab fares yourself."

"We've been through quite a lot together, my friend, these last few years. Perhaps you haven't grown fond of me, but you must admit that life would have been less interesting for both of us, if the other hadn't been around."

I wasn't entirely convinced, but I let it go.

"I'll doubtless see you at the Society," he said, as he made ready to leave, "when you're better. You can pay your subscription any time."

I let that go too, because it seemed not unlikely that he *would* see me at the Society, and Dupin too, whether the latter paid his subscription or not. For all Dupin's reluctance to fall in with thieves, the lure of the Harmonic Society's Archives would probably prove irresistible.

By the time I finally did get to see Dupin again, we were both entirely well, albeit still a little weak.

"I'm sorry that I couldn't come before," he told me, as we relaxed in the aftermath of a good dinner, "but Amélie can be a terrible tyrant, and the fact that she'd just been ill herself...we were afraid, for a while, that it might be cholera. We both lived through the epidemic of 1832, and we didn't need Thibodeaux's statistics to see that all the prior conditions are repeating: two consecutive poor harvests, with the consequent economic and political upheavals. If the Republicans do manage to get their way and topple Louis-Philippe—and it seems to me that he has too few friends left to save him—the consequent struggle for power will close yet more shops and bankrupt yet more businesses; and the cholera germ is waiting in the wings, ready to emerge on to the stage as soon as the time is right. History has a terrible tendency to repeat, even in the absence of any quasi-magical resonance of time, simply because of the inability of humans to learn from past errors."

"Will we ever overcome that inability, do you suppose?" I asked, thinking not so much about the patterns of famines and political upheavals, but the too-oft-repeated ritual of the Unknown Woman of the Seine.

"We must hope so," he said. "Whatever burdens we inherit from our past, in our blood and bones as well as in the echoes in our souls, we remain free agents—which leaves us room for hope, does it not?"

"I suppose so," I said, dubiously. Perhaps I should have told him, then, exactly what I had seen in Brocéliande, while the memory was still a little fresher in my memory than it was when I did feel able to tell the story—but he didn't volunteer to tell me what he had dreamed for a similar interval. We were both relieved to be well again, and were not yet ready to discuss the more intricate and vertiginous repercussions of infection.

I poured him a glass of brandy, for esthetic rather than medicinal or antiseptic use. We clinked our glasses, and drank a triple toast to Blaise Thibodeaux, Robert the Devil—the legend, not the opera—and Oberon the Fay.

I agreed with his judgment about our being free agents, once I had given it some thought. He had the force of reason behind him. And whatever the great logician had failed to see, or to understand, in the shadows of All Souls' morning, I knew that he had surely seen *something*.

ABOUT THE AUTHOR

Brian Stableford was born in Yorkshire in 1948. He taught at the University of Reading for several years, but is now a full-time writer. He has written many science-fiction and fantasy novels, including *The Empire of Fear, The Werewolves of London, Year Zero, The Curse of the Coral Bride, The Stones of Camelot*, and *Prelude to Eternity*. Collections of his short stories include a long series of *Tales of the Biotech Revolution*, and such idiosyncratic items as *Sheena and Other Gothic Tales* and *The Innsmouth Heritage and Other Sequels*. He has written numerous nonfiction books, including *Scientific Romance in Britain, 1890-1950; Glorious Perversity: The Decline and Fall of Literary Decadence; Science Fact and Science Fiction: An Encyclopedia;* and *The Devil's Party: A Brief History of Satanic Abuse*. He has contributed hundreds of biographical and critical articles to reference books, and has also translated numerous novels from the French language, including books by Paul Féval, Albert Robida, Maurice Renard, and J. H. Rosny the Elder.